Stone
Princess

By

Gabriel Klasing

Printed in the United States of America

First Printing, 2018

ISBN 0-9982173-2-8

Gabriel Klasing
915 Thomas J. Drive
Flint, MI. 48506

Dedication

In memory of my mom thank you for always believing in me!

To my husband thank you for supporting me.

∾CHAPTER 1∾

"Lily." Mom's voice rang through the house.

After a moment of irritation, not wanting to take my nose out of my book, I placed my bookmark and answered back. "What is it?" Trying not to sound agitated but failing miserably.

"Can you please run to the grocery store today and get the stuff on this list?" She asked politely. Even though I could not see her, I pictured her waving the list and money in the air then setting it on the table.

"Yeah, sure," I answered back more agitation creeping out of my voice.

I just didn't want to go anywhere today. Today was my first full day of being back home on summer break from college. I only have half a year left before I graduate with my bachelor's degree in Mechanical Engineering. I could not wait to get it over with and start my life as a full-fledged adult. For now, though all I wanted to do was sleep and read the book that I had picked up before coming home yesterday. However, I could not ignore all the sacrifices that my mom had made for me to even go to college, so I reluctantly wrenched myself from my bed and threw on a tank top and shorts, brushed my hair and applied a little makeup. I walked out into the kitchen and picked up the list and money that mom left me before she headed back to work. The voice inside my head grumbled at me. She owned her own store for Pete sakes. However, as I looked over the list, it is all things she didn't sell at her convenience store, salad, chicken, potatoes, and gravy. I headed for the door wanting to get this quickly over with. The book I am reading was getting to a good part where the girl was going to meet the man of her dreams. I knew that I would meet the man of my dreams too someday but I really was not looking, I wanted to finish school first. Before I could get out the door, my cell phone rang dragging me away from the thought. I looked down at the display to see Stephanie's name pop up. I already knew what she wanted, and I really didn't feel like going out tonight either but, so I debated about answering. On the last ring, I reluctantly answered the phone.

"Hey Steph, how are you?"

"I'm good." She said not wasting any more time she got to the point of her call. "Say me and some of the other girls are getting together tonight and going to the club. You want to go?"

"Steph, I would love to, but I promised my mom that I would spend some time with her tonight." I said lying through my teeth, I would have told her the truth, but she is the type of person that would come over and drag me out the door, kicking and screaming if she had too.

"Well, all right darling I will catch up with you later."

"Later." Then I tapped the call end button on my phone. I was thankful that she gave up easily this time, next time though, I knew it will not be that easy to get out of going.

After getting off the phone, I didn't waste any more time. I grabbed my house key and headed out to the grocery store. I was hoping that I would not run into anyone that I knew, hopefully making the trip quicker.

At the store, I picked up the things on the list. Chicken dinner, yum. I packed everything in my reusable grocery bag and started the short three blocks walk back home. On about the second block something black and shiny caught my attention. I bent down and picked it up. On further inspection, I noticed it was a stone. I was expecting the stone to be burning hot from sitting there baking in the sun, but it was cold. Cold like holding an ice cube in my hand cold, how peculiar. I opened my hand to get a better look at it. Looking at the black stone resting in my palm, I noticed one side was jagged but all of the other sides were smooth. The stone shaped almost resembled half of a heart. The color, mostly black with some white speckles. The shiny part of the stone seemed to be buffed to a mirror shine making the white flecks stand out against the black. The stone looked like it could be an expensive precious gemstone. As I was entranced by its beauty, it started emanating the smell of roses and bright white light.

The oval light grew bigger and bigger making some sort of white wall. Veins of silvery metallic liquid casting a rainbow-like effect made the wall shimmer and dance around in no particular pattern. The closest thing that I could relate it to would be like watching a soap bubble dancing through the air on a warm summer's breeze. The only difference is the white background. Every hue of reds, oranges, greens, and blues swirled inside swirled around looking like a melting rainbow. Hypnotized just like a young child, my feet are glued in place watching the bubble dance, fighting the overwhelming urge to pop it. I could not take my eyes off it even though everything in me said drop it and run. When the wall was large enough, it sucked me in and quickly closed behind me. I looked down at my hand, and the stone had vanished. A jolt of fear and shock ran through me. Where am I? Looking around at wherever the stone had taken me, it was much like the street I had just been walking on. Somehow though, I knew I was in a different place. I could feel it. I looked around for clues that would tell me where I am. Greenish brown grass sprawled out to my sides. Large brown tree trunks sprang up through the grass reaching towards the sky then branching out into a canopy of green cover. The sidewalk in front of me appeared to be made of same white concrete. The houses though were different from what I was used to. Usually a square box with some siding, windows, doors, and a pitched roof. These houses are shaped like giant silver bubbles that appeared to float over the ground, defying the laws of gravity. No windows, doors, driveways, pitched roofs and no electrical wires overhead. I stood there marveling at the houses. Am I in the future? Panic set in as I realized that I was not sure how to get home from here. Maybe I could ask someone where in the world I am. Looking around me I realize there were no people, cars, dogs or cats scurrying about. Where are the people? I would imagine they have to be here somewhere. Where is all the noise? It was eerily quiet. My heart started a fear induced beat like I was running a race, but I was standing still.

Something tapped me on the head twice. I quickly realized it was liquid as it drained into my hair and I could feel the cool wetness of it on my scalp. I had not noticed the rain coming before the drops hit my head. Then a few drops fell in front of me one-drop blue and another one yellow. What kind of strange place was this? I put my hand up to my head to wipe away those drops that had fallen on me. When I pulled my hand back and looked at it, I saw a smear of purple and green. I looked up to the sky. Darker storm clouds hung in the sky eating away at the bright sunlight. I watched the clouds trying to judge what way the storm is going. A bolt of lightning lit the blackened sky. With my observation of the direction the storm is moving and the bolt of lightning I needed to find shelter. I counted the seconds until I heard the thunder. One Mississippi, two Mississippi, three Mississippi, four Mississippi, then the thunder rattled through me. I had been told that if you count the seconds between seeing the lightning and hearing the thunder that you will know how far away the storm is from you. So, this storm was about four miles away and closing in fast. The need to find cover grew stronger within me. I looked at the silver bubbles but had no idea how I would get in. If I could not find cover soon, I could be struck by lightning and colored the same colors of the rainbow. I was sure the rain would ruin my favorite white tank top. Finally, my feet started to carry me slowly forward down the street. I scanned the area for a place to hide. A clap of thunder behind me made me jump, shoving my fear into overdrive. I started running as the urgency of the situation became real. My heart raced to the pace of my feet. I pushed myself even faster as a building made of brick and mortar appeared at the end of the street. It seemed like it took forever to get to the end of the short city street and to the building. It was an old building, but at least it was not some space age thing. It also appeared to be very abandoned but looked sturdy enough to provide shelter from the storm. I squeezed through a small gap in the chain link fence and jogged over to the front doors feeling relieved, but they were chained and padlocked closed. I jogged to the corner of the building. Looking down the side of the building, there are four garage doors, a regular door then three more garage doors. I decided to check all the doors, but I could not open any of them. I turned the back corner, but there was nothing on the backside of the building. I ran along the back to look at the last side. This was it if I didn't find anything here I was going to have to look somewhere else, and by the time I found something else I would be covered and soaked in a smear of colors. I peered down the side and noticed that one of the windows on this side was cracked open, just enough to climb through. Climbing through the window, I was met by darkness, not pitch black but darker than outside. Dust plumed up around my feet as they touched down on the floor. The dust made me sneeze. I closed the window all the way to keep the rain out. Looking around I found an old computer chair. I wheeled it over to the desk, sat down, leaned back in the chair and propped my feet up on a dusty, dirty desk.

The wind picked up and rattled some loose things outside against the building. It kind of gave me the creeps, but at least I was not out in the storm. It was raining hard now. It was spellbinding to watch. It was like watching a rainbow cry. Occasionally the wind would catch the raindrops just right, and it would hit the window providing a splash of color. Soon the window looked like stained glass, and I could not see out anymore. It was absolutely beautiful when the lightning lit the window. I watched and waited for the storm to pass, but it was clear that it was not going to be one of those quick moving storms. A yawn escaped me. I hate rainy weather it always makes me so tired.

∾CHAPTER 2∾

"What are you doing here?" The gruff disembodied voice said from the darkness, startling me awake.

"I was just trying to get out of the rain. I'm sorry, I will go now." I sprang from the chair and moved quickly towards the window, as I replied to the voice

I put my hand on the window searching for the latch to open the window when the voice came again. "No, once you are here you cannot leave." This time adding a creepy laugh.

I heard and felt his heavy footfalls coming towards me now like a slow and steady heartbeat. Every step he took closer to me echoed through the room, hitting me right in the chest, panic, and fear set in my heart raced, pounding in my ears.

I tried to open the window, but it would not budge, panic and fear rose to a new height within me now. I pushed on the window with all my strength, but still, nothing was happening. I tried one more time to lean into the window with all my weight. The window made a pop noise and started to open. However, it was too late I felt something on my shoulder. I didn't want to look not sure what I would see, visions of the bubble house flashed through my head. Whatever was touching me could be an alien or something else non-humanoid. Curiosity gripped me, and I just had to look. Gnarly looking fingers stained black with grease and grime, nails embedded in the skin, guessing from years and years of biting them greeted me. A jolt of fear ran through me, but for whatever reason, my mind was focused on seeing the rest of what was touching me. I forced my head and eyes to look past the fingers, to the wrist, and up the arm, forcing myself every inch of the way. They were extremely hairy, muscularly thick, with tight skin wrapping around the bones. I assumed from this point that a human man was touching me. When he moved his fingers, I could see each individual muscle ripple. Pressing myself to look farther, I passed the elbow and was to the shoulder when the muscles in his arm rippled again. I was still scared, but at least I knew this was a human and not some alien or god only knows what else. My mind didn't waste any time dreaming up other scenarios. Maybe this is an illusion, and when I looked at his face, it was going to be a big green alien head. Now I was curious and I just had to look and see for myself. Damn this human curiosity! I drew in a slow steadying breath preparing myself to look at his face. Ok, you can do this, I thought, trying to physic myself up. I counted in my head one...two...three. Forcing my head to move and my eyes to look up. I was relieved that he was not a monster or alien and that it was just a regular human just like me. He smiled, and I smiled back. He removed his hand from my shoulder, and I turned to face him. A tiny fragment of relief washed over me. The way his fingers looked suggested to me that he would have been a dirty old person but that was not the case. He was actually a young, clean, and handsome man. He had a boxy looking face with high cheekbones. His eyes though were something to behold. Even in the low light they sparkled like an emerald and looked as though they could light up the night as they twinkled at me. He had long flowing wavy blond hair about shoulder length. It was clean and brushed. He was actually very cute. You know that shy feeling you get when you see a cute guy and he talks to you. The butterflies filled my stomach.

"Hi, my name is Killian. I didn't mean to frighten you, but I could not help myself. I don't get very many visitors these days." He said in a deep husky voice with an apologetic smile. His bright white teeth gleamed at me in the dark.

I was putty in his hands, I had to look away for my brain to work again. My mind began to work again, and it was a rather weird thing for him to say but I dismissed it for now.

"Hi, my name is Lily. No harm done." I stuck my hand out for a handshake. He graciously took my hand and shook it then let it go. "Can you tell me where I am? I have never been here before." I asked remembering the silver bubble houses again. I was hoping that he was kind enough to help me out.

He laughed, an evil laugh, then grabbed my wrist and started pulling me out of the room. I pulled back planting my feet to the floor and leaning back with all my weight trying to break his hold on me. He pulled a little harder making my feet move from their location. I tipped forward throwing myself off balance. I stumbled a few times trying to catch myself before I face planted on the concrete floor. I had no choice but to relying on his grip to help steady myself again. As soon as I was steady, I tried to pull away back, but his grip was just too tight for me to get my arm lose. That didn't stop me from trying though.

I finally found my voice again. "Let me go," I demanded, screaming at the top of my lungs. I hoped that maybe someone would hear me, even though I knew there was no one around.

He didn't reply he just kept dragging me along behind him. It was darker in the hallway, and I could barely make out the shapes of chairs and doorways, and other miscellaneous things that cluttered the hallway. A set of double doors that have little windows in them came into view as we turned a corner. The windows shed very little light into the hallway, not enough to enhance visibility though. The doors resembled something you would see in a hospital surgical room.

Bile rose in my throat as I thought about what he might do to me. I swallowed it back down and tried my voice again. "Where are you taking me? I told you that I was leaving." I said hoping to get him talking again and just maybe I could talk my way out of this somehow. He didn't say anything, not even a backward glance at me.

I wondered what the hell had happened to the friendly person that I had just met. He pulled me through the swinging double doors and out to the center of a room where he finally let me go. I rubbed my wrist, it hurt from the struggling against his grip. He laughed a deep, guttural, disturbing laugh as he took something out of his pocket. It is long, thin, black and appeared to be made of cloth. He started to walk behind me, but I turned towards him, stopping his plan. Whatever he had planned for me I was not going down without a fight. He kept up the charade for two revolutions. We were on the third when he finally gained the advantage that he was looking for. I tripped over my own foot, momentarily losing my balance giving him the edge. Next thing I knew it was blackout dark and my hands were being tied behind my back. Tears fell from my eyes, and my heart pounded in my chest. I had no idea what he was planning on doing to me. A bunch of scenarios ran through my head, most of them ending up with me lying naked and dead in a ditch somewhere or the middle of the swamp while the alligators ate my body.

A rush of adrenaline shot through me, and I found my voice again. "What are you doing? I demand that you let me go right now!" I yelled as loud as I could, hoping still that someone passing by outside would hear me and rush to my aid. Then I remembered that I was in some other place and had not met another soul except for Killian. A thought occurred to me just then that maybe he was an alien wearing human skin suit and that is what he was going to use me for. The idea made me shiver.

"Oh, you do, do you?" He whispered in my ear.

I was not expecting him to be that close. I jumped as his hand touched my half-naked shoulder again. Damn, I wished that I had worn a tee shirt or something else besides a tank top.

"You are free to go anytime you like. That's if you can find your way out of here." He said with a small evil laugh his breath tickling the inside of my ear. Then he removed his hand from my shoulder.

"I promise that if you let me go right now, I won't call the cops," I promised though sobs not knowing if there were even police here.

My whole body shook with fear. However, as I shut my mouth and listened there was nothing in the room except for eerie silence. All I could hear now is a high-pitched ringing in my ears. I stood there shock waves of fear running through me. How did this go so wrong? At first, he seemed like he was a nice man but now I was just hoping to find my way out of here preferably not in a body bag. My felt frozen in the place I stood. I had to figure out how to get my body to react to my mind again. It has been like this since I was a kid fear just completely shut down my body. I knew it would be the death of me someday. I was guessing that today was that day. However, with the room being silent and I could not feel anyone watching me I somehow thawed enough to shuffled my left foot forward. I felt for anything that might be in front of me with my right foot. I could not feel

17

anything except for the floor. I wished I had gotten a better look at what was in this room before he blindfolded me. I knew that there was some big metal equipment somewhere in front of me, but I was not sure how far away or even if I was still pointed towards it. I shuffled my right foot forward this time then stretched out my left foot to feel for anything I came up empty-handed again. However, for whatever reason I was sure that the metal equipment was in front of me, I could feel it, but I was not sure how far away it was. I tried to bring up the mental picture of the layout of the room, I succeeded, but I was not sure how accurate the picture is, it is blurry. I knew though that I had to believe my mind was right. I shuffled my left foot forward again, but still, I couldn't find anything but the floor. I tried again with my right foot than my left foot until I finally found the big metal equipment, small victory. The picture in my mind became more evident at that point, and I knew what way I should run now. I turned to the right and put one foot in front of me to feel if that was the right way and it was because I didn't feel anything. I bolted and ran for the door in the picture in my head. I knew that I was almost at the door, I could feel the slight warmth of the sunlight on my body. Just as I was thinking I was taking my final steps something grabbed me, lifted me off the ground and for a brief moment, I felt like I was flying. I knew it just had to be me though there was no way we could actually fly.

The man's evil laugh is all I could hear in my ears; followed by a breathless "I don't think you are leaving just yet princess."

He set me down on my feet. I could hear his footsteps walking away from me, but then I heard something metal sliding across the concrete floor coming closer and closer until it stopped right next to me. I wanted to run, but my fear froze me in place again. Then I felt his hands on my shoulders trying to push me down to sit. I resisted locking my knees in place trying my best to stand firm. Something cold and hard pushed into the back of my knees hard pushing them forward, making them bend and easier to push me down. Not even a second passed before I was bound to the chair. Everything went silent again, nothing was moving anywhere, and the high-pitched ringing in my ears was back again. My mind overloaded with fear now, I just knew that this was going to be where I would die, in some other dimension tortured by this deranged man. If only I would have never picked that thing up, I would not be in this hell right now. I wanted to start begging for my life but refrained from doing so at this moment, besides I really didn't think that it would do any good. The questions began to flow again. What did this person want from me? How did this go so horribly wrong? I started to struggle against the restraints holding me to the chair, but I was not getting anywhere fast. The only thing happening is the wire or rope cutting into my skin. Pain shot up my arm as my wrist popped under the pressure I was placing on it trying to get free. I tried again then cried out in pain as another jab of pain seared through my arms and the world fell away.

~CHAPTER 3~

Holy shit that is cold! Was my minds first reaction to something cold and wet being dumped over my head. I yelled out and gasped for air. The liquid rolled down my body soaking my clothing. My eyes snapped open instantly, but all I could see was darkness. I thought that I had gone blind until I remembered the damn blindfold. My body started to shiver from being cold I could feel the goosebumps rise and crawl across my skin. I took shallow fast breaths trying to combat the cold.

"Oh good, you're awake," Killian said and let out a bellowing evil chuckle.

He genuinely thought that shit was funny. I wanted to tell him to go to hell, but I bit my tongue for now. I didn't want to make this situation any worse than what it already was. Squeaking of his shoes on the floor let me know that he had walked away. I heard a door open and then close, and I knew that I was alone again, dripping wet and cold. What the hell had been the point of pouring the cold liquid, that I assumed was water, on me? I concluded that he was an evil, evil man that made no sense.

A few minutes passed before I heard a garage door opener whirl to life. The sound of screeching metal wheels in their metal tracks screamed in my ears as it echoed through the room. I would have covered my ears if my hand were free. A burst of air hit me and sent a new wavy of chills over my wet body. I hoped that they would not leave the door open too long it was warmer with the door shut. I heard the doors motor whirl to life again, lowering the screeching wheels back down their tracks. Two sets of footsteps walk towards me now. I could tell one them was Killian, his shoes were still squeaking on the floor. I could hear their voices, but they were whispering to each other.

I could not make out what they were saying, until they got closer to me and said, "Here she is."

One of them touched my shoulder and then lightly ran his fingers over my neck, face and arms. His touch was warm, and I wished that he would pick me up and hold me against him just to warm up. This man's touch was different from Killian's touch. I don't know why but somehow this man felt kind, safe and gentle. He didn't feel evil like Killian did.

"She is perfect, and now she is all his." The man said to Killian, and they both laughed.

"I know the boss has been looking for someone like her. It was extremely hard to save her for him. It was really tempting not to keep her for myself." They both laughed again, Killian more so than the other man.

Then without warning, the whole chair lifted up with me in it. My arm rested against the man soaking up his warmth. Combating the goosebumps on that side of my body. I heard the sound of the garage door motor whirl to life, and the garage door was opening again. I felt a blast of cold air hit me, and it took my breath away for a second. I felt the goosebumps rise and crawl across my skin again, this time not as painful as last time. I heard the click of the car starter then an engine roared to life. I was loaded into what I assumed was a car. Lying on my back still strapped to the chair. The heat was blowing on full blast, and I could feel it combating the cold and my now shivering body. I know that it is summer but the rain earlier had cooled things off to about seventy degrees, to me that is cold. The door shut with a quiet thud then the front door opened which let in a small blast of cold air that I felt on my face, but the heat warmed it quickly. My driver shut the door put the car in drive and turned on some soft violin music, I think it is Bach. However, I could not really tell the volume was only loud enough for me to hear the upper registers of the song.

I wondered for half a second if Killian had sold me to this person and who the boss was that they had referred to. Maybe if I could get him talking he would tell me or, perhaps I could talk him into letting me go.

"Excuse me, can you please tell me where we are going?" I asked in a quiet, polite voice.

However, there was no reply just the sound of the car accelerating and the soft music of the violin. I wanted to know where we were going. I thought just maybe if I knew where I was going I could get out of this mess. My stomach growled with a low rumbling sound, and it was only one more reminder of how I wished I was home and had never picked up that stupid stone.

The car slowed, turned a corner and came to a stop. My driver cut the engine then I heard the car door opened then shut again as he exited the car. I waited for the door by my head to open, but it never did. After a few lonely minutes, the door opened again, and the man got back in the car. The smell of greasy potatoes and some fried chicken wafted in around him. My stomach growled even louder this time, begging for the food. As usual, the man didn't say anything and put the car in reverse, then in drive and accelerated. I could not take it anymore I was starving. I was just about to ask for the food when he stopped the car and got out leaving me there intoxicated by the smell of the food. I was not expecting the door by my head to open so when it did I jumped a little. I heard the paper bag crinkle then something brushed against my lips. I sniffed hoping that it was the food. I could smell grease, salt, and potato, leading me to believe that it was a French fry. I stuck my tongue out to taste it to make sure what was there. Dangerous, yes, but since I had heard the bag crunch, I was sure that it had to be the food. The salt bit into my tongue then a thin layer of grease coated my tongue and I knew that it was a fry. Without another wasted second, I inhaled it. We repeated this motion until the meal was gone. He shut the door and reentered the car's driver seat, and we were off again.

"Thank you for the food," I said hoping that maybe he would talk back to me but again he said nothing and kept driving.

Somewhere in the soft music, full stomach, warmth and hypnotic rhythmic movement of the car I fell asleep. I started dreaming about the world that I used to live in. The tall green grasses blowing in a warm summer breeze and the look and the earthy smell of the coming rain. I was dreaming about a time that my mom and I were at the lake house we rented in Michigan. My mind shifted to my mom, she must be worried sick about me. It was not like me not to come home, especially from the grocery store. The dream morphed into pictures of her smiling and laughing as she chased me around the yard. As fast as they had come, they were gone and the dreams warped into something else. All the beautiful stuff started turning into a terrifying nightmare. All starting with my mom's face turning into a demon like creature. Her kind green eyes replaced by terrifying red glowing ones, the kind that said I am going to eat you alive. Her usually short fingernails turned into long spikes that looked as if they could tear anything apart, even concrete. The image was so horrifying that it startled me awake. I was breathing hard, and my heart felt like it was going to explode. Even with my eyes open, all I could see was the image of her demon face, but it slowly started to fade away after telling myself several times it was just a dream and not real. As I began to calm down, I realized that we were still traveling down the road. I pushed the image hard to the back of my mind placing it under a stack of lovely photos.

I tried to make small talk with the driver again. I just needed a distraction from the nightmare. "Hi there, my name is Lily. What is your name?" Then I waited for a few minutes, but he didn't reply, so I thought I would try something else. "Where are you taking me?" Again, no answer, then I begged him to say something anything. He laughed a very short ha and then stopped. The laugh was so short that I almost missed it. Well, it was evident that I was not going to get anywhere with him. I could probably talk until I was blue in the face but I was sure that he would not answer or speak to me, so I gave up.

My back was starting to hurt, so I started to wiggle around trying to get comfortable again. This was a hard deed being tied to a chair. However, as I wiggled the blindfold began to slip off my head, so I kept wiggling until it completely fell off. The sun was bright, shining through the dark tinted car window making my eyes hurt. I squinted hard for a few minutes, slowly but surely my eyes opened wider and wider. Looking out of the window the only thing that I could see was the treetops whizzing by, and the light blue sky. The sky had no sign of any wispy, puffy or any kind of other clouds in site. I felt like I stared at the sky for forever but somehow, I felt at peace for the time being. After a while, the car started to slow and came to a stop. He turned right and then accelerated again. After what seemed like an eternity, the car slowed again this time making a left. We passed by a huge wrought iron gate as it stood to the side to let us pass. We drove up a very smooth and long driveway lined with huge oak trees. The trees shaded the driveway blocking out most of the sunlight. I am sure if I could see the whole thing it would look like one of those famous pictures of a southern plantation driveway. The driver started to turn to the left, and as he did, a humongous mansion came into view. Tall white pillars reached towards the sky stopping to hold up the balcony of the second floor. Then continuing to hold up the roof that ran the entire length of the front of the mansion. Dormers that boasted beautiful stained-glass windows broke up the roof line making the mansion more eye appealing. White railings ran between the pillars of the second-floor balcony and along the porch on the first floor. Planters overflowing with beautiful purple flowers reached down to the ceiling of the first-floor porch and swayed in the gentle breeze. The railing on the first floor carried the same stunning purple flowers. The purple flowers helped to break up the tan colored brick exterior. The front door is a site all within its self. Huge intricately carved wood doors surrounded by flower etched windows, you would have to see it to truly see its beauty. I would have given anything to live in a house like this back in my world. The home of my dreams. My mom and I had enough money to sustain us, and we lived comfortably but could never afford anything like this.

My driver got out of the car, and I could see now that he was dressed in a long-sleeved tee shirt and wore a baseball cap. His short black hair stuck out from under his hat. His black long-sleeved tee shirt fit tight on him showing off his muscles. I was hoping that he would turn around so that I could see his face, but he didn't and walked away from the car. I watched out of the window waiting for him to appear but there was nothing. I wondered where he had gone. Was he just going to leave me here? The inside of the car was starting to get hot, and I felt like I was beginning to suffocate. Then all of a sudden, the car door opened quickly, and before I could make out anything, the blindfold was back in place, and I could not see anything again. Ugh, this was so frustrating. Then the chair and I were hauled out of the car just as gently as when I had been put in the car. He untied me from the chair but then tied my hands behind my back and my feet together and threw me over his shoulder and was carrying me somewhere. I heard a door open, and I knew then that he must be taking me into the house, or at least that is what I was hoping. Someone greeted him at the door, I could hear him or her breathing, but no words were exchanged. He started walking again and by the way that it felt and sounded we were going up some stairs. Then I assumed down a hallway by the echo his shoes made on the floor. He stopped and opened a door. When he took me into the room, the smell of bleach permeated my nose, making it burn. The bleach smell quickly faded though giving way to the sweet scent of roses. He set me down gently on something very soft. I sank into it a bit, my fingertips could feel something soft. I let my fingers search for other clues of what I might be sitting on, but there was nothing, no hard or soft back to a chair, just absolute emptiness. The fear swelled in me as I realized that I must be sitting on a bed. What was he going to do to me? Images of rape, blood, and dead people flashed through my head. I started to sob uncontrollably. This was it, the end of my life. I wanted to escape but my hands and feet were still bound, and I could not find the door if I wanted to with this blindfold on. If this room was something that I had seen before the mental picture could have helped me get out. I took a few gulps of air trying to calm myself. I had to try to believe that I was going to be ok. I even repeated it in my head a few times. *Everything is going to be ok. I am going to get out of this.*

I heard the door open, and someone's light footsteps walked into the room. There were no words exchanged and now no more movements. The only thing I could feel was eyes staring at me. I wanted to move because they were making me uncomfortable, but I sat still as a statue my fear holding me there. I wanted to say something but could not get my voice to work, the same fear holding me still now captured my voice. I could not get out the words I wanted to say. *When, where and what are you going to do to me?*

A small knock on the door broke the staring from whoever was staring at me. Then someone with heavier footsteps walked into the room. There were still no words exchanged, this person with the heavier footsteps was in then out of the room quickly. A small draft swirled around me, and I knew that the door had been left open. I could try to run I thought. I didn't hear anyone else in the room, and the eyes that had been boring into me were gone. I bounced up from my seated position with the help of the bed's springs. I tried to shuffle my feet forward, but this only resulted in me falling. I would have done a face plant on the floor, but I was mindful enough that my hands were still tied and threw my shoulder to rotate my body. Even despite all the noise I had made there was still silence in the room. No one had rushed in or moved to help me. I rolled over on my stomach, using my forehead and knees, I managed to sit up on my knees. Now I just needed to get from my knees to my feet. I moved my left knee in front of me. To my surprise, it seemed to be easier than trying to get to my feet. I also noticed that it was more stable than trying to walk on my bound feet. I shuffled my right knee forward until the binding rose up my calf muscle and started to cause pain. It didn't matter to me how I got across the floor the only thing that mattered was just that I needed to make it. But, where are you going? My conscience asked me. While I was pondering the question, I kept moving forward and decided the answer to that didn't matter right now. I lurched forward as I lost my balance banging my head on something very hard and unforgiving. I rolled onto my side and could feel the ache of the blood pooling under my skin. Then I could feel the blood start running from the cut. I moaned out in pain. Hands on my shoulders gently flipped me on to my back then cradled my head. Something wet touched my forehead where the blood had run. Slowly edged its way towards the cut that was still spilling blood all over. Then I realized whatever was sopping up my blood was not abrasive like a cloth. Whatever was touching me was soft and slightly wet. A sound similar to a dog drinking water caught my attention. It was at that moment I knew what I felt was a tongue licking my wound. What kind of sick, sadistic, twisted person licks someone's blood? The tongue

licked over the wound again that was it for me,
everything faded to black.

∾CHAPTER 4∾

When I awoke, I tried to move but quickly realized I had been tied up. Both my arms stretched upward and out to the sides with each wrist bound by what felt like thick leather straps. I extended my fingers up wrapping them around a taunt, scratchy, thick ropes. I pulled hard on the ropes, but there was no give in either of the ropes or anchors. I gave up on pulling quickly and decided to try my feet. Not quite sure what I would do with my feet but I was sure something would eventually come to me. However, I found my feet are bound in the same manner as my hands. There was a little more slack in these ropes that allowed me more movement, but not enough to get a good jerk to see if the rope would break. Using my stomach muscles, I pulled with all my strength on all restraints at once, hoping that something would break, but nothing happened. This rope was not anything that would be broken easily and whatever I was tied to was solid. The more I thought about it, the more I realized I was actually quite comfortable. This led me to believe I was tied to a bed. Before I could dwell on that little piece of information, I wondered if anyone was in here with me. I lay there completely still now just listening for signs of someone anyone, but all I could hear was the deafening silence of the house. The silence was so loud it seemed as though my head was going to explode. Speaking of my head, the wound pulsed with pain. The memory of the tongue licking my wound came back to me. I thought about how strange it was. Gentle like a kiss but it also seemed to take the pain away. I had no explanation in my mind of how that worked, or maybe my brain had just made up the last part. Then without warning horror struck me, what if this was some sick twisted game and these people were cannibals and just tasted me to see if I tasted good. On the other hand, maybe they would make me bleed on purpose to fulfill some weird blood fetish. This made me cry out in fear. Right now I just hoped that they would end this quickly if that were their intentions. I wondered how long my body could take being bled and how long it would take for me to die. Could I really endure this for months? The thought of them being cannibals resurfaced, and I wondered if they would knock me out before they started to cut up my body, or did they want to hear me scream. I gasped at the thought and cried out again. A sharp pain crossed my forehead from the wound as I scrunched my forehead as the tears pricked my eyes.

My cries caught the attention of someone because the door opened. I heard the light footsteps come into the room and for the first time, he spoke to me.

"Don't cry, my child… Don't cry everything will be ok." His voice sounded soothing somehow.

I could tell it was a man by the deep throatiness of his voice. Even though his voice sounded strained, it was even more soothing and welcoming somehow when he spoke again.

"Can I get you anything?" He asked after a few seconds. His words were light and quiet like his footsteps.

"You can get me the hell out of here!" I snapped back shouting with all my anger, fear and frustration as my emotions finally outweighed his soothing tones.

"Yes, I know you would like to go home, but you are mine now. So please let me make you as comfortable as possible." He said not changing his tone and ran one finger down my cheek trying to soothe me again.

I was repulsed by his touch but really could not do anything about it. His words stuck out to me now, what did he mean that I was his? I let it fall away for now deciding to ask about other things that were more important to me. "Ok, then can I be untied? And, can we please do something with this blindfold? Oh, and I'm hungry and thirsty." I snapped back, but I quickly gave up on being so angry and started to sound a bit nicer when I got to the hungry and thirsty part. I was hoping that if I dropped the anger, he would do at least one of the things I was requesting.

"One thing at a time, one thing at a time." He said in the same hushed voice still trying to calm me, stroking my face with his hand. "To answer your first question, no I don't think that is a good idea just yet. For your second question, the blindfold should stay just for a little bit longer. For your third question, I will have someone bring some food so that I may feed you."

I heard him get up and walk lightly to the door. He opened it and then closed it without saying anything more. He was only gone for maybe two seconds when I heard the door open, and his footsteps enter the room again. He sat on the bed next to me again this time lightly caressed the back of my hand but not say anything. Then he gently touched the wound on my forehead, the touch was so light I barely felt it. "That is a horrible gash I will have someone look at it."

Then he said nothing and I was about to break the silence between us but heard a knock on the door and whoever it was entered the room without a word being said. I heard something being set down on a nearby table and it sounded like dishes by the way that they slightly rattled against each other. Then in a matter a second, I could smell the food. It smelt delicious, I wished my hands were untied, and I could just start eating it right now. If I were untied, I would have forgone the fork and spoon and just used my hands to stuff huge bites into my mouth. I heard the person's heavy footsteps leave the room and then his voice broke the silence between us.

"I hope you like it. I have some chicken, corn and mashed potatoes. I will feed it to you in small bites." He said and then curled one hand behind my head lifting my head up a tad. "Are you ready?"

I nodded in response and opened my mouth wide. I pictured a baby bird's mouth wide-open waiting for momma to feed it. I hoped it was not scorching hot as he placed a bite of chicken in my mouth. It was tender, juicy and practically melted in my mouth. It tasted a lot like a rotisserie chicken. Herbs with a hint of lemon flavor flooded my taste buds. It was delightful and left me wanting more. As soon as I chewed and swallowed I opened my mouth for more. He placed another fork full in my mouth. I chewed the food quickly, swallowing it, and opening my mouth for more. He obliged and on we went until it was all gone. Then he placed a straw next to my mouth, and I gulped down the water.

"Thank you." I said in a small tired, but a content voice.

"You are most welcome." He sighed in relief. "I can hear that you are tired and you should sleep now."

I wanted to protest, but my eyes were heavy with sleep again. I didn't want to go to sleep I wanted to ask questions about what he was going to do with me. Just before my mind shut down, I wondered if they put some kind of sleep aid in my food so that I would be calm. There is no way that I should be tired, but before I could say anything, everything went black.

∽CHAPTER 5∽

I awoke to a sharp jabbing pain in my arm. I screamed as the pain became too intense to bear. However, as fast as it had started, it went away with no lingering pain. This was curious to me. Did I dream the pain I wondered? No, I could not have I thought. But, I still felt groggy and convinced myself that I had imagined it. I listened carefully to see if anyone was there just to be cautious but didn't hear anything. My heavy eyelids carefully caressed me back to sleep.

When I slept, I dreamt about my mom and her beautiful green eyes. Her long dark locks that framed her sweet, innocent, happy face perfectly. I reached for her hand and took it in mine like when I was a kid. We walked down a sidewalk, me skipping along to keep up with her hurried pace. I was skipping and whistling a television show tune, the one that belonged to Jeopardy to be precise. I didn't see the unleveled sidewalk and tripped scraping my knees on the hard-unforgiving concrete sidewalk. Ouch, that hurt and I started to cry. My mom, however, stood there unmoving and almost like stone. This was not her usual response to me getting hurt. I looked up, my mom had morphed into some kind of monster. Her eyes black elliptical orbs that seemed not to see anything. However, her face was the same. Her skin was pale like it always had been. Her nose was still small and pointy. Her cheekbones raised and perfectly holding her eye sockets. The only difference is her eyes. I tugged on her arm and screamed out "mommy, mommy. Can you hear me?" She didn't move just stood still. I tried to free my hand to get in front of her to shake her. Maybe she would wake up. However, I could not remove my arm from her grip. Let me go I demanded but still nothing. I started looking around to find help, but it was deserted not a sole in site. Finally, after I had given up trying to get free, a car sped around the corner. I stood perfectly still not really knowing if I should flag them down or let them pass. It looked like a police car, so I decided to flag them down. I put my free arm up in the air and started jumping up and down to get their attention. It worked the car came to a screeching halt. It took a few seconds for anyone to get out of the car. When they finally got out, they had masks that covered their faces. One person yelled at the other "get the kid." As the person approached, I became scared. I had made a mistake. The closer he got I could see that the mask not only covered his face but also covered his eyes. I could not make out anything about this person's, or things face except where the nose is. "No, get away from me." I screamed, but I was ignored. The person was standing in front of us now, reaching for my arm that my mom was holding onto. Then he had me in his grip. His hold on my arm was so strong, it felt as though it would crush my bones if I moved just right. Nothing was said, and my mom's hand let me go. The next thing I knew it was dark and I was screaming and screaming hoping that someone, anyone would hear me. I must have been screaming in real life because the screaming jolted me from my sleep. My eyes popped open, but all I could see was darkness. I was hyperventilating and drenched in sweat. I tried to move one of my hands to wipe the sweat from my face, but it was no use I was still tied up.

I felt a hand on my leg, it startled me, and I jumped. "Are you alright?" He asked quietly, brushing the sweat from my forehead for me. "Your wound is looking good it is not going to leave a scar or anything."

It took me a long second to recover my voice. "No, no, no, I'm not alright." I said getting louder with every no.

I struggled with the restraints again trying to get up. I didn't care if he saw me or not. He put a cold, clammy hand on my arm this time to stop me from pulling. I pulled hard one more time but then relaxed.

"You are fine, I'm here with you. No one can hurt you now." He said in a soft whisper.

The voices in my head were not ok with what was happening to me.

"What can I do to make it better?" He asked in a soft but pained whisper.

He really was asking me this question again. "For starters, you can let me go." I said, and the voice that protruded from me sounded more like a snarl, with a menacing bite to it. I waited a moment for a response, but he said nothing. I knew he was still there because I could feel his hand on my leg. I calmed myself a little fighting back any urges to sound venomous this time. Maybe if I played nice, he would give me a little more freedom. "Okay, okay, I know that you are not going to let me go." But can we at least take off the blindfold so that I can see your face?" I ask, but again he didn't answer. I decided to try for something different. "Can I have a shower? Can you at least let one of my limbs go?"

I felt his hand lift from my leg my heart sinking thinking he was going to leave. However, moments later his hand gently rested on my face. I stopped all questioning, in hopes that maybe he had some compassion and was actually going to do one of the things I asked. He touched the blindfold lightly, tracing the outline with his fingers. I got excited thinking that he was going to remove it and at least I could see but instead his hand moved away, my heart fell. Then I felt his fingers tracing the restraint on my left arm I got my hopes up again, but he moved on to my right arm and traced that restraint there, but still didn't do anything. He moved down to my ankles and traced the restrains there too. My left ankle was the last place he touched. He took his hand away, and I could feel nothing touching me but knew he was still there. I could feel his eyes staring at me and wished that I could see his face maybe I could tell what he was thinking.

"Please." I begged, hoping that he would at least do something. Instead, he got up and softly walked away from me. I heard him fiddle with the door handle, and I knew he was going to leave.

In a last-ditch effort, I called after him. "Please, don't go." I say in the kindest, sweetest voice I could muster. Then when he didn't respond I begged again, the tears started to roll from my eyes soaking the blindfold. It was no use though. I heard the door open then the soft click of the door latch as the door shut.

I started furiously pulling at the restraints at my hands and feet. I heard the bed groaning under my every move. I was trying everything I could to get free, but nothing worked. Somehow, in the struggling, the blindfold started to slip off. I carefully pulled myself up, careful not to touch the back of my head on the pillow. I hoped that this would keep the blindfold from rolling back down. Now that I was up as high as the restraints would let me go I firmly planted my head on the pillow and pressed down as hard as I could. Pulling my body down with my legs, the blindfold rolled up a little more. Finally, after a couple of times of doing this, the blindfold was at the top of my head. I pushed my chin up and worked the blindfold the rest of the way loose. Then shook my head side to side to get it off my face and finally, the blindfold was off.

It was so bright in the room my eyes burned. I had to squint really hard to keep most of the light out until my eyes could adjust to the light. After a few seconds, I forced my eyes to open fully. Yes, it hurt my eyes as my pupils dilated but everything became clearer. The restraints holding me in place were tied to a canopy bed. The pillars on this bed were as big around as a medium size tree trunk. There was no way I was going to break free from them. Even though the pillars were robust, they boasted a beautiful ivy vine and leaf pattern. The vines and leaves ran up to the top of the pillar where there was a Greek Corinthian style capital. On top of the capitals sat cross beams, they looked more like crown molding right out of the renaissance era. Draped over the canopy was red satin material that hung over the sides but only hung down about a quarter of the way. The headboard was also made of solid wood with the same ivy vine and leaf pattern on it. In the middle of the headboard was a circle but I could not make out what was in the circle at the moment. This bed looked like it belonged to a king. The same red satin material of the canopy also made up the sheets. The white pillow like comforter lay underneath me giving me extra cushion from what I could see. The rest of the room decorated in old World Victorian era facade. To my left and below my feet glass walls stood running from the floor to the ceiling. A Victorian style couch the same red color as the canopy sat facing the windows. The sofa appeared to be made of velvet instead of satin though. This couch sat between the bed and the huge windows and looked perfect for relaxing and reading. To my right wide double doors stood taking up most of that wall. The doors were shut, and I assumed that this was the entrance to this room. The doors looked old, thick and heavy but had a very detailed delicate carving on them of flowers and more ivy vines. The wall the headboard was on, had a door to my left halfway between the bed and windows. To my right on the same wall, a door tucked almost in the corner between the double doors and the bed. The walls were painted white, and from what I could see of the floor, it was dark wood that matched the bed.

I heard footsteps outside the door. My head snapped in the direction of the door but whoever it was didn't come in right away.

"Close your eyes." He commanded.

"And if I don't?" I spat back at him not wanting to close my eyes for a second now that I could see.

"Well if you don't then I will be forced to make you wear it again." He barked back at me mimicking my tone. For the first time, it sounded like he was getting testy with me.

Without saying another word, I closed my eyes. It was so hard not to open them as he sat on the edge of the bed. He lightly brushed my arm with his hand and mumbled something incoherent under his breath.

"How are you?" He asked still lightly stroking my arm. The sensation tickled slightly, but I tried to ignore it so that I would not burst into laughter.

"I'm fine." I replied keeping any and all sarcasm and anger from my voice. The light strokes on my arm helped me to achieve this.

He was silent. I think that he was waiting for me to yell and scream like I had been doing. I just didn't feel like doing that anymore besides it was not getting me anywhere. Even though my eyes were closed, I still felt freer than I had been in what seemed like weeks. I didn't want to do anything that would jeopardize him putting the blindfold back on me.

"I want to try something." He said and then placed a finger on my cheek tracing the outline of my eyes with one finger.

It was so hard to keep my eyes closed, but I managed to squeeze them to keep them shut. Then as if he had been called away, he was gone in a flash. I knew I could open my eyes when I heard the door shut. I thought about how bizarre it was that he wanted to try something then ran away without saying another word.

I stared out the window for a short time before I heard a knock on the door. I immediately clamped my eyes shut just in case it was him. However, I could tell by the footfalls that it was not him and I opened my eyes. A big burly woman stood beside me holding a tray. I could smell the mixed palate of food emanating from it. The smells that stuck out the most are roasted potatoes and chicken, yum.

The woman was dressed in a plain light green dress and wore a white apron over the dress. Her hair braided in long thick pigtails. She looked like a Viking maiden. The only thing missing was the metal helmet with horns sticking out of it. I stifled a giggle, as I imagined her wearing the Viking helmet. She peered down at me with her big brown eyes. I smiled back at her kindly. I had to say something to break the ice.

"Is that for me?" I asked, but she didn't speak she just nodded.

"Are you going to feed that to me?" I asked and pulled on the restraints to reinforce the idea that I could not do it by myself. She still didn't speak and just shook her head no.

I tried one last time to get her to say anything, anything at all. "My name is Lily." I said and smiled at her again. She just stared at me blankly, set the tray down and started for the door.

"Wait please don't go. I'm starving, and the food smells so good." She hesitated at the door slightly but then exited without saying anything or glancing back at me.

A few seconds later, the door opened, and his voice rang through the room. "Close your eyes."

I did as I was told because I knew that he was there to feed me and my stomach agreed with my decision. He didn't say anything as he sat on the edge

44

of the bed. I heard him pick up the spoon and carefully scooped something off the ceramic plate. The bite of food entered my mouth, roasted potatoes with a hint of herbs and spices, yum. The hunger in my belly was starting to fade just after one bite. Since he would be busy feeding me, now was my opportunity to get a quick look at him. I just had to know what he looked like. I waited for the right opportunity. He placed a bite of food in my mouth, and I knew that he would be looking at the plate to scoop up some more food, this was my chance. I cracked my eyelids open ever so slightly, and though my vision was a little blurry trying to see through my eyelashes, I could tell he was gorgeous. I didn't get too many details about him though because I had to close my eyes again quickly as he started towards me with another bite of food. What I did see was his long, straight and as black as coal hair. His eye seemed to sparkle in the dim light. I wished that I could have seen their color. His face was clean-shaven. The profile of his nose was small and fit his face well. For whatever reason, that little glimpse of him excited me. I didn't mind being his prisoner right now. I mean really, he had taken care of me for the most part and has not tried to do me any harm so what should I be scared of. I decided that maybe I should try and talk to him when I was done eating. I would do it now, but it would be rude and very un-ladylike to speak with a mouth full of food.

"Last bite." He sang to me.

I chewed and swallowed it quickly so that I could talk to him before he left me again. "I think we may have gotten off on the wrong foot. I was, and am, scared because I don't have any idea what you are going to do with me or to me. I am hoping that we could start again. My name is Lily." I said dubiously. "May I ask you, kind sir, what your name is?" A long moment passed before he answered me. I'm sure he was trying to figure out my angle.

"I guess I don't see any harm in telling you my name." He said pausing again.

I'm sure he was thinking about the consequences of telling me something as simple as his name. What could I possibly do with just a name? Was he worried that I had heard of him before? In the quick glimpse that I caught of him, I was sure that I didn't know who he was.

"My name is Lucian Stratton." He said pulling me for my questioning in my mind. He touched my hand and traced my long skinny fingers with one of his fingers. "Can I get you anything?" He asked sweetly.

I didn't have to think about what I wanted. I knew what I wanted and that was to be let go, but I knew that was not going to happen. However, maybe I could convince him of a bath or shower, maybe one hand or foot lose. I decided to try for something that would get me completely free first.

"I would really like a shower or bath." I said pausing then quickly following up with. "I will be good, I promise, I will not give anyone a hard time. I will not try to escape. Please." I begged, sticking out my lips to pout. Hoping that would win him over. I wished that I could see his face again to see what he was thinking.

"Ok, I will let you take a bath. If you are lying to me, you will be caught, and this time your capture will not be so nice. I trust you will do the right thing. Please don't let me down. I would really like to keep you around for a while. I do need something from you before I will let you do this though." He said with an undertone to his voice that I didn't quite understand. However, I ignored it as my mind jumped to the fact that he was going to let me go.

"Sure anything." I replied without hesitation. Then I thought better of it. I should not have promised that I would do anything. I could be sealing my death certificate.

"Ok hold still and keep your eyes shut. This may hurt a little bit. It will be quick I promise." He said.

He grasped my hand and my elbow gently in both of his strong hands. In the middle of my forearm, I felt two pricks of pain but if I focused on something else I could ignore it. It was like getting a shot. My curiosity was sparked, and I wondered what kind of drugs he was giving me, but I didn't feel anything enter my body. Then I thought that maybe he was a doctor taking my blood to run tests on it, the thought of an alien crossed my mind again. Then another thought occurred to me, maybe, he was putting stuff in my food and needed a blood sample to check the dosage. Oh, I so badly wanted to open my eyes and see what the hell he was doing but knew that if I did the trust that I had just built with him would be gone. Then I surely would be stuck here until I die or he kills me. After a few short seconds, he gently let my arm go massaging the area gently.

"Are you ok?" He asked.

"Yes, I'm fine. But what were you doing?" I asked.

He didn't answer then I felt something wet on my lips. It was not a lot and didn't taste bad. However, I instantly forgot about the question that I had asked him and all of a sudden, I needed to sleep.

My dream consisted of him chasing me through the woods. We must have been playing because I didn't feel like I was in danger in the dream. He caught me, slung me over his shoulder, and climbed to the top of a one-hundred-foot-high tree. This may be slightly exaggerated I am not good at guessing heights all I knew is that it was very high. At the top, he wrapped his arms around me then leaned in for a kiss.

∾CHAPTER 6∾

"Lily, Lily, Lily." Someone was yelling at me and shaking me. My eyes popped open without even thinking about if it was Lucian or not. To my relief, the Viking woman was waking me. She started towards my left hand to undo the buckle on my leather bracelet.

She hesitated for a moment looking down at me. "He told me to run you a bath and that you promised that you would be good. Please don't make me hurt you." She said in a husky voice that sounded like it should have come from a man, not a woman.

She eyed me, and I could see in her eyes that she was not kidding she would hurt me if need be. My conversation with him came back to me. I had promised him that I would be good.

"That is true." I said after a few moments of silence.

With my confirmation of what I had told Lucian, she finished untying my arm. She gently and carefully helped me put my arm down to my side. My shoulder ached from being stretched above my head for so long. She moved down to my feet and untied them. In the meantime, I was trying to make my spaghetti noodle arms to move around. I found that I was stiff from laying here like this for days or had it been weeks I was not sure anymore how long it had been. She had both of my feet free by the time I got my arm to start cooperating with me. With great effort, I brought my knees up so that my feet were flat on the bed. All my joints ached now. I wanted to roll to my side and get off my back, but this was going to take the most effort to do. I started rocking my body back and forth building up momentum. I swung my right leg over my left making my hips all the way up to my shoulders follow. Finally, I tried to sit up but failed. Everything ached, groaned, and cracked at me protesting the movement. The Viking women disappeared into the door on my left leaving me laying there. I heard the water running and knew that she was getting my bath water started. It was going to feel so good on my aching body.

I placed my hand flat on the bed and pushed with all that I had to get my body upright. As I sat up my head, started pounding and things began to spin. I fought the urge to lay back down. I slowly made progress, my feet dangling over the edge of the bed now. The Viking lady walked back into the room, she eyed me for a moment then offered a hand to me. I graciously took it. She pulled me to my feet letting my hand go quickly then stared at me. Now that I was standing on my feet I could feel the weight of my body pulling on every joint. It is kind of like when you have the flu, and all your muscles and bones ache. I took a step and about fell flat on my face, but she caught me. She took my arm, wrapped it around her shoulders, her other arm wrapped around my waist, and she helped me walk to the bathtub. She carried most of my weight for me.

Steam rolled off the white cloud of bubbles coupled with the scent of roses, it looked so inviting. She looked at me again, and without saying a word, she let me go. I stood there feeling the full weight of my body on my legs again. I just wanted to sit down, but I forced my legs to hold me for now. I stripped off my plain supposed to be a white tee shirt, that I had no idea where it had come from, and threw it on the floor. I hoped that I didn't have to put it back on it smelled horrible. I took my bra off and threw it on top of the shirt. I slid the sweatpants down along with my underwear to the floor, again having no idea where they came from. I stared at the pile of dirty clothing wondering how long I had been wearing them, and how I had gotten them on in the first place. The thought quickly passed and was replaced with embarrassment, I was standing naked in front of someone that I didn't know. I put my arm and hand over my breasts trying to cover them. My other hand was covering my area, region, woo-hoo, my lady parts. All I wanted is to hurry up and get in the bubbly water for cover, but it was not ready yet. I had not realized that I had been staring into the water trying to shut out the embarrassment until she shut off the water and cleared her throat to get my attention. I looked over at her as she gestured for me to climb in. She turned her back towards me giving me privacy. I put one foot in the water, I could feel the stinging, burning sensation, the water is hot. Not hot enough to cause actual burns though. The hot water was turning my skin red, but it felt good at the same time on my aching bones and muscles. I slowly sank down into the water letting the heat sink into and relax my body.

I closed my eyes, sunk all the way down, and let the water cover my face for a few seconds. When I emerged, I started looking around the room. The room was painted white. Three huge windows ran from the ceiling to the floor overlooking a forest. Tall trees boasted a thick green canopy of leaves. Then I notice there were not any window coverings. I guessed they figured the windows didn't need it because one, we were on the second floor or higher and two, the trees blocked any direct views in or three, the window was one-way glass, I could see out, but no one could see in. The bathtub was not like anything I had ever seen before. Well maybe except in a magazine once but I had never seen one in real life let alone sat in one. There was enough space in this tub for four people, and it sat in the middle of the room. The water was filled to the top, and it was deep enough for me to sit upright and the water would still cover my breasts. I noticed the water spill over the edge of the tub as I moved. Out of habit, I check to see if there was a towel on the floor to soak up the water that I had sloshed. Then I noticed that the tub would take care of its own overflow through the stone ledge that lined the outside of the tub. The porcelain or whatever material it was made from felt smooth under me. To my left dark wood cabinetry held up two glass bowl sinks with huge mirrors that had flowers etched around the outside. The two glass sinks were held up by a beautiful black with white veined granite counter top. To my right, there was empty space and just the door. Behind me was a massive shower with a glass front. The inside was covered in the same black and white granite. The shower looked like you could fit four or five people in it. The bathroom was every girl's dream except it was missing some varying tones of pink. Just in front of the shower on the left side was a door. I wondered where the door led to. I wished I could go look but the bath was still hot and I was not ready to get out. Movement by the windows caught my attention, and I found myself staring out the window watching the clouds race across the sky and a slight breeze making the treetops sway. It was hypnotizing and peaceful to watch. A knock on the bathroom door surprised me, and I jumped with a gasp.

"Lily, are you ok?" Lucian asked from the other side of the door.

"Yes, yes, I'm fine." I answered back immediately not wanting him to think for one second that I was being bad.

"Ok, I was just checking on you." He said.

"Do you want me to get out now?" I asked trying to be on my best behavior. If I wanted to escape, I was going to have to try to play my cards right.

"No, you are fine, please take your time. I will be waiting for you when you get out. I have a surprise for you." He said

What could he have for me I wondered. While I wondered, I began to wash. When I was done, I asked Viking lady for my towel she obliged handing it to me. As I dried, the towel ran across two scabs where Lucian had stuck me with something earlier. I thought about it for a second but then moved on quickly. I hoped that my surprise awaiting me was a chance to go home.

I wrapped the towel around myself then looked down at the pile of dirty clothes. "Do you know if I have another set of clothes? Or do I need to put these ones back on?" I asked the Viking lady as I pointed to the clothing on the floor.

She didn't say anything but pointed to a red dress that was hanging on the back of the door. It was a plain red satin dress, and it looked more like a fancy nightgown than a dress. I looked at the tag sewn in the dress, not a name I recognized but it was my size, and I slid it on. It fit my long skinny frame well. I opened the door that went into my room. He was standing there as promised with his back to the door. I immediately clenched my eyes shut, tilting my head to the floor. Viking lady unplugged the tub and gently pushed past me. His hands were on me after she left the room. He touched my shoulders and my wet hair. Then he touched my face and gently and slowly trailed his fingertips down my neck circling a couple of times. Then with one finger, he traced the top of my collarbone out to the edge of my shoulder and back up to my face. His touch was so light that it tickled a bit. The whole time though I was good and kept my eyes closed. He spun me around so that my back was up against him. He wrapped both arms around me. His body was hard against mine but soft at the same time. When he had me securely wrapped up, he made me walk a few feet then stopped.

He leaned down and whispered in my ear. "You may open your eyes when you want to. I should warn you though what you see maybe scary."

I was so scared that I decided that I didn't want to see his surprise anymore and kept my eyes clamped shut. What if I opened my eyes and my beautiful room hand been transformed into a torture chamber. What if...

"Are you going to look or not?" He said, sounding like he was growing impatient.

I slowly peaked out of one eye. In front of me was a mirror. Ok, this is not so bad, so I opened both of my eyes. I saw me standing there in the beautiful red nightgown. I saw his arms folded around my midsection. I took in all of me in the mirror from my feet up to my head. I was kind of hoping that I would see him in the mirror but he was hiding behind me, and all I could see was his black hair sticking out just above my headline.

"See how beautiful you are!" He said into my hair.

I nodded not sure, where he was going with this.

"Someone as beautiful as you should not be tied to a bed. They should be able to enjoy this little space you have here. If you promise that, you will be good I will not tie you back to the bed. As soon as you are ready, I will let you know who I am. I still expect you to close your eyes when I'm here." He said and lifted one hand from my waist and put it over my eyes.

I got the hint that I was supposed to close my eyes now and did. He removed his hand from my face resting it on my shoulder for a moment before sliding it down my arm grabbing my hand. His other hand and arm slowly fell down my back as he led us away from the mirror. Gently he guided me across the room and carefully sat me down on a chair or couch by the feel of it. It felt so good to be sitting up.

"Can I ask you a question?" I asked unsure if I should or not.

"Of course, you may." He said

He was being so nice, and I hesitated to ask my question, but I just needed to know. "I'm just wondering what you are going to do with me? I mean are you going to kill me. I'm just terrified and am hoping that you can help me overcome this fear." I said hoping that he would give me some sort of answer. He sighed heavily, and a jolt of fear ran through me. Scared that I might have angered him, I quickly said. "I'm sorry, I just…"

"No, it is quite ok." He said interrupting me. I understand what you must be going through. However, the answer to your questions lies within you. Well, I must be going now. I will see you in a little while." He said and brushed my cheek with his hand. This startled me a bit, and I jumped. He giggled at my reaction.

The door opened, closed and I opened my eyes. I got up from the chair, walked over to the window, and stared out at the night sky. It was so dark here, only the silvery light of the moon lit the room enough for me to see the shadows of things, so I didn't trip over them. I don't know how long I stood there, but I had watched the moon float from one side of the room to the other. I decided it was time to get some sleep. I didn't go to bed though, I grabbed the comforter and a pillow off the bed and curled up on the sofa. It didn't take me long to fall into a deep sleep.

~CHAPTER 7~

Small noises in my room awakened me from the best sleep I had had since I had been here. No dreams just sleep. I could not tell who was there. I knew I was not supposed to see him, so I stared out the window not saying or moving a muscle anything. As my eyes adjusted to the light and I looked closer into the window that was acting like a mirror now. The image of the room was very faint, so faint that it gave the person in my room a ghostly appearance. I could not tell if it was Lucian at first, but when the man turned, I knew it was not him. This man wore a beard on his face that was big and bushy. I could not make out exactly what he was doing, but I knew now that the small noises were coming from him.

Then I heard Lucian call to me. "Close your eyes." I did, and within a second, I could feel his hand on my face softly caressing it. "Give me your hand." he said. I raised my hand, and he clasped it in his. Then he pulled me to my feet and wrapped his arms around me. "Come we shall dance."

Music that I didn't recognize started to play. It was a string orchestra playing a sweet slow-paced piece. It sounded amazing. He slowly twirled me around once, it was hard to keep my eyes closed and not get dizzy.

When he pulled me in close to his body again, I confessed to him. "I don't really know how to dance."

"I will teach you." He said softly back in my ear with his arms around me. "You are a beautiful dancer so far."

I stifled a laugh, I knew that was not true. He released me into a slow spin and then pulled me close to his body. He leaned me back on one arm, leaned in, and kissed my neck. He continued trailing kisses down my throat and along my collarbone. He pulled me up and pulled me in close to him again. I could smell him. He smelt like the woods at dusk. It was tantalizing and calming all at the same time. I could have stayed right there smelling him for forever keeping time with the music though he sent me away again. Pulled me close one last time before leading me to a chair and sitting me down while the song came to a crashing close.

"Thank you for the dance." He said softly.

"Who is this?" I asked without skipping a beat. I felt like he was going to leave again but for whatever reason, I didn't want him too.

"This is Escala." He said

"I really like it. Can you stay? I would like to get to know you better." I said.

I could not believe the words coming out of my own mouth. I was asking my captor who's face I could not see. Also, the same person who didn't answer my question to wither he was going to kill me or not. The only answer I had gotten out of him was that it was up to me if he killed me or not to stay. What the hell was I thinking? Oh, that is right I had to gain his trust in hopes of getting a little more freedom to make my escape easier.

He hesitated but finally, I heard him sit down to my left. "What would you like to know?" he asked sounded guarded and unsure if he wanted to sit through my line of questioning.

Without saying anything, I rose from my chair and slowly felt my way to where I thought he was sitting, for whatever reason I wanted or had to be next to him. Maybe I was trying to show him that I was not afraid of him anymore. Finding the arm of the couch but not him I sat down and slowly reached a hand towards the other side of the sofa where I thought he would be, but I didn't feel anything. He must have noticed that I was looking for him because he gently touched my hand stopping it from flailing around like a fish out of water.

"Would it be ok if I lean on you?" I asked.

You know the saying keep your friend close but your enemies' closer, maybe that is what I was trying to do subconsciously. Without saying a word, he pulled me over to him. He put an arm around my neck so that I could rest my head against his chest. I could feel his muscles tense and relax after I settled in place. I was struggling inside myself though. The voice inside my head said what the hell are you doing cuddling up to someone that is going to kill you eventually? I shut that voice down quickly I didn't need to hear it right now if I was going to pull this off. I started to wonder if I was starting to have feelings for my captor. It sounded so weird, but there was just some kind of connection happening. He really had not given me a reason not to like him. So far, he had treated me better than most of the boyfriends that I have had. My subconscious yelled at me, but, he tied you to a bed. Recanted but he also fed me when he could have let me starve, and he has been nothing but gentle with me.

"Lucian, can I ask you what your intentions are for me?" I asked, and he tensed up immediately, and I could tell that he was uncomfortable with the question. However, I kind of had him where I wanted him. He was stuck behind me although it was not impossible for him to escape but, I could also feel that he didn't want to go anywhere. There just was something there that was not there before now.

He was silent for quite a while before he spoke. "My dearest I am planning on keeping you around a long time. But before I reveal my true self to you, I need you to trust me first." He said, and I could hear the truth in his words, then he added. "You are beautiful, and I can't imagine a life without you."

This was the sweetest thing that anyone had ever said to me, I melted like ice in a fire. I reached my hands up above my head and slowly moved them towards his face. He didn't protest and let me feel his face. Rough whiskers bristled at my fingertips first. I felt my way up across his face his skin and lips were smooth I could not feel even the slightest flaw in his skin. I was trying to get a mental picture of what he would look like, but it was not working. Then I ran my fingers through his soft hair then clasped them behind his neck. He kissed both of my arms softly. We just sat there not saying anything else just enjoying each other's company. My arms did get tired, and I pulled them down after a few minutes. I searched for his hand and then twined my fingers with his. Since this whole thing started, this was the first time I felt safe with him. This situation was getting so weird. I am being held against my will but yet I was falling for the man keeping me here. I had no idea what to expect from him. I wanted to cry and be happy all at the same time. My emotions were all over the place and out of control. Somewhere in our silence, I fell asleep. I dreamt about him chasing me through the woods again. This time he caught me and crushed me in his arms. I pulled back to see his face. When I did, I was shocked at what I saw his eyes were glowing red. Then his face began to morph into that of a demon with horns. I screamed as he opened his mouth. My screaming awakened me from the dream. I was surprised that he was still there holding me.

I quickly shut my eyes as he whispered. "Are you ok?"

"Yes, I'm ok, just a bad dream." I said still panting with fear.

"What was your dream about?" He asked.

I thought carefully about the answer and decided to decline to tell him the truth at this point. "It was nothing just an old memory." I said and snuggled back into him.

"Well, I must be going." He said and started to move out from under me. "I will be sending dinner up to you soon."

"Wait please don't go, I want you to stay. Please eat dinner with me." I begged.

"I'm sorry, I have to go and take care of a few things. Tell you what; I will be back in about two hours. Would that be ok?" He said adoringly touching my cheek.

"Yes, that will be fine." I said back with my best pouting face.

"Ok, then I will see you in a bit." He whispered against my forehead as he kissed me then he was gone.

Well played I think he actually bought it. My plan of being nice was starting to pay off. I now was untied and free to roam this room, and I had a time frame of how long he would be gone. One thing that I still needed to know is when shift change was for the guards at my door. The door seemed like the only way out of here since the windows in the room didn't open. For now, though I took the time to snoop around the room. I walked over to the dresser and looked through all the drawers they were all empty. I proceeded into the bathroom and snooped through the vanity, but there was nothing in there either. I opened the door across from the shower to reveal a toilet, no help there. Only one more place in this room that I could go. One single door sitting in the only darkened corner of the room. I placed my hand on the doorknob and took a deep breath just hoping that this door would take me somewhere. As I started to turn the knob, I heard a commotion outside the main doors. The Viking lady must have been here with my food. I leapt over the bed and settled on the couch just as the door swung open. As usual, she didn't say anything just set my food in front of me and left the room. I opened the silver lid to reveal a bowl of soup and some warm bread and crackers, it looked very delicious. I devoured it knowing that she would be back shortly to get my empty dishes from me. I got the feeling that if I didn't eat it now, she would have sat and stared at me until I did. She gave me the impression that she knew what Lucian wanted me to do and was going to make sure I did it. Right now, though all I could think about was the door. I wanted to look now my curiosity building within me, but I sat there until she came back and picked up my empty dishes. As soon as she left the room, I was back at the door. I slowly opened the door peering into the darkness. I felt the wall on the left looking for a light switch but didn't find anything. I felt the wall on my right finding the switch and flipping it on. I think that my jaw hit the floor as the lights blinked on. The room was the same size as my room, but it was a closet. This would be any girls dream closet. Rows and rows of clothing hung from the bars that were barely noticeable through the hangers. Underneath the hanging clothing stacked two boxes high and lining the closet floor where shoe boxes. In one corner, a three-way mirror stood from the floor to the ceiling. However, before I could go any further, I could feel his presence coming. I ran to the door and closed it softly behind me. The main door handle began to rattle slightly and move. I jumped on the bed and closed my eyes as the door swung open.

"Lily, it's me are you awake?" I heard him whisper from the door.

"Yes, I'm awake." I said in a tiny voice that almost sounded like I just rose from sleeping.

He cuddled up behind me on the bed and wrapped me in his arms. "Lily I need you to give me something." He whispered in my ear.

What could I possibly give him I didn't have anything here in this world.

When I didn't say anything, he said. "I need you to give me your promise that you will not run. I don't mean you any harm, and you seem to be ok with me." He tightened his arms around me again, and I could tell that he was going to tell me something that hurt or pained him somehow. "I want you to see my face." He said each word slowly like honey being poured from a jar.

My pulse quickened for a moment then settled. "Tell me when you are ready." I said not sure if I really wanted to see his face clearly for the first time. I kind of liked the mystery. My mind found something in his words, he said promise not to run. Maybe his face was disfigured, or he was really an alien, my mind was frantic with the possibilities. He had let me feel his face and the glimpse that I had stolen of him, he seemed perfect. What could there possibly be that would scare me?

It took him a long moment, but without saying a word, he began to help me roll over so that I could face him. First rolling me onto my back where he kissed my cheek. Then on to my right side to face him, he kissed me on the lips this time. He caressed my cheek with his hand and slowly and softly whispered. "You may open your eyes."

I slowly opened my eyes first thing I saw was his full perfectly pink lips. Very kissable I thought. Then his nose that was small but seemed to fit his face well. His eyes were perfectly symmetrical along with the rest of his face. His eyes were closed though so I was not able to see the color. His forehead was crinkled a little bit, but these little wrinkles were also perfectly symmetrical. His long black hair started in just the right place above his forehead. His hair fell across his face a little bit, and I hesitantly reached up and brushed it back behind his ear. His jawline was perfectly square, and his cheekbones were high.

There was no doubt that he was beautiful almost angelic like. I could not figure out why he had hidden himself from me for so long.

"You are so beautiful." I whisper to him gently sliding my hand down the side of his face barely touching his flawless skin. Butterflies swirled inside me fluttering around in my stomach.

He let me admire his beauty for a few seconds before he spoke. "Lily, please don't be scared. I'm going to open my eyes."

However, before he did anything, he grabbed onto me tightly and held me in place. I thought about shutting my eyes, but for some odd reason, I wanted to see what he was going to show me. What could be scarier than what I have been through in the last week or two, or however long I had been here? He slowly started to lift his eyelids. His eyes were this most amazing translucent blue, almost as if they were glowing. I began to laugh instantly. My mind had conjured up some awful things like he had no eyes or they would be red like in my dreams. He looked at me strangely for a few seconds then smirked.

"Why are you laughing?" He asked me.

"Well Lucian, I'm laughing because I was expecting to be scared and when I was not scared, I don't know, I thought the whole thing was funny. I am sorry if I hurt your feelings. The truth is that you are just beautiful." I said trying to smooth things over with him. He did appear to be a little angry or disappointed with my reaction. I could not help it he kept telling me please don't run and that I was going to be scared. There was nothing scary about him. In fact, he was just plain out beautiful.

He leaned in and kissed me. This ignited a passion deep down inside me. I wanted him and had to have him. I kissed him back and placed my hands in his hair. Before I could even grasp what, I was doing, I was lost in him. I don't know how we ended up in the shower, but we did. The water started to run cold, and we got out. He could not keep his hands off me though. He wrapped me in a towel and carried me off to bed. I fell into a deep sleep with him cuddling me.

∾CHAPTER 8∾

I awoke alone and naked. I searched for the nightgown that had been provided for me, but I could not find it anywhere. My thoughts turned to the closet. I wrapped the sheet around me and went into the closet in search of something to ware. I guess the last time I was in here I had not realized that it was mostly full of dresses. I searched through ball gowns, sundresses, cocktail party, and casual dresses before finding pairs upon pairs of jeans. Like the dresses, there were a variety of jeans as well. After pawing through a few pairs, I finally found a pair that I really loved. They were on the fancy side of things with beautiful designs scrawled on the pockets with imitation gemstones. Above the jeans were skirts, all different styles, long, short, very short and also in a variety of colors. Turning around to look at the wall behind me, I found the tee shirts, blouses, button downs, and sweaters. I looked through the tee shirts and finally settled on one that had a V neck with some pretty flowers printed on it. Looking at some other clothing hanging here I realized that they were all my size. At that moment, shock speared through me as I realized that no one would spend this amount of money on clothing for someone that they were going to kill. I stood there with a new feeling of hope that I would eventually be able to escape from my prison. As the moment passed, my next task was to find some undergarments. In the built-in drawers on the far side of the closet, I found what I was looking for, panties and bras. A variety of panties greeted me, colors and styles, ranging from grandma style to sexy lacy thongs. Checking the size, I realized that these to were a perfect match for me. I slipped on a pair of underwear and sat down in the chair that faced the mirrors. Holding the clothing in my lap, I was so exhausted from just that little bit of movement. I was going to have to ask Lucian for a treadmill or something that I could exercise on to build my strength back up. I should not be this tired from just looking for clothing. I glanced up in the mirror to see if I looked as tired as I felt. That is when I saw two small scabs on the side of my neck. Looking down at my arms, I saw the same little wounds on both of my arms. Holy shit what the hell had he done to me. I studied my reflection a bit longer in the mirror and saw that I was a little paler than usual. I let out a gasp then a scream. I pulled my legs up to my chest, wrapped my arms around them and started to cry. All my renewed hope replaced by fear because now I knew that he would kill me one day soon. Then I wondered what the small circular wounds were from. Had he shot me up with some kind of drugs? Was that why I was so attracted to him last night? Just a day or so ago he had given me something or taken something from me. It is the only thing that made sense in my mind.

It was only a matter of seconds before he appeared before me. "Lily, it is ok, I'm sorry. I…I…got carried away. Please, we can talk about this." He said begging me to listen to him.

I could feel the sorrow and pain emanating from him, but I didn't care he had hurt me.

"Go away... Just go away." I said crying into my legs not lifting my eyes to look at him.

However, he didn't leave me. He picked me up and carried me to the bed. He let me cry, but he didn't leave my side. I really just wanted him to go away though. I was crushed how could I have been so stupid. He kissed my naked shoulder, and a shiver ran down my spine.

"We can talk about this now if you would like." He whispered in my ear.

I didn't say or do anything. "Lily," he started "I want you to know that I'm not going to hurt you. I have fallen for you baby please." He begged me again to forgive him.

Finding some kind of courage, I asked him "What is this?" I held out my arm for him to see.

He leaned in to kiss the spots, but I pulled away from him. I pushed him away from me, sprang out of bed, and ran to the bathroom slamming the door behind me. I leaned my back up against the door, sunk down to the floor and placed my forehead on my knees. I was still not sure what all of this meant I was scared. I cried until I could not cry anymore then I gathered the last of my whits, stood up and opened the door. I was expecting him to be standing there, but he was not. I searched the whole room, but he was nowhere to be found. I went to the main doors, pulled one open, and ran out into the hallway. My brain had pieced everything together, and the answer rose up to the surface. How could it be I pondered while I ran. I think I know what he is but I needed him to tell me. Then I questioned myself if I really wanted to know.

"Hey wait." I heard shouts behind me.

I refused to stop though, I was out of here. Of course, they ran after me, but I was faster than they were. I was pushing myself to my limit to run as fast as I could. I rounded a corner, and he was standing there. I skidded to a stop barely managing to maintain my balance as my socks slid on the hardwood floor. Surprising enough I kept myself upright. The guards caught up with me and were about to grab me but I managed to dodge them and run towards him. The guards either gave up or he waved them off I don't know which but they were not a problem anymore.

"Lily, what are you doing?" He asked me.

Since I was caught trying to escape, aided in my split-second decision that running towards him and not away was a better choice. Who knows what he would have done if he knew what I actually was trying to do. I didn't answer his question, I was too busy gathered my thoughts while I ran towards him. What was I going to say when I finally got to him? I could not let him think for one second that I was trying to escape. Words escaping me I simply opened my arms, jumped up wrapping myself around him.

Holding on for dear life to him I finally said. "I…I… just had to find you. I'm sorry I was not trying to go anywhere I just wanted you." Then I kissed him as passionately as I could manage. "I need you to tell me what is going on here." I said breathlessly against his lips.

He must have believed me because he wrapped his arms around me and carried me back to my room but didn't say anything.

"I'm sorry Lucian, I'm just so scared. I feel like you are going to kill me at any minute." I said starting the conversation that needed to happen now. For the dramatic flair, I started to sob.

He crushed me closer to him and sat down on the bed still holding me. "Baby, I'm so sorry. I should have told you before last night happened. You know the legend of Dracula?" He paused and waited for me to acknowledge what he said.

I slowly nodded to let him know that I did. I knew all about the legend of Dracula, I owned the book.

"What if I were to tell you that it is not a legend and in fact, it is true that there are vampires in this world."

I didn't know if I wanted to laugh or cry at this moment as I remembered what Dracula did to the women in the story. Since he had bitten me, does that mean I'm going to change into a vampire now? My head started to spin with questions.

"Baby." He said paused and pulled me up tighter against him. Holding me with one arm now he used the other hand to pull my face up to look him in the eyes. "I am a vampire." He said slowly articulating every word.

I felt all the blood drain from my face and I felt faint.

My nose is on fire, every breath taken in burned more and more each time. My eyes popped open to see that he was holding something by my nose. He quickly took it away when our eyes met. I stared into his eyes as he stared back into mine. I faintly smiled at him as I collected my thoughts.

"What happened?" I asked, but then I remembered before he could tell me again. "You told me you were a vam…pire." This time instead of fainting, I busted out laughing.

I was laughing so hard I was crying. I raised my arm to wipe my eyes and seen the little round scabs again. I stopped laughing instantly. He smirked at me. I stared blankly back into his eyes again.

"Ok, so I need proof that you are a vampire." I said. Everything in this world is built on proof. This is a primary part of engineering.

Even though I loved vampires and wished that they were real, I just could not believe that he was telling me the truth. I mean really, they supposedly existed for several hundreds of thousands of years, but there has never been real proof that they exist.

"Really you need proof? Are the small little scabs not enough?" He said pointing out the ones on my arm sounding very annoyed.

"Yes, I need you to prove it to me. I don't remember anything about getting the little scabs, so that is a moot point." I retorted sounding every bit as annoyed as he had.

"Well ok, I will prove it to you. Please don't be scared of what you see."

He looked away for a few seconds and then back into my eyes. Nothing had changed except his expression, which seemed to be playful. He slowly placed his hand on my cheek then slowly parted his lips and closed his eyes again. Opening his mouth wide I watched as his fangs dropped into place. When they were fully extended, he opened his eyes they were still the same blue that they had always been. However, I could not help but stare at the two needle-like teeth that looked like they could pierce through anything. My mind told me to run, and I pushed away from him with all my strength but then relaxed as he hid his fangs from me.

I stumbled over the words.
"Oh…Oh…mmmmyyyy god."

That was all I could get out of my mouth. The shock had set in, and my mind now questioned everything that I knew to be true about the world that I had lived in and this new world.

"Baby, it is ok, you're ok. I'm not going to hurt you. You have my word." He said in a rush of words.

I could barely understand his words and just needed to get away from him to think.

After a few seconds, I finally managed to say. "I need time to think about this. I'm going to take a bath."

I pulled away from him and walked stunned into the bathroom right to the tub. I mindlessly turned on the water letting the tub start to fill. I quickly stripped off my clothing and got into the inch of water that had collected in the bottom of the tub. I leaned back against the tub wall, not minding how cold it was as I sat there in shock. My mind could not string anything together. The only that it was doing was repeating vampire over and over again. I just stared blankly at the ceiling not paying attention to anything going on around me. I don't know how long the water ran over the side of the tub or even if it did. I vaguely remember seeing Lucian turn the water off. My whole life I really was into vampires and wished that I could meet just one. I had promised myself that if I did meet one, I would do everything I could to become one. But now, that it was so close to me, I was not sure how I felt.

"Do you want some company? He asked.

Not wanting to talk I ignored him and just sank my head under the water. He pulled me back up instantly. He must have thought I was trying to do myself in.

"Ok whether you want me to or not I'm going to join you." Not waiting for an answer he was undressed and sitting behind me holding me. "Please say something anything." He said finally after a few moments of silence.

The truth was that I didn't know what to say. The shock started to wear off, and I found my voice again. "Are you going to make me a vampire too?" I asked cutting right to the point. I could not believe that I had said that out loud. I wanted to take it back as I feared what he would say.

"No... no... I don't plan on it. I would not wish this on anyone." He said wrapping his arms around me. "Please understand you can ask me anything you want. I will try not to laugh."

Eased a little by his answer a slew of questions erupted from me. "Ok, so what about coffins? What about crosses or holy things? What about the sun burning you to a crisp?" I said remembering things from vampire novels that I had read.

"No, no and no." He said. "I'm pretty much like you except I drink blood instead of eating food to stay alive and I'm immortal and will not die of old age. The only other thing that I can think that is different is that I don't have to breathe."

I took in all the information and all of what I thought I knew about vampires and threw it out the window leaving me only one other question to ask. "How old are you?"

"Today is my birthday, and I am celebrating my one thousand eight hundred and thirty-fifth year. I was turned when I was twenty-three years old."

I turned to face him. "Well happy birthday." I said, caressing his face. He closed his eyes and leaned into my hand. I leaned in and kissed each one of his eyelids, then the tip of his nose, and finally his lips.

"That feels nice." He said when I pulled my lips away and rested my forehead on his.

"Lucian." I said hesitating, not sure; I wanted to know the answer to this question. "Are you hungry now?" I ask swallowing hard to keep my fear pushed down inside me.

He instantly popped his eyes open and looked at me curiously. "No, I'm not, besides I can't take any more blood from you right now."

I wasted no time to say. "How about never again."

He eyed me curiously again. "How about right here right now I will make a pact with you. I will not drink from you unless you allow it. I will not do this again." He said as he pointed to the tiny scabs on my arms.

"That is agreeable." I said then I rose and got out of the tub. I put on the bathrobe that was hanging on the back of the door. He slowly started to move to get out, but I put a hand on his shoulder. "Please let me wash your hair."

I grabbed the cup from the counter and found the shampoo. I lathered it into his hair and rinsed it out. He got out of the tub and threw a towel around his waist. I found a hairbrush, and we headed to the couch. He sat in front of me and let me brush and brush his hair while we talked about insignificant things like our favorite colors. We didn't talk about vampires the rest of the night.

At some point in our nonsense conversation, we moved to the bed he tucked me in and held me close to his body. I don't know how long we laid there until I fell asleep.

∾CHAPTER 9∾

The nightmare of him chasing me through the woods didn't repeat itself tonight. That dream was replaced by a new nightmare. In the dream, he leaned into me for a kiss. I kissed him back of course, but then everything went haywire. The first sight of blood awakened me. For a moment, I didn't see the room all I saw was blood everywhere like I had put on a pair of solid red contacts on my eyes tinting everything red. I was gasping for air.

"Lily, Lily, Lily are you ok baby?" He asked putting his hands all over me. "Are you hurt anywhere?"

"No, I'm fine." I said as I sat up and wrapped my arms around my knees trying to catch my breath.

"Do you want to talk about it? Maybe it would help." He said wrapping his arms around me trying to soothe me.

"Nope… I don't want to." I leaned back against him for a second before I twisted until I could face him. "Please, I want you now more than ever." I pressed my lips to his.

Without saying a word, he surrendered to me. I was his, but he was mine. We ignited into the throes of passion. He kissed me all over my body, but he did refrain from biting me tonight. Laying there panting when it was all over, and crushing myself to his body so tight that we were breathing as one for a moment until he moved rolling half on top of me. He ran his hand through my sweat-drenched hair and lightly kissed my neck caressing it with his lips.

"You, taste, delicious, just simply divine." He whispered each word individually into my neck with each kiss.

I could hear the undertone in his voice though he wanted just a little taste of my blood. However, after yesterday I knew he was not going to ask for it. He wanted me to willingly give it to him. Could I do this, could I let him have some just for a moment? Will it hurt? Of course, it would hurt; he would be puncturing your skin you idiot, a small voice in my head said. He did just give me what I wanted. How can I deny him something he wants? I didn't say anything and turned my head to the side exposing my neck to him. He sighed and lifted his head away from me. Then he went back to his own pillow. I guess he didn't get the hint that I was willing to give him my blood.

"Lucian." I said softly turning my head to look into his eyes. "I will try if you want me too."

A look of confusion washed over his face. "Try what?" He whispered after a few silent moments.

I really didn't want to speak the words out loud and was not sure that I could get them out of my mouth. I had to try though. "Lucian, I…I… want you to drink from me." I said softly but in a rush before I could not say the words.

He didn't say anything else and moved back to caressing my neck with his kisses. I turned my head away allowing him unrestricted access to my neck.

"Ok, are you ready?" He whispered into my neck in small tiny breaths.

I nodded not saying anything afraid that I would fall apart if I did. He started nipping at my neck, and then a shockwave of pain ran through me. I arched my back slightly pushing my stomach against his arm that was there holding me in place. It was like pushing up against an iron bar. I wanted to thrash around but knew that it would cause me greater pain and maybe even death. I could feel every time he took a mouth full of my blood. However, after a few seconds, the pain dissipated and it became erotic quickly blocking out the pain and turning it into pleasure. This was how I had not known he had bitten me the last time we had sex. All it had done was made the sex that much better. It felt like only a split second passed before he was done then he slowly removed his fangs from my neck and lightly licked the wounds until they stopped bleeding.

"Are you ok my love?" He asked, his voice was timid and unsure with a hint of I'm sorry.

"Yes, I'm fine." I said keeping my eyes closed not wanting to give up the moment just yet.

I had done it, given him his pleasure. I opened my eyes to peer into his eyes. They were begging for forgiveness and full of sorrow.

"Don't be sorry, it was actually quite pleasurable." I said and reached out for his face to caress his worries away.

He realized then that I was telling the truth and a small smile reached the corners of his mouth. He pulled me in close to his body draped one arm over me and the other arm underneath my head. My forehead was resting on his chest and moving with every breath he took. Now I was exhausted and needed sleep, and it didn't take long.

Before I was sleeping, he placed his lips on my head kissed me lightly and whispered. "I love you." I was too weak to answer right now but did manage a moan to acknowledge him.

No dreams the rest of the night, and I woke up to the sun shining through the windows on my face. I wondered what time it was, but in reality, I really didn't care. I was still wrapped tightly in his arms. I didn't want to move because I was not sure if he was still sleeping or not. I laid there for a few seconds before my bladder reminded me that I was human and needed to get up. I tried to slip out of his arms undetected, but he was not having it.

"Are you ok? Where are you going?" He asked softly.

"I'm fine, but I really need to go to the bathroom." I said, and he immediately let me go.

I rushed into the bathroom and did my thing. He was still lying on the bed when I came out, and I decided that I wanted to cuddle back up to him.

"Did you have a good sleep?" I asked after I snuggled back in.

"We don't sleep, I watched you sleep." He said, kissing the back of my head and my shoulder.

I turned over on my back. "Did I say anything in my sleep?" I knew that I had done it several times in the past; my mom would tell me about them.

"No just a lot of snoring." He said, smiling big, he was joking with me.

I smiled back and turned towards him. I winced a little because my neck hurt a little bit from the bite. I buried my face in his chest and just laid there not saying anything or moving. How could I possibly have fallen in love with this thing? Not human, a monster that has no meaning of life and kills for fun, maybe not fun but food. I wondered what would happen if he didn't drink. Then a small part of me didn't care anymore. I would give him my blood without any afterthought. Then on the other hand, what if he grew bored of me and decided that one day he was done with me. Obviously, he would not just let me go he would definitely kill me and that I knew for sure. What if it was not like that at all, maybe he would change me into a vampire too. Would I want that when the time comes? I would say no right now, but as my bond with him grows, I might change my mind.

He interrupted my thoughts. "Lily, I have to go take care of a few things. I will be back soon my love." He leaned down to kiss the top of my head. Then got out of the bed and started dressing. He looked down at me and said. "How about I get you out of this room tonight, for dinner with me?"

"That would be great." I exclaimed, I wanted to act like a kid and bounce up and down on the bed but refrained from doing so. "What should I wear?" I asked not sure if it would be fancy or not.

"There are a ton of things in the closet, surprise me." He said, sitting on the edge of the bed putting his socks on, then standing up grabbing his pants putting them on as he walked to the door. He grabbed the handle but turned to me. "Sweetheart, please be good and stay here." Then without another word, he disappeared in a blink of an eye.

∾CHAPTER 10∾

I laid there for a little while longer breathing in his sent. I finally decided that I should start getting ready or at least go to the oversized stuffed closet to find something to wear. I opened the door and turned the light on. I browsed the dress section. There were slim fitting dresses, big ball gowns, short, slim fitting dresses, and sundresses. I decided on a slim fitting dress that was made of green satin material. My mom had always said green was my color. I knew she was right because every time I wore green, I felt happy. I pulled the dress from its place, found the underwear again, and then decided that maybe I should skip this part. I headed towards the bathroom, but the Viking lady stopped me in my tracks.

"Do you need anything?" She asked eyeing the dress and me.

I could tell that she approved of the dress by the look on her face.

"I could use someone to do my hair. Do we have anyone here that can do it?" I asked.

"Of course, we do." Then she pointed to herself.

"Great." I suppressed a groan.

What could she possibly do with my hair? Put in braids like hers?

"I'm going to take a shower, then if you would do my hair that would be great." I said, half smirking half smiling at her.

I was trying to be positive about the situation. An upside to this is maybe this is my opportunity to get to know her better.

"Sure, no problem just let me know when you are ready." She almost sounded like a girl instead of a burly man this time.

In the shower, I turned on the hot water, as hot as I could take it. This relaxed my muscles, and it helped ease the pain in my neck. It felt great. When I had washed everything twice, and the hot water was about gone, I grabbed my towel and wrapped it around me and invited Viking lady in. She had gone and retrieved a bunch of things, curling irons, a blow dryer, hairspray and a bunch of hair accessories. There are so many accessories to choose from. This is going to be hard to figure out what would go best with my dress. Then one stood out from the rest, a gold hair comb that looked very old and had green emerald stones inlaid in it. That was the one I wanted, I pointed to it. She nodded at me and picked it up laying it on the vanity. I sat down in the chair facing the bathroom and not the mirror. I didn't want to see anything until she was done. I did feel better about her doing my hair now that she had brought all of this stuff.

"So." I said pausing not sure what to say next or if she was going to talk to me or not. When she acknowledged me with a sigh, I went on. "Do you think that I could know your name?" I asked trying to learn something about this mysterious woman.

"I can't see how it would hurt now that you and the master are getting along. My name is Marcella." She said.

I almost lost it when she called him master it just sounded funny coming from her. No matter at least she finally told me her name. I didn't have to secretly keep calling her Viking lady. I knew that I would slip up one day and call her that. That would be so embarrassing.

"So how long have you been working for Lucian?" I asked.

Wondering how she would take me calling him by his name. There was no way I was going to call him master. No matter how long we could be together. However, it didn't faze her.

"I have been working for master for about twenty years. I do know what he is, you know." She said as her voice lowered to almost less than a whisper. "You know he is really into you, or he would have killed you by now. I have seen it happen to a few women that ended up here."

This information sent chills down my spine. I actually felt fear for the first time since he told me what he was. Of course, my mind started to run wild with what ifs. What if he was going to kill me tonight, and that is why he is taking me out of the room. I had to shut this train down quickly because that was not important right now. What is important is getting the layout of the house to make my escape. Even though I was starting to have feelings for him, I still wanted it to be on my terms. I pushed down my thoughts of dread and fear and locked them away somewhere deep inside me. Focusing on what I needed to do to get away. A little whisper of a voice inside my head said, maybe you should just stay and let him love you until he kills you. I shook that voice from my head. This was turning out to be like the beauty and the beast. I wanted to run away, but the more I had gotten to know him the more I liked maybe even loved him. No matter that fact, I was still being kept here against my will, and I wanted to go home.

After a long delay, I managed to finally respond with, "Oh."

After a few moments of awkward silence, she said. "You're all done."

I rose from the chair and turned to look in the mirror. She had done a beautiful job, part of my hair up and part down with lots and lots of curls straggling here and there. She had dappled my hair with little shiny diamond barrettes, each one holding just one medium size diamond that sparkled under the bright vanity lights. The comb that I had picked out was tucked between a small loose bun and the back of my head. The comb stuck up slightly off my head giving the appearance of a backward crown. As I admired my hair, she pulled another bag from her stuff. Getting the feeling that she was not entirely done with me yet, I sat back down in the chair. I waited as she applied the makeup to my face. When she was finished, I looked in the mirror again and could not believe my transformation. I was absolutely stunning. I could not recall a time in my short life that I looked so beautiful.

Marcella gathered her things and left me standing in front of the mirror admiring myself. After a few seconds, I turned, gathered the dress and slipped it on carefully over my head trying not to mess up my hair or makeup. I was thankful that the dress provided a wide opening for my head to fit through easily. The dress was plain except for the spaghetti straps. Four separate strings made up the straps in front and the back they joined together at the crest of my shoulder. The neckline plunged down to a V. As for the rest of the dress it hugged me in all the right places. I looked at my hair one more time to make sure that I had not messed up anything. My hair still looked perfect.

Marcella had surprised and impressed me. I would have never guessed that she would know how to do any of this. The thing that surprised me the most is that I had not seen her wear makeup, yet somehow, she knew what to do with my face. My hair though was the most shocking part. I had only seen her wear the pigtail braids.

I looked back in the mirror one more time before I exited the bathroom. When I opened the door, he was standing there, dressed to the nines in a tuxedo. He looked like someone that had stepped out of a movie wedding. He had the look of awe in his eyes and a smile exposed all of his beautiful pearly white teeth. He pulled one single red rose out from behind his back and started towards me from across the room.

With each step he took, he said. "This rose is for you, I wish I could have found a more beautiful flower but, to be honest, there is no flower that is more beautiful than you tonight."

Handing me the rose, he placed one hand on my cheek, and the other under my chin, and pulled my lips up to him. He kissed me deeply, passionately but gently.

I was flabbergasted that was the most beautiful thing anyone had ever said to me. This seemed like a new side of him that I was seeing and I felt for the first time that maybe he was not going to kill me. I stood in front of him speechless and staring at him. I wanted to say something but the words would not come. We stood not moving and staring at each other for a long moment until he pulled away and offered his arm for me to take.

We walked out of my room, down the long hallway, and to the right down another hallway that led to the grand foyer complete with a double set of arched staircases coming up to greet us. We slowly descended the staircase down to the foyer, where we turned to the left at the bottom. Then we walked thru a short hallway in-between the stairs into a room that opened up into a two-story great room. I will call this room the white room. Everything in this room was some shade of white, it was beautiful but lacked color, and I really like color. On the opposite side of the room, we took another hallway. Then to the left again and down a short hallway to a set of double white doors, that had a carving of a bear with a ring of flowers around it. Some of the flowers had gold leafing done to them, making them shine in the dim lit hallway. Doormen stood on each side of the doors. They waited for Lucian to nod before they pushed and held the doors open for us to walk in. When they pushed the doors open it revealed a small table set for two in the middle of a medium size room. The whole room lit by candles. The candles burned in sconces hanging on the walls and a very old looking chandelier that hung over the table. The chandelier was three tiers and made of silver and crystals. It was absolutely stunning to watch the flames dancing in the crystals reflection. I felt like I had taken a step back in time before electricity. Three candles set in a candle opera on the table. These candles though were different from the ones everywhere else, two red and one white the white one had not been lit. I briefly wondered what it symbolized but quickly got distracted by the rest of the room. Three tiers of red roses rested against the wood-paneled walls, making the square room feel circular. A vast stone-faced fireplace rose from the floor to the ceiling, with a small fire burning in it. The fireplace must have been every bit of ten-foot wide. The room was just absolutely breathtaking. Soft classical music was playing in the background I think it is Beethoven. We slowly walked to the table, and he pulled the chair out for me to sit. Then he poured me a glass of wine before he seated himself across the table from me. He could not keep his eyes off me for a minute. I didn't know if he was scared that I was going to run or if he was admiring my beauty, maybe a little of both. The door quietly opened and a person that I had never met before brought in a plate of food. The tall, longhaired blond girl set the plate down in front of me then as quietly as she had come she left. The plate had a piece of steak and a baked potato with sour cream, chives and bacon bits on top. It looked delicious. The door quietly opened again, and the girl brought a simple gold chalice to Lucian. He eyed me and took a sip from the chalice. I was slightly revolted knowing what was in the cup, and I wondered whose blood he was drinking. A pang of jealousy hit me. It should have been my blood and my blood alone. The voice in my head reprimanded me for that thought immediately, you are a stupid girl; stop it you must get out of here.

I must have stared too long because a look of worry came over his face and he said. "Do you not like the food? I will get you something else." Then he started to get up from his chair.

"No, it is wonderful. I just was too lost in your beauty to eat." I said.

Looking down at my plate, I cut off a tiny piece of the stake with the knife and started to eat it slowly, but it tasted so good that I began to eat faster and faster. I wanted to act like an animal, pick up the meat, and chew it off the bone. I refrained though because I knew that this was not the time or place for that, I needed to maintain being ladylike. However, the food was so good, and I had not realized how hungry I was. I ate every bit of food on my plate then I was so full my stomach hurt a bit. I grabbed my glass of wine, sat back in my chair slouching, and took a sip. I sat there not saying anything just looking around the space. There must have been one thousand dozen roses in this room, and they were all perfect shape and size.

"Did you get enough to eat?" Lucian asked me, pulling me from my observations of the room.

"Yes, it was delightful." I said with a smile that touched each ear.

Then as if on cue the song that we had danced to before started playing, and he rose from his seat. Slowly walked over to me, extended his hand towards me, and said. "May I please have this dance, beautiful girl?"

If I were made of chocolate, I would have melted into a pile of goo on the floor. I didn't say anything and took his hand. The only fear I had now was crying because he was so kind to me.

He led us to a spot right in front of the fireplace. He held me close and spun me around in a slow circle like he was admiring how my body moved, and I supposed he was. He was an excellent dancer, and he moved me around the floor with ease, as if I am weightless. When the song was over, he released me, and we walked hand and hand back towards the table. I could not help but stop and pick up one of the beautiful roses. Ouch, the thorn pricked my finger and blood started to ooze from the tiny poke. He slowly and carefully raised my finger to his lips licking the blood off my finger. This ignited something in him, and he picked me up flinging me over his shoulder and rushed me upstairs to my room. The ten-minute walk that it had taken us to get down there only took a fraction of a second to get us back to the room, he moved so fast. Setting me down on my feet he leaned in and kissed me tenderly. Trailing kisses down my neck and back to my mouth.

"I want you, can I have you?" He whispered against my lips.

I stopped everything by pulling away a bit. "Can you define what you want from me?" I don't know what snapped in my mind just then, but it was instantly racing as I waited for his answer. Was he going to kill me now? Wine them and dine them type of killer. Did he just want a drink from me? Did he just want sex? On the other hand, did he want to make me a vampire too? The questions were coming in rapid succession in that split second that I waited for him to answer me.

"I'm sorry if I scared you." He said softly placing a gentle hand on my cheek. "I just meant that I want to take you to bed, no drinking or killing."

He said almost as if he could read my thoughts then he pulled me in close to him again. "I would never hurt you, besides I promised."

Something in his voice felt sincere, and I felt relieved and somewhat foolish now. I started to apologize but he pressed his lips to mine, and I could not talk back. When he pulled back a bit, I whispered, "Of course you may."

∾CHAPTER 11∾

The door flew open.

"Master we have a problem."

It was Marcella, she was wide-eyed, breathless, panicking, and her eyes filled with fear. This big, brawny lady was actually afraid, this must be big. I heard scuffling breakout in the hallway and looked at Lucian's face. His face too was that of panic. I wanted to ask what the hell was going on but Lucian beat me to it.

"Marcella, take the girl through the secret passageways stop when you get to the end of the tunnels. If anyone comes after you, use the stakes. Be careful, you must keep her alive." He said then he turned to me. "I love you, just remember that, do what Marcela tells you to do."

He kissed me quickly as Marcella grabbed my hand, pulling me into the closet. At the back of the closet, she pulled a switch hidden under a dress. A door opened, and we went through. She closed the door softly grabbed my hand again, and we started to run. We ran through what looked like concrete boxes. We came to a fork and took the left side. We ran a little further until we ran into another fork taking another left again, then another left, then a right, and another right, and finally a left until we ran into a concrete wall. We had no choice but to stop now. Going up the side of the concrete box was a ladder that led up to a steel door. The door had a wheel that you turn to unlatch and open it. This was it, my chance to escape. I could run now but where would I go, I don't even know where I am, plus if memory serves me correctly, I was in another realm or world. I knew though that this was my chance I had to do this now or be stuck here forever. I remembered what my ex-boyfriend told me. The ex-was big on survival skills and had taught me a few things mostly about knocking someone out. I didn't know if this was going to work, but I was going to try it anyway. I mentally got ready. If she didn't go down, then I was going to be in big trouble. Gathering my nerve, I walked around to face her. It was clear that she was not expecting me to do anything.

"I'm sorry." I said.

I threw an uppercut and hit her square under the chin. While her head snapped back, I took two fingers and hit her in the throat. Then as a final blow, I kicked her in the side of the head and boom she fell like a ton of bricks. I stood there for a second in shock that it had actually worked. Knowing that I didn't have much time left, I grabbed one of the steaks that she had been carrying and went for the ladder. The door at the top was locked shut, but only with the wheel that I could turn. I turned the wheel until I seen the lock mechanism unlatch then pushed with all my might on the steel door to get it to open. I squeezed my body out under the heavy metal hatch and on to the cool damp grass. All I could see was darkness poorly lit by the full silvery moonlight. I was surrounded by a dark shadowy forest. I didn't know what direction I should run but had to pick away quickly. I ran what I assumed was south out of the clearing and into the forest. I tried to run in a straight line, but the trees and brush made me deviate quite often. Finally, I found a small creek. I had been told by the same ex-boyfriend that if you follow a creek or a river that eventually you will find a city or town. So, I followed the creek hoping that he was right. I walked for what seemed like miles and miles, and it probably was. The sun started to break the horizon fading the silvery light into a beautiful burning orange glow. I was very thankful for the sun consuming the darkened landscape and offering much-needed light to be able to see better. I hoped that I had not missed any crucial ways out of here. Finally, I spotted something, a tent, then another tent and a camper. It appeared that I had found a campground. Oh, thank god. I saw a pair of jeans and a plain grey tee shirt hanging on a makeshift clothesline, and they appeared to be my size. I quietly walked over and grabbed them from the line. The clothing smelled fresh, and I assumed that they had been freshly laundered. A building standing tall in the middle of the grounds caught my eye. I approached the building to find that it is a bathhouse and proceeded to go in. It was not anything special just three stalls with wooden painted plywood doors, a row of older looking sinks, and a little hall that led to two showers stalls. I looked up into the mirror, my face was covered in dried mud that had started to crack and fall off. I looked down to my arms and found the same thing. It must have been when I slipped a few times and fell in the mud along the creek. A shower was definitely in order. I made my way over to the showers stripping off my dress and stepping into the far shower. Using the soap bottle from the sinks I tried to scrub everything away, Lucian especially. I felt violated and vulnerable right now and wanted to sink to the floor and cry my eyes out. The only thing that I had going for me right now was the fact that I was still alive. I knew that I needed to keep moving. Something inside me told me that if Lucian found me that would be the end of my existence. Stepping out of the shower I realized that I didn't have anything to dry off with, so I turned the mud caked dress inside out and used it for my towel. I realized that I was putting dirt on my clean body, but it was the least of my worries. Throwing on the clothing that I had swiped, and throwing the dress in the trash I walked out of the bathhouse. I stood still at the door for a minute as I pondered what way I should go now. In front of me was where I came from so I decided maybe I should follow the road. Perhaps it would take me to the main road. Maybe I could find a car or hitchhike my way back home. If it was even possible to get home from here. Rounding the corner of the building a man stood casual leaning up against the building. His presence startled me, and I froze in place not sure if this was one of Lucian's henchmen or not. His dark green emerald eyes locked with mine. He wore no expression on his face, not even a faint smirk. He stared at me for a moment longer, and it was starting to creep me out.

"You smell like vampire." His deep slow voice articulating every word he said to me.

My breath caught in my throat, and I started slowly backing away from him. How would he know about vampires unless he is one, or one of Lucian's henchmen? Whatever the case I knew that I had to get away. Standing in the middle of the dirt road I glanced around for options keeping one eye on him. I was hoping for a car coming or a person walking around that would have been nice, but everything was eerily quiet. He didn't make any advances towards me, but that didn't mean he was not waiting for the right moment. A thought occurred to me, maybe he was the kind of person or thing that liked the chase its prey. Like a cat playing with a mouse, grab it then let it go then grab it again playing the game until the mouse is dead. The thought of this made my blood run cold, I scanned the area again for some sign of life, but there was still nothing. If I screamed, that would surely wake up any of the campers but would I be sealing their fate to die if, in fact, this was one of Lucian's people.

I finally managed to find my voice. "What are you talking about? There is no such thing as vampires." I said trying to play the dumb card hoping that maybe I could convince him that I knew nothing about vampires or had spent however long with one.

He moved his foot, and that was all that I needed. I started to run on the dirt road, but I didn't get far until his arms were around me. He spun me in his arms, and now we were face to face, and I could feel his hot breath on me, then he sniffed me. I tensed under him getting ready for the fight of my life. I somehow managed to get my hands between us. I tried to push him away but he was too strong for me, but I wasn't going to give up. I pushed harder getting my hands up by his face I was ready to start clawing at his face if need be. However, he was one step ahead of me grabbing each wrist in each hand. I tried to free my wrists, but his grip was too tight.

When he knew, he had me secure he spoke. "You are not a vampire though. Where did you come from?" He asked curiosity shining in his eyes.

I knew right then that my previous thought was incorrect about him. It was clear to me now that he was not one of Lucian's henchmen. I knew I should still be afraid but somehow relief washed over me. All I could feel now was a sense of safety, kindness and caring. I was on the edge of breaking down into tears because I knew that I was safe for a moment anyway.

After a moment of silence, he went on to say. "I'm not the enemy it is my duty to protect humans." He eyed me like I was supposed to pick up some hidden meaning in his words.

I knew he wanted me to say something but, at that moment, I was unsure what to say, if anything.

My mind was overloaded with feelings. I didn't know if I wanted to hug him, run from him, or just plain outbreak down and cry. The only feeling I was sure of right now was not to answer any of his questions, for fear of what Lucian would do to him when he found me. If I didn't tell this man what had happened to me and made sure that Lucian knew that I had not said a word about it then maybe, Lucian would let him live.

The thought of Lucian killing him made me say. "I should be on my way."

He let me break the hold he had on me, and I turned and started to walk in the opposite direction of him. I checked to see if he was following me but he did not. His actions reinforced the fact he was not one of Lucian's people. This built more trust in me, and my feelings for him grew stronger. It was crazy, I have heard of love at first sight but never thought it was real. Ok, maybe, it is not love at first sight but a mixed-up emotion of feeling safe.

"Wait, please, I know of a place that you can rest. I really would like to help you." He said. I could hear the plea in his voice.

He sounded genuine, and for a moment, I thought he felt the pull too. I quickly shook the thought from my head again blocking out my feelings for him and decided to stick to what was factual. The facts were that I knew he would not do me any harm and I was exhausted and had nowhere else to go. Really was I going to go sleep under a tree in the woods? I doubt that.

I turned back to him and warily accepted his offer. "I will take it."

He gestured for me to follow him, so I did. He led me away from all the campers and to a small little shack in the woods. Everything in me was say run away, all the horror movies that I had ever seen in my life popped into my head. That's how they all start, in some little shack or house in the middle of nowhere. He is possibly going to bring me here and cut me up into small little pieces and feed me to the wild bears if they had any here I thought. However, he had not made any moves to support that theory. I let it go and decided at this point that I really didn't care because somehow, I knew that if I didn't stay, I would die for sure. I opened the small wooden door, found a light switch to my left, and flipped it on even though it was daylight it was still dark in the little shack. The place was small, but it had a bed that appeared to have clean bedding on it. It really was not that bad. I relaxed a little when I closed the door, found the lock and locked it. I shut off the light and plopped myself on the bed. My head was swimming with thoughts of this new man and thoughts of Lucian. It didn't take long though before exhaustion took over and I fell asleep.

∾CHAPTER 12∾

I opened my eyes to see the inside of the little shack, the sun waking me as it beat down on my face from the small window by the bed. The sun was still approximately in the same spot as when I laid down. I figured that I had only slept for ten minutes because I was still so tired, I rolled over covering my head with the blanket slightly and drifted back to sleep.

An ear-piercing wolf howl jolted me out of my sleep. It was right next to the little shack. I could hear it sniffing at the door, but then it was gone. I sat up in bed trying to catch my breath, I was terrified, what if the wolf went to get his friends. I climbed out of bed and slipped on my shoes, I just had to get out of here. I looked out of the tiny window next to the door, and everything seemed clear. I went to the door and slightly opened it keeping most of my body behind the door for protection. I still didn't see anything or anyone. I opened the door all the way, ready to run back to civilization or at least the campground.

"Where are you going?" A voice asked from the blind side of the shack.

I jumped what felt like ten feet high, and my heart felt like it was going to beat right out of my chest. Oh, my god, Lucian found me, but Then I realized who it was. He had scared the crap right out of me. If he only knew what I had been through, he would not have done that.

"If I would have been that wolf you would have been eaten." He said chuckling to himself like it was some kind of joke.

I was still trying to gain any composure that I had left to answer his question. I wanted to snap at him for scaring me but decided against it.

"W…w….well I was going to the restroom, and then I am going to find something to eat." Then I stormed off towards the campground with a huff.

"I can help you with that. However, you are going the wrong direction." He said smugly.

I turned to see him leaning against the cabin smirking at me. Hastily I walked back towards him and past him without looking at him as I passed by. I was embarrassed, and I wanted to smack him. I decided that would not be a good idea since I had no idea where I was going, obviously. Then it dawned on me that I also had no idea where to get food let alone buy some so I decided to keep my mouth shut and hands to myself. Another thought occurred to me just then if I had some money would it be accepted in this other world. I glanced over my shoulder to see that he had caught up with me. I was still furious with him, but it was quickly fading, I could not hold it against him. He had no idea what had happened to me.

"Look I'm sorry, I didn't mean to scare you. I was just trying to have some fun."

I glanced at his face, and he seemed sincere, so I let it go.

On the other side of camp, there was a little convenience store. It was a quaint little place. Huge windows sprawled across the front of the store, revealing the old but beautiful inside. The outside of the store was still the old-time wood siding painted a pale-yellow color. At one end, a ten-foot section that didn't have any windows. In this space, someone had drawn and painted the store logo. A big circle half yellow and half green fading with a black silhouette of a bear standing on top of the green hill. I think the yellow part of the circle resembled the rising sun over the green hill. The bear posed on all four legs and appeared to be looking at you. Around the outside of the yellow sun in big black letters are the words *Bear Paw*. I assumed that was the name of the store. The inside of the store appeared to be nicely kept and smelt like cleaner and cooking food. The floors sparkled and shined like they had been freshly waxed. The food made my stomach growl. Normally I would not have thought this, but the smell of hot dogs cooking on heated rollers smelled delightful. The shelving stood in neat evenly spaced rows, and they were filled with all kinds of goodies. The woman working the counter smiled as we entered and I returned her smile. What a wonderful way to say welcome to my store, I thought. On closer inspection of the store I found that they sold pizza, popcorn, nachos and of course, the famous not sure I should eat that taco rolls. I was starving though, and at this point, I didn't care I would have eaten the taco rolls no questions asked.

"Please get anything you would like." He said to me then walked over to the woman behind the counter and started conversing with her.

I wanted to ease drop, but they were speaking so low I could not make out any words unless I were to stand next to them. I would see the woman look at me occasionally, and I wondered if they were talking about me. It didn't matter right now though I was too hungry to care. I grabbed one of everything that was hot even a taco roll, a soda from the fountain dispenser, some beef jerky, regular old plain potato chips and finally a snack cake. Trying not to drop anything, I made my way back to the counter. I set all the stuff on the counter, and the woman began to ring up my items. When she got to the end of my order, she asked if I would like anything else.

"No this will be plenty." I said feeling a little self-conscious, but I really didn't care I was starving.

"Will that be all for you Bill?" The woman looked up from the register and asked. He nodded his head yes. "The total is eighteen dollars and fifty-six cents." The woman said with a smile.

"Mrs. Woods, would you please put that on my tab." Bill said. She nodded and placed a few of the items in a bag and handed it to me.

"Thank you." I said to the both of them, while I started stuffing the hot dog in my mouth.

I felt a little guilty for getting so much food and not being able to pay for it, but I was starving. I told myself that I would repay him somehow, trying to make myself feel a little better about how much I spent. I was not the type of person to take advantage of someone. My mom raised me better than that.

As we walked out of the store, I took another a considerable bite out of the hot dog. I almost moaned at the taste of it. Surprisingly it tasted good for a convenience store hot dog. We slowly walked down to the riverside and sat at a picnic table on an empty campsite. I pulled some items from the bag and started eating them immediately. He paid no attention to me and just stared into the water. I wondered what he was thinking, but for whatever reason was too afraid to ask. When I was finished with what I had, I turned and stared into the water as well. Now that I had time to think and reflect on what had happened to me, I started to break down. I pulled my knees up to my chest and wrapped my arms around them. I started rocking back and forth a bit trying to help soothe the pain that I felt deep in my heart. Lucian could have killed me or changed me into a vampire was my first thought. Worse than that, he could have kept me chained to that bed for forever. Yet even worse than that, I thought that maybe just maybe with some love I could keep him. He really didn't treat me that badly. A motherly scolding voice started to yell at me. *What the hell is wrong with you? You were just some kind of love slave, and when he was over you, he was going to kill you.* Even though the voice was probably right, I tried to ignore it for now. Then there was just a few days ago when those people broke in, and I got the opportunity to run. I wondered who those people were for a moment. If Lucian was an all-powerful vampire, then why was I running from people that he could destroy in a matter of seconds? I pondered on that for a minute. The thoughts though soon faded as my mind didn't come up with any reasoning. After that, an overwhelming feeling of wanting to go home and see my mom took over my body. I began to sob and clutched my knees tighter to my chest. However bad I wanted to go home I could not because I didn't know how to get back to that world without that stone or whatever it was that got me here in the first place. I had no idea where to even find it or get it back. I had not seen it since the day that I came here. I was lost here forever, and I was just going to have to come to grips with that. I was startled when I felt someone put their hands on my shoulders. I lifted my elbow and threw it back but didn't connect with anything.

"It's ok, it is me Bill." He whispered quietly. "Do you want to talk about it?" He asked

"No, I don't want to; can you show me back to that cabin?" I asked feeling tired but mostly just wanting to be alone with my thoughts and try to sort through everything.

"Sure, but there is another cabin that is vacant, and it has a better setup than that shack in the woods. Would you like to go there?" He asked.

I didn't say anything just nodded my head in reply. We walked back to the store, and I waited outside as he went in. In a few seconds, he was back out with keys in hand. We walked a few feet to the cabin. He placed the key in the lock and started to turn it when a wolf's cry sounded through the air. He stiffened a tad but proceeded to open the door.

"Come let's get you inside." He said and pushed the door open and let me enter first.

The cabin was small but cute. An old fieldstone fireplace stood proud and tall against the wall to my right. Two little couches facing each other with a coffee table in between them sat on a beautiful tan rug a few feet away from the fireplace. As I took another step in, the wood floor creaked under my foot. The walls were covered with a knotty pine that had a shiny finish. One huge picture of an old cabin hung proudly on the far wall. On my left was a small kitchen complete with a stove and refrigerator. Straight in front of me were two doors. One led to a bedroom and the other to a bathroom. I wandered in further as he shut and locked the door behind us.

"Can I get you anything?" He asked.

"No thank you." I said softly, he had already done enough for me. "If you don't mind I'm going to take a shower." I said slowly feeling like I was in a haze of emotions that were all over the place.

One minute I wanted to cry and the next I wanted to run. I just needed some time to myself to get my emotions in check. I practically ran to the bathroom not waiting for an answer from Bill. I shut the door and leaned back against it, I stood there and reminded myself to just breathe while I pushed all my emotions back into their proper corners. After I had almost everything pushed back and relaxed a bit I turned the water on and let it get hot. I stood in the hot, almost scalding water, just allowing it hit me then drain off my body for a few minutes hoping that it would wash away the leftover emotions. I put the soap in the washcloth and lathered it up, then scrubbed my body as hard as I could, I repeated the same thing with my hair. The water started to turn cold before I wanted to be done. I quickly rinsed off, shut the water off, grabbed my towel, and wrapped it around me. I heard the front door open and close.

"Bill is that you?" I called from the bathroom my heart beat rapidly waiting for him to answer.

"Yes, it is I." He replied without missing a beat.

I instantly felt relieved, I don't know why but I just did. I guess he just felt easy to be around. Maybe it was the invisible strings that leaped out from me and connected to him. This feeling puzzled me but, then again maybe I was mistaking it for some other emotions. Perhaps it was a coping mechanism helping me to come to grips with what had happened to me these past few weeks or months.

I pulled my dirty clothing off the counter in front of me and slowly put them back on. If I were home, these would be clean clothing, but right now this was all I had. Just one more reminder of wanting to go home. I opened the door, strolled to the couch, sat down putting my feet up on the edge of the coffee table, leaned my head back against the sofa, and closed my eyes and just took deep calming breaths. I wondered how long I had been gone from home. I tried to count the meals that I ate when I was chained to the bed. Then I tried to count how many days I had been untied, two, three, maybe four. I was coming up with one week, two weeks…

His voice broke me out of my thoughts. "If you need to talk I'm here. I know you don't know me very well, but I'm pretty good at listening." He said as he sat down on the couch across from me.

I didn't know what to say or if I should say anything at all at this point.

"I really don't want to talk about me or my issues with a stranger." I snapped and immediately regretted it. I could see on his face that my words stung him and that stung me.

This man had done a lot for me even though he didn't have to do a thing. I felt horrible. I tried to reword my response trying to take back the sting.

"I mean I'm not really ready to talk about any of it yet."

If I were to tell him what happened to me, he most likely would think I was insane. Even my vampire loving friends back home would think that I finally snapped.

He acknowledged me with a nod of understanding and then said. "Maybe you can tell me your name and where you're from."

I could tell by the look in his eyes that he wanted to know more about me so, I thought about it for a moment. I could tell him a little bit about me. Maybe, it would help me mentally to remember who I was before all of this craziness.

"My name is Lily, and I come from a different world than here." I said, and then the unexpected happened. It felt so good to talk that I started rambling on and on about how I got here and what had happened to me. I didn't mean to tell him everything, but I just could not stop the flow of words coming out of my mouth. By the time, I got to the end of my story I was crying, and said, "I just want to go home."

For whatever reason, he didn't think that I was insane, instead, he came to me and gently wrapped his arms around me to console me, and I let him. Something about his touch helped heal me somehow.

"It is ok we will get you home. Can you tell me where you lived in that other world that you're from?" He asked as I wiped away a few tears and tried to stop crying before I answered him.

"I lived at eight hundred thirty-two St. Peter Street in New Orleans."

Thoughts of my mom flooded my head. I could not hold back any longer and let everything go, crying so hard that it was difficult to breathe. I tried to slow my crying by taking deep breaths, but it was not working. The seam that had been holding me together had finally come unraveled. I desperately tried hard to grab the strings to stop it, but they kept slipping out of my hands. Finally, after the fourth attempt, I was able to catch the strings and hold on tight. I pulled hard and slowly started to lace the gaping hole back up.

"I may know someone that could help you, but it is going to take me a little bit to get a plan in action. We currently are about a ten-hour drive away from there." He said.

This news instantly lifted my mood a bit, and that helped me to quit sobbing. I could not believe in this dimension that they still called it New Orleans, but then again, it is an awesome place.

Somewhere in the warmth of his arms, I fell asleep. I dreamt about home and my childhood. I made it through the part where some lunatic wielding a gun killed my dad right in front of me. The lunatic would point the gun at me then at my dad then back at me. It was obvious that one of us would die no matter how much money my dad gave him. At the very last moment, the gun pointed at me, and I heard the pop of the gun rattle around the room. In slow motion like in a movie, I saw my dad slump to the floor. He had jumped in front of me and took the bullet that was intended for me. People started to shuffle down the sidewalk towards us, and the man ran. In my dad's dying breath lying on the hard-concrete ground, he whispered to me. "Always love you" then he was gone. The paramedics arrived and tried with all they had to revive him, but I knew he was in heaven now with my grandparents. The police took me home to my mom, and that was that. The funeral was two days later. After the incident, mom didn't like me going anywhere without her, she was afraid of losing me next. I cannot say that I blame her, I was scared of losing her too. This lasted until I went off to college, but I still talked to her every day. The thought of her being home alone while I was away at college made me sick. In fact, I didn't want to go, but she practically begged me to go. I saw the argument we had about it over again. Then my dream suddenly morphed into Lucian chasing me through the woods again, and all I could see of his face were his red glowing eyes.

My eyes popped open. Bill had propped me up on some pillows and covered me with a blanket. I realized that I was all alone when there was a knock on the door. My heart started racing, and I could not control it. My thoughts instantly jumped to Lucian. Oh no, he found me. I laid there not moving frozen with fear and the hope that maybe if it was him, he would just go away.

"Lily, honey, it's me Mrs. Woods from the store, I thought you could use some clean linens." She said through the door.

I jumped to my feet and raced to the door feeling a little embarrassed that I had kept her waiting. I started apologizing right away for making her wait.

She just smiled and said, "That is okay, dearie."

She handed me the stack of towels and without saying anything more, turned and walked away. I took the towels to the bathroom and decided another shower sounded good since I had been drenched in sweat from my nightmare. In the middle of showering, I heard the loud grumblings of my stomach, complaining about wanting some food. I made it a quick shower and decided that maybe I should go visit Mrs. Woods and see if I could exchange some work for some food. I could not have Bill paying for anything else for me. I hated owing people anything.

∾CHAPTER 13∾

Mrs. Woods was sitting on a stool by the cash register looking half-awake and half-asleep when I walked in. She greeted me with a lopsided smile. The place looked like it could use a little cleaning today in my opinion.

I didn't waste any time and got right to the point of my visit. "Hi Mrs. Woods, would you be interested in exchanging some work for food? I could help you clean the floors or something." I said glancing around the store.

A smile turned up the other corner of her mouth. "That would be lovely dear. Come I will show you where the cleaning supplies are." She gestured to a doorway to her left.

I followed behind her as she showed me all around the kitchen area first before we got to the back corner. A half wall jetted up from the floor and stood serving as a divider between the cleaning supply area and the kitchen. I started towards the broom, but she stopped me.

"First you must eat something. Please go find something out there to eat." She pointed to the sales floor.

I turned to protest but she looked like she would ninja chop my head off if I went against her directions so, I opted to keep my mouth shut and do as I was told.

I eyed out a piece of pizza, one of those hot dogs and a small bag of chips. Meanwhile, Mrs. Woods had found a chair and pulled it up to some empty counter space that she had behind the cash register. In-between bites I thanked her for letting me do this. I devoured the food, cleaned up my small mess, and went for the broom again. I swept every nook and cranny and then went for the mop. When I finished mopping, the floors were all shiny and clean again, I took the bucket in the back to empty it. I heard the door chime, and I was hoping that it was Bill.

I was on my way to the front when I heard a man with a gruff voice asking Mrs. Woods "I'm looking for someone. She has long mahogany color hair, green eyes and about this tall."

It took me only a split second to realize that he was describing me. That stopped me dead in my tracks. The curiosity in me wanted to run out to the front and see who it was but something inside me was screaming stay put. I wished there had been one of those one-way windows that I could see through. Then I thought I could try to peek around the corner, I slowly edged my way to the doorframe being careful not to make a sound.

I heard the door chime again and heard Bill greet Mrs. Woods and then the man that was asking about me.

"I'm going to go back there to start making pizzas for that big order." Bill said to Mrs. Woods.

As soon as he appeared, I started towards him, but he held up his hand to stop me. He slid over to the counter where he could still see out the front and started rattling stuff around. For a moment, I thought he really was going to start making pizzas. I wanted to run to him now, I was terrified. My legs had started to shake, and I was not sure how much longer I was going to be able to stand on them without falling.

I finally heard Mrs. Woods say "I'm sorry I have not seen anyone that fits that description. However, if I do see her would you like me to give her a message?"

"Yes, could you please tell her that Lucian is looking for her and he would really like her to come home." The man said.

"Sure thing, I will let her know if she comes my way." Mrs. Woods replied.

The door chimed, and the man was gone. I ran to Bill, threw myself around him, and started to cry. "He is going to find me, and take me back to his prison again. What am I going to do; I just can't go back there." I said through sobs.

"Don't worry you are safe with me. I will not let anything happen to you. We do need to get you out of here though. Something tells me that he will be back. Do you know who he is?" He asked wrapping his arms around me in what felt like a protective bubble.

"No, I have never heard his voice before." I said.

"Mrs. Woods, could you please lock the door, bring your shotgun and come here?" Bill asked.

Within a matter of seconds, she emerged standing in front of us looking more like a worrier than a fifty or sixty-something woman.

"I need to go and check if the coast is clear I have to get her out of here. These people are bold, and I need to find a safe place for her until Friday when I can take her back to New Orleans." Mrs. Woods nodded in acknowledgment.

He disentangled from me giving me a don't worry look then slipped out the back door.

"He really likes you." She said when the door closed. "He wouldn't be going through all of this trouble if he didn't." She said as she walked over to a television set and turned it on.

When the screen came on, I could see off all four corners of the building in all directions. There were no signs of anyone moving about. It felt eerily quiet and strange. It felt like that feeling you get just before something horrible happens where everything slows down. I peered at the screen and wondered where all the campers were. Then I realized maybe it was a weekday and everyone had gone back to the mundane everyday hustle and bustle of life. But then again, the two days that I had been here so far, I could not recall seeing anyone at all. All though I had not been outside much either, my mind reasoned with me.

My mind drifted back to her comment from earlier, and I found myself staring at the door waiting for it to open and Bill to walk in holding a bouquet of flowers. From what she had said I thought that maybe he felt the same way about me as I did for him. There was definitely something there that we both were not ready to commit to.

Mrs. Woods grabbed my shoulder and pushed me back behind her as a knock on the front glass door pulled me back into reality. I tried to peer around her at the screen to see who it was but she had me pinned up against the wall where the screen was just out of sight. Then I heard some screams or cries of murder, and it chilled me to the bone. The back door flew open and slammed hard up against the wall making the small building shutter in protest. Mrs. Woods raised her gun in the direction of the intruder pointing the barrel at him.

"Stay back, or I will shoot." She yelled at the man.

I recognized him at once of course, it was Lucian. My blood ran cold in my veins, and my heart pounded in my ears. Time slowed to a crawl.

"I don't think so, lady. You are going to be the first one to die." He said, and then looked at me cowering behind Mrs. Woods.

His eyes glowed translucent blue, and it terrified me. This was the first time that I had seen him like this. Even back at the house, I could not remember his eyes turning the translucent blue, soulless orbs. No matter though I knew this was going to be the end of the road for me. I knew that the gun that Mrs. Woods was holding would not kill him as I gathered my knowledge from vampire books that I had read. I realized that the only thing to do would be to turn myself over and maybe he would let Mrs. Woods live. I forced my way out from behind Mrs. Woods.

"Lucian, wait, please don't hurt her. You can have me, but please leave her be." I begged

He pondered that for a second. Then slowly he moved towards me as I pushed the gun towards the wall lifting the other hand for him to take.

"Oh, Lucian." I cried out. "I missed you, but I wasn't sure how to get back to you or even if it was okay to come back." I said trying to distract him from Mrs. Woods.

I started to move away from her and towards him when I saw something move out of the corner of my eye. A shadow figure now stood in the doorway.

"I wouldn't do that if I were you." The female voice rang through the room.

Without even looking at her, he stopped his advance and said. "Oh, and you are going to stop me?" Fury filling his eyes again.

"Well, as a matter of fact, I am going to stop you. How would you like to die? Would you like to be burned or bound and buried?" She asked. Then in the matter of a split second, she was in between our outstretched hands.

"What are you doing?" I shouted at her. "He is going to kill you." But then she shoved him hard, making him fly out of the door.

The next thing I knew Bill was standing in front of me with his hand out towards me to take. "Come let's go."

I took his hand without hesitation and let him pull me along through the woods. We didn't stop running until we came to a house and he pulled me inside and locked the door. I put my hands on my knees trying to catch my breath. When I finally caught enough breath, I started to shake. I just knew that the two women were going to die because of me.

Bill put an arm around me and walked me to the couch. He sat, pulling me down into his lap. "Don't worry she can handle herself." He said almost like he could read my thoughts then he let out a slight giggle.

I didn't think it was funny though. The idea of her fighting a vampire that would kill her in an instant just was not funny to me.

Four rhythmic knocks on the door sent a shiver down my spine, as fear rose in my throat ready to scream. Bill set me aside then jumped up to answer it. In came the woman who saved Mrs. Woods and me. I felt relieved as she walked in with Mrs. Woods in tow. Feeling emotional, I jumped up, ran to them, and gave each of them a big hug. Then I thanked the woman profusely for saving us.

"No need to thank me," the woman said with a small smile, then she pointed at Bill and said, "Can I talk to you?" She hesitated and looked over at me then added. "Outside."

Bill nodded at her and gave me a quick glance. Then they went out the door. Mrs. Woods came and sat next to me on the couch.

"That was the most fun I have had in a long time." She said and started to laugh.

What the hell was with these people laughing about a cold-blooded killer? However, as fast as she had started, she stopped. I think she realized that I was not laughing with her but was shaking. She put an arm around me and pulled me close to her. I lost it and started crying again.

She stroked my hair and said, "It's ok, you are safe, and no one can hurt you here." I felt her genuine promise and felt as though it was a true statement. I had to grip onto something other than gloom and doom.

She pulled a blanket off the back of the couch and draped it over me. The blanket was soft and warm. I leaned on her shoulder, and she just continued to stroke my hair not saying anything. The adrenaline started to wear off letting my body shut down and I was sleeping in a matter of seconds.

The scene at the store replayed itself over and over again in my mind. I tried to control the dream and make it something else, but it was not working. So instead, I started to change the outcome of the scene. The first ending I put myself back with Lucian in my bedroom at his house. As the scenes progressed and ended, he killed me. However, just before he was going to kill me, I made the dream start over again. This time I had Mrs. Woods shoot him with the gun she had. It didn't stop him though all it did was piss him off and he killed her after one more shot passed through his body. He didn't drink her blood though he just squeezed her head until it popped open spilling her brain on the floor. Then he grabbed me his eyes glowing red. This terrified me; it was like looking into the soulless eyes of a demon. I didn't like this ending either and changed it one more time. This time though I was able to get the dream outside any buildings. Standing in the middle of the woods, I heard wolves howl all around me. They sounded like they were closing in on me from all sides. I got my first glimpse of the wolves. However, they were not facing me they had their butts towards me. They were protecting me. As the circle closed in, I saw the glowing red eyes of Lucian appear in the darkness. However, as I turned away from him I seen other vampires appearing one by one out of the shadows. We were outnumbered, and there was only one way out. I could let the wolves fight, and they would surely die, or I could surrender to him and save their lives. He beckoned to me. I closed my eyes for a second then ran and leapt in front of the wolves. I turned my back to Lucian for a second to look at the wolves and to say sorry without actually speaking the words. I saw a tear run down one wolf's face but quickly turned away towards Lucian. I ran towards him as fast as I could grabbing a strong pointed stick that I hoped was sharp enough to pierce his heart and kill him. As I drew closer to him, I pretended to trip and maneuvered the sharp end of the stick between him and me. I felt the stick hit his flesh, but I just didn't have enough strength to make it pierce him. He grabbed me and started to squeeze my head. Just before my head popped, my eyes slung open as I gasped for breath a few times. I had heard at some point in life that if you died in a dream, you died in real life. I wondered if that was true?

Bill had traded places with Mrs. Woods, who now sat across the room from me. The other woman sat in a chair next to her. I wondered why these people were protecting me. I didn't have anything to give them in return. I had to get out of here before they ended up dead. Peering around the room, everyone seemed to be sleeping. I slowly and carefully slipped out of Bill's arms and very quietly rose to my feet and started for the door.

"Where are you going?" A woman's voice came from behind me.

Her voice startled me. I hung my head for a second. I knew that I had been caught. I turned to look at her, swallowing down the sadness I felt.

"I'm sorry, but I must go." I said in a whisper as the tears started to flow down my face. "I don't want you to die because of me. My life is not worth your life." I said and turned back towards the door, placing a hand on the knob. "He is not going to stop until he has me back and all of you will be dead." I just could not face her right now.

I felt Bill's hand on my shoulder. "Please don't go. We can protect you." He said and spun me away from the door into his arms. "I really would like you to stay with me. I can protect you I promise." He whispered into my hair.

The tears flowed in a continuous stream down my face. "Bill, I would love to stay with you but I know that this is going to end in death for the both of us." I tried to turn away from him and proceed out the door, but he had a tight grip on me. His arms felt like iron bars holding me in place. It felt so safe and secure making my decision even harder to follow through on.

"Please stay; I was planning our trip for tomorrow. You know the one where we go to New Orleans. It would get us away from here and away from Lucian." He said smiling down at me.

My mind burst into yes, yes, yes, I will stay with you but my heart said no, no, no, you should go and leave him and these other people alive. My conscious was winning the battle though. It was telling me that I should stay and that I was safe here.

I decided to go with the three yeses'. "Alright, as long as you think that we are safe here I will stay with you."

Bill's face lit up, and he pulled me back into his arms not saying anything. He walked me back over to the couch, and we sat down. The room was silent. The woman across from me stared out the window by the door, and Mrs. Woods had her eyes closed and looked like she was still fast asleep. I cuddled up next to Bill as he wrapped his arms around me. I was almost falling asleep when the door flew open and thudded against the wall. I must have jumped a mile in the air, breaking Bill's hold on me.

"It's ok." Bill said trying to calm me. "It is just Aidan, Mrs. Fox's husband." He gestured to Aidan and the woman.

I relaxed after a second, but my heart was beating way too fast. I took in some deep breaths trying to calm my nerves. If I smoked, I would surely need a cigarette right now.

"Hey Aidan," Bill called out to him. "Are we all set to go in a few hours?"

"Hey bro I heard you had some problems at the store and yes you are all set to go the car is filled with gas." He said as he draped his arm around his wife and pulled her into a kiss.

I looked away trying to give them a private moment. All I could think about at that moment was kissing Bill like that. I suppressed the sigh that almost escaped me. Bill draped his arm around my neck, and I snuggled back into him. My thoughts were spinning with the prospect of going home or at least I was hoping that it was home. Somewhere in the somber moment, I drifted to sleep.

∾CHAPTER 14∾

The next thing I knew Bill was waking me. "Are you ready?" He asked.

I was still groggy and didn't know what he was saying to me at first, but that quickly gave way to excitement. I jumped to my feet proclaiming that I was ready to go. I was hoping that this trip would leave all of my problems behind. However, at the same time, I was anxious to leave unsure of what I would find. I may or may not be in the same world I used to live in. If I were not, then I would figure it out from there. I was still holding on to my hope. Bill stood up after a few seconds of me standing there staring at him. Without saying a word, he grabbed my hand and led me towards the door.

"I'll see you guys in a few days." He said, putting his hand up giving them a little wave.

In unison, they replied "Later" and I think I heard a "Be careful."

He opened the door to reveal our chariot. A silver Audi A8, the windows were tinted so dark you could not see in the car. The car looked like it was fast just sitting still. Bill opened the door for me to get in. He was such a gentleman. I climbed in on the leather seats and admired the interior as it took him a quick second to get in himself. We both buckled our seat belts, and he started the engine, it roared to life with enthusiasm. He switched the gears to drive, nailed the gas and spun the car in a small circle, giving me a minor heart attack. I reached out for something to grab hold of but found nothing at first until I found his arm. A jolt of electricity ran through our touch, and I felt his pull again. A deep-down feeling in the pit of my stomach said you are his. I was not ready for any of these feelings so, I did my best to ignore it.

I released his arm quickly and breathlessly said. "Can we please not do that again?" Terror trickling through my voice and making it shake. I searched the interior again for something other than him to hold onto, but there was only the door handle. It was going to be a long ten-hour trip if he drove like that the whole time.

A smirk crossed his face then he said. "Sorry I just wanted to make sure that the car was in good working condition." Then he busted out into laughter that almost deafened me.

Once we reached the blacktop road, he relaxed into his seat and was paying attention to the road and behaving himself for the most part, except for the speeding. About twenty-five miles down the road, he pulled into a restaurant and into a parking space.

"Come we are going to eat."

Before I could get my seat belt off, he was at my door opening it for me. He stuck his hand out for me to take. I placed my hand in his, and he pulled me up and out of the car. He wrapped one arm around me keeping me in place like I was going to run away or something, and closed the car door with the other. He pulled me along into the small greasy spoon restaurant. A waitress met us at the door, then walked us to a booth in the back of the restaurant. She sat a menu down for me and handed Bill one. She took our drink order then went to fetched them for us. When she returned, she asked for our food order. I ordered a hamburger and fries. Bill, on the other hand, ordered a burger, fries, onion rings, and deep-fried mushrooms. After he was finished ordering, he looked at me. I must have had a look on my face that said are you really going to eat all that. He grinned at me sheepishly and nodded his head yes. It seemed like only seconds passed before the waitress brought us our food. I slowly moseyed my way through my hamburger and fries. I watched Bill devour his food in a matter of what seemed like seconds. If I had to compare it to something it would have been a dog that had not eaten anything in days. I could not believe that he ate it all and that quickly. I asked for a box for the rest of my food. We paid and were out the door, back in the car and on the road without incident.

The silence in the car was driving me crazy, so I turned on the radio and flipped through the stations, but there was nothing on really, so I just left it on a hard stone station. Then Leaned back in the seat and watched as the darkness flew by the car. The darkness was hypnotizing and made me very sleepy despite my anxiety. The next thing I knew the car was slowing down and I opened my eyes to see the sun rising above the trees in the sky.

"Oh, good you're awake, we are going to stop for gas."

I nodded still trying to get the sleepiness out of my voice before I spoke.

"Did you have a good snooze?" He asked eyeing me as if I was going to run away or something.

"Yes, I did." I answered as he pulled up to a gas pump.

"Do you need or want anything from inside?" He asked as he put the car in park.

"Actually, I am hoping they have a restroom." I said as I undid my seatbelt and opened the door to get out.

I walked into the store and asked the clerk for the restroom he pointed to a door between two walk-in coolers. I opened then shut the door, locking it behind me. After I was finished using the toilet, I washed my hands. I looked up into the mirror at a woman I didn't recognize. My hair was a mess and knotted in various places. My face looked shallow and dirty. Black circles enveloped my eyes. I looked like I had not slept a wink in days or I was on some kind of drugs. I splashed some water on my face trying to wash it all away. The water dripped down my neck and revealed two round circular scars that

Lucian had given me. The thought of him sent a shiver down my spine. I decided that if I washed my face with soap that maybe just maybe I could wash him away. I lathered up some soap in my hands scrubbing my face. Then I splashed water on my face to rinse it. I reached for the paper towel and dried my face a bit before I stood up and opened my eyes. That's when I saw Lucian standing behind me. I tried to scream, but my voice just would not work. I was frozen with fear. He stretched his hand out to reach for me. A knock on the door though made him disappear into thin air.

"Lily are you in there?" I heard Bill's panic laced voice come through the door.

It took me a second to find my voice and take the two giant steps to the door. I flung it open and jumped on Bill throwing my arms and legs around him.

"What is going on?" He asked eyeing me speculatively. He knew something was wrong.

I looked around and only saw the clerk in the store, and he seemed to be paying attention to what was going on. I whispered "Lucian" to Bill and said nothing more.

He must have gotten the hint that I was not going to say anything until we were out of earshot of anyone listening. I didn't want the word vampire hanging in the air for the clerk to hear. He would think I was crazy and had escaped from the loony bin. I guess I looked like it too.

"Ok, we will talk about it in the car." He said then gestured to the coolers. "Would you like something to drink?"

I walked over to the cooler and found some sweet tea. He wrapped an arm around me, and we walked to the counter to pay for our stuff. I felt relieved when we were back in the car, buckled up, and on our way.

"Ok talk, what the hell happened in there." He said in a demanding voice, no not demanding, by the look on his face, it was more that of concern.

I started spilling my guts about what I saw and what happened just before I saw him. I could see that he was thinking about it trying to put the pieces of the puzzle together. Then he picked up his cell phone and called someone. He explained the situation then asked whoever it was if this was possible and if vampires could do that. Then there was just a series of yeses and okays. Then he was off the phone but didn't say anything to me, but had a puzzled look on his face. I was dying to know who he had talked to and what was said. So finally, I asked after I realized he was not giving up any information without me asking.

"So… What did they say?" I asked looking at his face that was still deep in thought.

"That was my sister." He said, paused for a long moment before continuing. "She has never heard of such a thing happening."

His sentence caught me a little off guard as I thought about it. I wondered how she knew so much about vampires. If she knew so much about vampires, was she one? Then another thought occurred to me if she was a vampire was Bill a vampire too? As I realized this, I could feel my heartbeat increase and terror spread over me. I quickly calmed myself though and realized that I was being irrational. I had seen Bill eat food. Most vampires according to books, and what I knew about Lucian, food would have made them sick. Besides what were the chances? Bill reached for my hand and I hesitated but took it anyway.

"Are you okay?" He asked.

"Yeah, I'm fine now. "I said trying not to give away anything with my voice. But my voice betrayed me and broke on the word fine.

"It is ok, you know. You are with me I will not let anything or anyone harm you." He said as he lightly squeezed my hand three times.

Something in this comforted me, and I felt like I could ask my question.

"Bill, I have a question. You said that your sister had never heard of that happening before. How does she know stuff like that about vampires?" I asked slowing down on the last part not really sure I wanted to hear the answer. I felt somewhat weird for asking the question at all.

"Okay..." He said and paused.

I think he was contemplating what he wanted to tell me.

"I could lie and sugar coat this but eventually you will know the truth, and I really don't want to hurt you so here we go. My sister is a vampire." He said pausing waiting for that to sink into my head.

My heart started racing.

"But she is the good kind of vampire. She is not like sick twisted Lucian. She actually saves people, don't get me wrong she kills to stay alive, but she only goes after bad people and takes them out of this world so that they can't hurt anyone else." He said pausing again. "You actually met her you just didn't know it. She is Mrs. Fox."

I didn't know what I was feeling right now, betrayed, hurt, anger he could have told me sooner. I knew that was false though because I knew in my heart that if he had told me sooner, I would not be sitting in this car with him right now.

"Please say something." Bill begged me.

I was looking for the words to say but didn't know really what to say. I opened my mouth but shut it before anything came out. I tried again, and my subconscious took over. "So… are you a vampire too?" I said the words in a rush not sure if I could get all of them out before my mouth locked shut again. I stared at his face as a wave of emotions washed over it. I could tell he was trying to decide to tell me the truth or a lie. And I knew right then and there that he was a vampire too.

"Lily… yes, I am. But I will not hurt you. I'm not Lucian I don't want your blood." He said in a calm rush of words.

This was all too much for me to take in right now and my brain denied everything and shut down. I pretended that I had not heard any of it. Everything started to swirl around me, and I could see the little white balls of light dancing through my vision. How the hell is this possible was my only thought before blackness dragged me under.

∼CHAPTER 15∼

Bill shaking me a bit awakened me. "Lily, please wake up we are here."

I stretched and rubbed the sleep from my eyes. "I had the craziest dream. You said you were a vampire and had a vampire sister." Then I started to laugh hysterically.

He laughed too but not quite to my extent. I finally quit laughing when I could see the city lights of New Orleans. My laughter replaced by excitement. I was home. I wanted to start jumping up and down. Everything looked the same as before I was pulled into that other place. Nothing had changed there was no bubble looking houses. This raised my excitement level through the roof. I was home, finally home where there were no monstrous Lucian's.

"Our exit is 235A then we will turn left on Orleans Avenue." I said as we approached the exit from highway 10. He did exactly what I said. "Ok turn left here, and then turn right there." I said As I point in the direction, I wanted him to take. "My house is the next block down on the left."

My house came into view. Big and blue with white Victorian style trim. I could not wait to get out the car. I almost jumped out before Bill had a chance to put the car in park. I ran up to the door and tried to turn the door handle, but it was locked. I absent-mindedly reached into my pocket looking for my key but then remembered that it was probably in the clothing that I had worn to Lucian's. I grabbed the rocking chair and stood on top of it to reach the spare key that we always kept on the sill above the door. I tried to stay steady on the chair but it rocked quickly throwing my balance off, and I started to fall backward. Bill caught me before I could injure myself. His face inches from mine. I saw his eyes dart down to my lips, but then he quickly set me down on my feet and reached for the key. Once he had it, he then handed it to me. I quickly turned before his eyes found my face and noticed the blush staining my cheeks. I shoved the key in the lock and started to turn it.

His hand quickly covered mine and said. "Wait are you sure that we should just enter the house?"

What a weird thing to say but then maybe he was afraid that my mom would shoot me or something. "It's fine my mom does not carry a gun or anything like that." I said and pushed the door open and walked in. Everything was just the way it had always been. "Mom, are you home it's me, Lily." I said, but there was no response. She was apparently not home.

"What is today?" I asked Bill and turned to look at him waiting for his answer. He had a funny look on his face but answered my question.

"Today is Wednesday."

"Oh, she is at Church and should be home around nine. Make yourself comfortable. Would you like something to drink?" I asked and started towards the kitchen.

I opened the cupboard where we kept the glasses, pulled two from the shelf, walked over to the refrigerator, and fill the glasses with ice and water. I sat down on the couch next to Bill turning on the television. Nothing was on as usual, so I turned it to a movie and just relaxed leaning against Bill. The clock on the wall started to chime, letting me know that it was nine. My mom should be walking in the door at any minute. I was excited to see her, so I got up and started pacing by the door waiting for her to walk in. A minute passed, but it seemed like an eternity before I heard her small footfalls on the porch walking up to the door. I grabbed the handle and ripped the door open. Her face lit up with surprise as soon as she saw me standing there.

"Lily, is that really you?" She screamed with excitement. Then wrapped her arms around me so tight that I thought she was going to break me. Then she held me back from her and took me in. "You have lost some weight, are you hungry?" Then we both burst into tears pulling each other close again.

"Oh, mom I missed you, I love you." I managed to get out between sobs. She tightened her arms around me and kissed my cheek.

"I thought that you were gone forever. Where did you go?" She asked. I was not ready to tell her where I had been. Bill came to my rescue clearing his throat behind me.

"Mom, I would like you to meet Bill. He brought me home." I said, and I knew that he did more than just bring me home he fought off an evil vampire. The thought sent a shiver down my spine. I quickly shook it off though and pretended like nothing was wrong.

"It is nice to meet you Lily's mom." Bill said then continuing after a few moments of awkward silence. "But I really should be going."

"No, you should stay and have dinner. I'll call and order some pizza." She trilled.

Bill didn't protest he just went and sat down on the couch. My mom went to the phone to order the pizza, and I sat down next to him.

"Thanks for saving me just then, with my mom. Thank you for saving my life and bringing me back here. Where are you going though?" I asked not sure why he would want to leave already. I definitely was not ready to let him go just yet. I reached up and touched his face. He leaned gently into my hand, and I felt a static charge run through me.

"Well, I did what I said I was going to do. That was getting you home safe now it is time for me to go home." He said sheepishly smiling at me.

I don't know if he was testing me to see how I felt about him in that moment or what. But, I just could not bear the thought of him leaving me just yet. A thought ran through me, maybe he didn't like me like I like him or maybe he didn't feel the same pull I felt when I was with him.

Whatever the case, I was not ready to let him go just yet, so I settled for begging. "Please, don't go I would really like to show you around while you are here. Please stay for a few days. Please, please, please." I said giving him the most pitiful pouting face I could muster.

"Ok, ok, I'll stay for a few days but then I must go home. I have some business to attend to there. I do however need to make a few phone calls I'll be right outside on the porch." He said and smiled wholeheartedly at me this time. He kissed my forehead and walked out the front door.

My mom came back in the room and sat down next to me on the couch. "It is so wonderful to have you home. I still want to know where you have been for the last month. I thought you were…" She trailed off and started to cry.

Holy shit, I had been gone for a month. I put my arms around her, squeezed her tight, and said. "Mom I'll tell you someday where I have been but for now let's just say I'm home safe and that is all that matters." I eyed her seeing if she was ok with that. She must have been because she dried her tears and smiled at me.

A knock on the door startled both of us, making us jump, then we giggled at our responses. "That must be the pizza man." She said rising to her feet to answer the door. "Where did Bill go?" She asked as she realized that he was nowhere to be seen.

I pointed outside and said. "He had to make a few phone calls. Oh, and you don't mind if he stays here a few days, do you?"

She shook her head no, as she answered the door to get the pizza from the pizza man. She handed the man the money in exchange took the pizzas, and then she shut the door and waltzed into the kitchen to set the pizza on the table. "Come let's eat." she trilled from the kitchen.

I walked over to the door and opened it so that I could tell Bill it was time to eat. I poked my head out the door looking for him, but I didn't see anyone. I called him. "Bill, where are you?" I said loudly but trying to be quiet.

He popped up from around the corner of the house as he put his phone in his pocket. He sighed slightly, looked up at me, and smiled, but it quickly faded. He looked like something was wrong. I walked out on the porch shutting the door behind me.

"What's a matter?" I asked as he walked up the stairs towards me.

"Nothing, maybe just a little homesick." He said and changed his frown to a small straight-line smile.

I wrapped my arms around him kissing him on the cheek. Then took his hand and pulled him into the house. We all sat at the table as my mom shared embarrassing stories about me. We sat there for hours talking about everything under the sun except for where I had been. I just thought that it was best that I not share any of it with my mom or anyone else for that matter. This was something that I was going to take to my grave with me. The clock started to chime signifying three in the morning, I was getting tired, and I could tell my mom was getting tired as well. She looked as though if she closed her eyes for a split second that she would fall asleep.

"Mom we should go to bed." I said followed with. "I'll be here in the morning, I promise."

She nodded sleepily, then got up from her chair came over to me and kissed and hugged me. "Love you and see you in the morning." She mumbled sleepily in my ear. Then she left the room heading to her bedroom.

I stood and grabbed Bill's hand and led him to the couch. Then went to my room and grabbed a few pillows and a blanket, taking them to the living room for him.

"Lily, will you stay right here with me?" He asked. I shot him a look, and he said. "It's not like

146

that I just want to make sure you are safe." He smiled at me and opened the blanket for me to get in. I glanced back to my bedroom where I really wanted to sleep. In my own bed but decided that maybe just for tonight I would sleep with him. Besides I knew if I slept alone the awful dreams of Lucian would come back to haunt me. Not to mention I didn't know how long he was going to stay. I wiggled in beside him, and he wrapped his arm and the blanket around me. It was not long before I was asleep. The next thing I knew it was morning and the sun was shining in the windows. I was surprised to find bill sitting in the recliner and not behind me on the couch. I wondered how long he had been awake.

"Good morning." I whispered as I wiped the sleep from my eyes with the back of my hands.

I stretched and moved to get up as he mumbled his good morning to me. I sauntered to the bathroom then to the kitchen to make some coffee and to find something to eat. I was starving. When I got to the kitchen, my mom was already up and had made coffee. She was sitting at the table drinking a cup and looking at the newspaper. On one of the pages, there were the charred remains of a building. A headline saying something about vandalism at a state park in Georgia. I grabbed the page and started to read the report. It didn't say anything more than a band of thieves and arsonists broke into the store, stole hundreds of dollars, and then burned the store to the ground. It also said that anyone with information about the crime should call the police department. My heart skipped a beat for a second as I realized that I was involved with what happened. How do I go to the police department and tell them a vampire attacked me and was going to kill me if I didn't go with him? They would never believe my story they would put me in the asylum for sure. My heartbeat was rising I could hear it and the more the scene came back to me the faster my heart started to beat.

Bill startled me when he put his hand on my shoulder. "Are you hungry? Please let me take you all out for breakfast." He said looking at my mom clearly inviting her to go with us.

My mom folded her paper and placed it on the table. "That sounds like a wonderful idea." She said but then her face turned apologetic, and I already knew what she was going to say. "I would love to take you up on that offer, but I really must get going to work."

"Ok, Lily's mom." He said and then turned to me. I just shook my head yes.

My mom spoke up just then. "You can call me MaryAnn." She said with a giggle then she nodded at me, excused herself and waltzed into the bathroom.

I let out a laugh. "She likes you." I said standing, letting the paper fall back to the table and forgetting about it for the time being. "Come let's go get some breakfast and then I can show you around a bit." He pulled me into his arms and squeezed me a bit then released me and took my hand.

148

I stopped by the bathroom door. "Mom we are leaving, I'm taking the spare key since I lost the other one. I will see you later tonight. Love you."

She replied with "love you too" then we were out the door.

Bill started walking to the car digging the keys out of his pocket.

"You should put those back in your pocket, we are walking where we are going." I say beaming a big bright smile at him.

He reached for my hand, and I graciously took it. We walked two blocks down from the house to The Old Coffee Pot Restaurant. I had eaten here many times and loved their food. It was so delicious. I just knew Bill would like it too. We sat down at a table, and Bill's phone rang. He picked it up and answered it with an apologetic expression on his face. He didn't say much other than okay several times. The expression on his face changed from apologetic to happy then to anger. He hung up the phone and reached his hand across the table for me to take.

"Sorry about that it was my sister. She has been keeping me informed about what is happening back at home." I was going to ask about Lucian when the waitress came to take our orders but as soon as she left the question came out in a flurry.

"Has there been any more trouble with Lucian?" I asked and held my breath until he answered. I was hoping that he would say no.

"There was a little the day we left, but there hasn't been anything since then. Please don't worry about it right now. The thing that is bugging me is how you were tricked into thinking you were in another dimension when really you didn't go anywhere. I wish you had whatever it was you picked up that day. My sister knows someone that helped her out a several years ago, and she lives here somewhere. The only problem I have is I don't know where she is or where she lives." He said smiling at me.

"Well we could take some of this delicious food to my mom she knows a lot of people around here. Do you know what this woman looks like?" I asked the smile fading from my face as I realized that I might have to tell her what happened to me, to explain why we are looking for this person. Maybe she will not ask though she is not the nosey type. She is just happy that I'm home and safe, my mind told me.

"No, I don't, but my sister could describe her to me." He said answering my question.

We ordered my mom some food, paid and walked out on to the street. The sun burned my skin, but it felt terrific. The hot, humid air filled my lungs making me feel like I was underwater trying to breathe. However, it was still nice to be home. We walked the block back towards the house making a right-on Bourbon Street where my mom owned a little store called Voodoo Blues. She had bought the place after my dad had been killed. He had an excellent insurance policy that paid off the house and left her with enough money to buy the store. So far, it was a good investment for her. It paid the bills and put money in her bank account for when she retired. Mom was stocking shelves when we walked in. Without saying anything, I stuck the food out for her to take.

~CHAPTER 16~

"What a pleasant surprise." She said taking the food and wrapping me in a hug. "Thank you." She said mostly to Bill.

We followed her to the breakroom taking a seat at the old vintage table and chairs from the sixties. Mom had fallen in love with the set and vowed to keep it forever. Mom dug into her food.

"I have a question." Bill started with. Mom stared up at him blankly but nodded for him to go ahead. "I don't know how to start the conversation without sounding weird, or like some kind of freak." He said pausing for a moment. I was sure that he was trying to figure out how to ask the question.

I jumped in just then. "Mom, what Bill is trying to say is this. I picked up what I thought was a pretty stone. When my hand warmed it, something happened, and I felt like I had been transported into a different world." I went on to explain what I saw but stopped when I got to the abandoned building. I really didn't want her to know the rest of the story, well not right now at least.

She looked at me then at Bill then back to the door. She slowly excused herself from the table and shut the door resting one hand on the door and the other on top of the door handle. She paused and waited a minute before she turned around. She came and put a hand on my shoulder. In all of my twenty-five years, I had never seen her act like this.

"I have only heard about this happening one other time in my life. It happened to me just before I met your father." She said, "I don't know what it was, but I looked for an explanation for years. I saw the same things that you just described. I ended up by an abandoned warehouse."

Images of the warehouse flashed through my head as she spoke.

"I tried to get in, but it was locked. I ran away from that place and eventually found shelter from the storm under an umbrella that I found. I tried to go home, but it was no use. Finally, I found a quiet place that was somewhat out of the way, rested my back against the wall, and fell asleep. Your father is the one that woke me up. It was bizarre, I thought that maybe I dreamt it at first, but then realized that it was real and that I had been temporarily transported to a weird world. Afterwards, I sought out someone that could explain what happened to me. A year went by with no word or explanation of what happened. Your dad and I had gotten married. One day though when I was walking to work this lady passed me and whispered I know the answer. At first, I thought the answer to what. The puzzled look on my face must have given me away because the next thing she said was. I know where you went. The images of that other world flashed through my mind. I just knew that I had to talk to this lady. What do you know? I asked her. How do you know that? She looked into my eyes and took my hands. I can't tell you on the street there are too many people listening. She said as she glanced around wildly looking for anyone that may have been listening to our conversation. Meet me back here after work, and we will talk about this. She said and then she disappeared into a darkened alley. I walked the rest of the way to work at a quick pace and the day slowly went by. I couldn't wait I was going to find the answers to my questions. I practically ran back to the spot where I met the lady. She was already waiting for me. Follow me she said. We walked to a house that had purple shutters, things hanging in the windows and broken glass hanging on strings. I think she said that these things were too ward off evil spirits. Anyway, I followed her into her house, we sat at her dining room table drinking tea, and we proceeded to talk about what happened to me. She told me that it was some kind of Black Magic and it was supposed to trap me in the illusion that I had been transported to a different world. However, when I was there, I didn't do what I was supposed to so I ended up sitting in that alley. When she touched my skin, she said that she could feel the place I was in and that it was full of darkness and it was supposed to lure the bride of darkness. Of course, I didn't know how to take all of it, but eventually, I just dismissed it, and figured she was crazy." Mom said.

I started shaking as she said the last sentence. This would mean that I looked into the face of darkness. I escaped from the darkness. His name was Lucian. Bill noticed my shaking and took my hands to help me hide it from my mom.

I had so many new questions that I wanted to ask, but there was a knock on the door interrupting our conversation. "Mrs. Martin, there is a lady out here that is requesting your presence." Sarah said through the door. Sarah has been my mom's helper since she bought the place.

"Tell her I will be right there dear." My mom kissed my forehead, unlocked and exited the little breakroom without saying another word. I was sure that we could pick up the conversation later back at home. I looked up at Bill, and he looked at me, his face an unreadable mask.

Then he rose from the chair and said. "How about we get out of here." He reached for my hand, and I slowly placed my hand on his, and he pulled me to my feet.

We walked out into the sales area, and my mom was talking with a lady in one of the isles. I hated to be rude, but I wanted to tell her that I was leaving. As we approached, the lady looked up. The color fell from her face, and she started to walk backward, saying something incoherent at first. Then it began to make sense one word at a time. The first word I could make out was doomed. The next word was vampire. Then she said a whole lot of other words, but I just could not make it out at all, as it was in another language. It was weird though as fast as she had lost it, she regained her composure. Her stare pierced the air and space between us, her eyes locked on Bill.

"Hello, Bill. I see your sister did something right." She said. I was totally lost what in the world was this lady talking about. Then she looked away and back at my mom. "MaryAnn, you should come see me tonight. I'll make your favorite dinner." She said.

My mom looked at me then said, "No thanks not tonight Eva, I am going to spend some time with my daughter and her boyfriend."

I didn't recall telling my mom that Bill was my boyfriend. And as a matter of fact, I didn't think we were quite there yet.

Eva's face appeared to be stunned by the news that Bill was my boyfriend. "Well, suit yourself and be careful you never know what may be lurking." She said eyeing Bill again. Was she warning us, or him, or what was she doing I wondered. Then she was gone.

"Mom, what was that all about? She kind of was giving me the creeps."

The day was getting weirder by the second.

"Oh, that is just how she is." My mom said giving me an apologetic smile. "We will talk more when I get home tonight. Love you."

I gave her a hug and said. "See ya later, love you too."

Bill and I walked out of the shop and onto the street that was becoming packed with people. He reached for his phone then looked at me. "Um… Do you mind if I make a quick call?" He asked me and smiled softly at me. I knew he was calling his sister to talk about the crazy lady in the store.

"Sure, go ahead." I said and stared off into space. Eva, however, was not gone. While Bill was busy on the phone, she started rambling on and on to me about vampires and werewolves. She was talking so fast that I could barely understand any of it. She would point at Bill and say vampire then all was lost. She was trying to tell me something. At the last moments of being alone with her, she said something intelligible. "End of Vampire world." Then she quickly excused herself and was gone again before Bill could get to my side. For an old lady, she sure could disappear fast.

"What was that all about?" He asked me

I shrugged. "Most of that was unintelligible, but the only thing I got out of it was the end of the vampire world." I said as a chill ran down my spine.

I quickly changed the subject and started telling Bill about the places as we walked down Bourbon Street. He was listening to me, but he would stare off into space, his mind was somewhere else, and he seemed distant. I knew he was probably thinking about what the crazy lady said, but I really needed a dose of normal right now before I jumped back into crazy. I kind of felt like Dorothy in the

Wizard of Oz. Lucian was the wicked witch. I had my three friends the tin man who is Bill, the scarecrow who was Mrs. Woods and, the Lion was Bill's sister. Of course, this was after we saw the wizard and he gave them their brains, courage, and heart. Everything seemed so crazy, I wished I could click my heels together three times, and all the vampires would go away. My life would be normal again. We walked down to the little city park and sat down on a bench.

"Bill, please tell me what you are thinking about."

I asked hoping that he would open up to me. I had opened up to him, and I was really hoping that he would take this opportunity to open up and talk to me.

"Lily, I'm not sure what I'm thinking right now. I'm trying to put everything in perspective. There is a key element that I am missing somewhere." He said not really looking at me.

I scooted closer to him making him put his arm around me. We sat there not saying anything just staring into the abyss, both of us just thinking back on the day's events. All I knew was that I needed Bill, vampire or not. I knew that fate had put us together somehow. Then I wondered if he felt it too. I was about to have this conversation with him but decided that with everything else going on I just could not take his rejection, if, in fact, he didn't feel the same way about me. Buzz…buzz… Bills phone rang pulling us both out of our thoughts. He reached into his pocket and pulled it out.

"Hello" then there was a short pause. "What the hell." He said and jumped up to his feet and started pacing. "I'm on my way back now." He said and hung up the phone. I could tell he was heated about whatever was going on. "Lily, I have to go back home. I'm asking if you would like to come with me?"

My mind started spinning. I could not leave, not right now, I needed answers to what was happening to me and why. Besides my mom and Eva seemed to know something about what was going on. Which brought me to another question my mind had been holding on to, what secrets was Bill hiding from me. When we ran into Eva, she said something about his sister did something right. I was not sure if I could ask him what she meant by that. But if I don't go would I lose him forever? Would he come back for me? My mind was a whirlwind of activity. It is just I had only known him for a short time, but I felt tied to him somehow, and the thought of losing him made my stomach turn.

He calmed down a little bit and sat back down next to me. "Lily, I know that it is not fair to ask you to come with me. I would like you to come with me, but I understand if you want to stay with your mom. After I take care of the problem, I could come back." He said. It was almost like he could read what my mind was thinking.

"Bill." I said placing my hand on his. "I really would like to stay here. Maybe my mom can give me answers to what happened to me. How long do you think you would be gone?" I said fighting back the tears that were coming. I had spent so little time with him, but somehow in the pit of my stomach, I knew that I loved him.

He placed his hand on mine. "I would only be gone two maybe three days."

"If you promise that you will come back then I will stay here." Then the unexpected happened, and the words fell from my mouth before I could stop them. "Bill, I love you." I said to him. He looked stunned, and it took him a minute to regain his composure.

"And I love you." He said wrapping his arms around me and lightly kissing my lips. I sighed as his lips pressed mine softly. I was stunned and elated that he had said it back. I knew now that he did feel the connection. "I'm sorry to break up this moment, but we really must get going back to your house."

My selfish side of me didn't want to let go but knew that I had too. I chose the quickest way back. We walked up to the car, and he got in. I felt a moment of terror pass through me knowing that he was going to be away from me, my love, my protector, was leaving me. Many things could happen in three days. Nevertheless, I was going to do this, and I was going to talk to Eva and my mom. I had to find out what they knew about all of this.

He rolled down the window. "I promise I will be back in three days. Please be careful."

I leaned into the car window hoping to steal another kiss and was successful. He paused before rolling up the window and putting the car in drive. He looked at me one more time I smiled and made a heart symbol with my hands and placed it over my heart. Then he slowly pulled away. I stood and watched as the car disappeared around a corner. Saddened that he was gone, but I knew there was nothing I could do about it. I turned and slowly walked up the steps and on to the porch. I sat down in the rocking chair and stared off into space. These three days were going to be so long without him here. I wished that he would have given me his cell phone number so that I could call him. I was depressed now, and I just wanted to sit here and not do or talk to anyone. Maybe a nap would do me good I thought. I got up from the rocking chair and put the key into the lock.

"Wait, wait, wait." I heard from behind me.

It was Eva, I could instantly tell by her voice. I pulled back from the door and walked towards her. "I have so many questions for you." I said. "What were you talking about the end of vampire world?" I said way too loud. A panicked look sprawled across her face and she began to look around wildly.

"You mustn't talk like that here, too many ears. Come we should go to my house where it is safe. It is not safe here." She said as she grabbed my hand and pulled me down the sidewalk a bit before releasing me.

This was getting weirder by the minute.

"Can I please stop and tell my mom not to worry?" I asked starting to second guess going anywhere with her.

"Yes, but please don't tell her that you are coming with me though. We have some private matters to attend to." She said still watching everything going on around her. It is as if she could see stuff that was not there it was so bizarre.

"Ok, I will just tell her that I am meeting up with a friend."

We stopped at the corner, and I walked the half a block down to the store. I poked my head in the door, and my mom was standing at the counter.

"Oh, hey mom, I'm going to go to Shelly's house. I'll be home later. Oh, and by the way, Bill had to go back home and do a few things so he will be gone for a few days." I said then blew her a kiss.

"Okay darling, I will see you later tonight. Love you, have fun." She said and blew me a kiss back.

I turned and walked back to Eva. We walked in silence for what seemed like forever until we came upon a house with purple shutters. It was exactly how my mom had described it. Eva opened the door to reveal a place that didn't look like it was used as a house but more of a center for voodoo. I instantly thought what the hell have I gotten myself into, this was insane. There were sculls some with black candles and some with red candles placed in the eyes and mouth. The wax had melted on them at some time, and now they looked like they had been bleeding black or red blood. Old looking books cluttered the shelves. She grabbed my hand and quickly pulled me along before I could really see anything else. She pulled me down the hallway. The only other thing that stuck out was the five-foot mask that hung on the wall. It appeared to be made of wood and had strategically placed paint lines on it. It was very nice looking but had a scary nuance coming from it. Finally, we reached the back of the house where it opened up into a kitchen. The whole kitchen looked like it had not been updated since the nineteen sixties. I stood there for a moment just admiring the look before Eva gestured for me to take a seat on the opposite side of the table from her. I slowly walked over and pulled the chair out and sat down.

After I was seated and looking at her, she spoke. "I need to know where you went child." She said softly almost whispering the words.

I wondered if it was safe to talk here. I didn't have time to dwell on safety though. The question loomed over me taunting me. I didn't want to answer, I didn't want to re-live all the horrors again. Something inside me told me that I had to tell her though and I had to tell her everything, even about Lucian. "Well, I'm not sure that I should be telling anyone what I have seen you will probably think I'm insane or hooked on some kind of drugs."

"Honey it is ok you can tell me, I'm sure that I have heard this before."

And with that, I proceeded to tell her the whole story describing everything in detail. I told her about Lucian and how he is a vampire and showed her the scars on my neck from him. She didn't interrupt me and just let me talk. She didn't even stare at the scars when I showed them to her. To say the least her face didn't even show any signs of shock when I told her vampires existed. She just sat there and took in every piece of information that I gave her. Not showing one ounce of surprise at any of it. I guess I was hoping that she would at least tell me I was crazy. Every time I mentioned Lucian's name out loud though it sent shivers down my spine and an image of him would pop into my head. I tried to dismiss them as quickly as I could. I never wanted to see his face again.

When I was done telling her my story she got up from the table and walked over to the counter and poured herself and me a glass of sweet tea. She placed the glass in front of me and gestured for me to get a drink so I did and it was the best sweet tea that I had ever tasted in my life. Then she reached for my hand, and I pulled back from her.

"Please, I'm not going to hurt you." She said and smiled sweetly at me. "Lily, I know that it was hard for you to tell me all of that but you must know that I knew vampires existed for some time. So that part doesn't shock me. The part that peaks my interest is the black stone looking thing that you picked up.

Do you happen to still have it? I would love to examine it." She said looking a little greedy.

"No, I don't still have it. I couldn't even begin to tell you where it would be. Heck for all I know it could be in the same spot where I picked it up the first time." I said looking down at my hand. I wished I did know where it was. It would solve a lot of mystery in my life right now, not only for me but for my mom as well.

"Do you think you could take me back to the place where you picked it up?" She asked, and I could tell that she really wanted me to take her there.

"Sure, I could do that." I said as I racked my brain trying to remember where I was that day.

I reached into my memory to find the place, and it all came back to me like I was doing it all over again. The room that I was sitting in went dark around me, and all I could see was the sidewalk and the shiny black thing gleaming in the sunlight just begging for me to pick it up. I reached down to pick it up when I heard Eva yell at me no, don't. But it was too late I already touched it and was cradling it in my hand. Eva hit me, and I dropped it, and everything dissipated back into the kitchen. But not before I saw red glowing eyes come out of the darkness. I looked up at Eva she looked panicked. Why was she freaking out? It was almost like she saw what I saw or she knew something more than she was telling me.

"Eva, what is going on?" I asked, but she ignored me and started chanting something that I could not understand. The doors and the windows started to rattle, and now I was scared. What the hell was happening? She pulled a bunch of stuff off some shelving and placed them on the table. Two of the items were white candles, a bowl with bones in it, a stone and some other objects that I didn't recognize. Then she said a name as she lit the candles "Jaxson." Then she muttered incoherent stuff again. All of the lights except for the candles on the table went out, and the room fell into darkness. A bright white light came into the room flooding it like the sun shining through a window in the middle of summer but brighter. I didn't see a figure, but I could hear a man's voice.

"Eva, you have called upon me. What can I do for you?" He asked in a deep booming voice. His voice, sounding a bit like a Greek god was speaking.

"I seek your protection and wisdom. It seems that our little friends are back and I need you to help me this time." She answered back to the voice.

What was she talking about our little friends, I was hoping that she would elaborate but she didn't.

"I see, I will do my best to help and protect you. Who is your little friend? She reeks of vampire. Is this whom you need protection from?" The voice asked.

I was totally creeped out now when I realized that he was talking about me.

"No, no she is not the one causing the direct problem, and she is not a vampire yet. However, she is the direct descendant of a very powerful vampire though. You may have heard of him, Marcus." She said then paused for the dramatic effect before continuing. "It seems as though Lucian Marcus's partner in crime was not killed years and years ago. He lives as a vampire, and he wants her. The only question is why?" She said.

How did she know all of this stuff? I wanted to go running and screaming from the house now, not sure that I wanted to know any more information. I tried to move but I was frozen in my seat, I don't know if it was fear or something else that held me there.

"It's simple she holds the key to total domination of the vampire world, even if she doesn't know it. It is all there in her. She will know the answers when the time comes." Then as fast as he appeared, he disappeared with a final warning. "Whatever you do little one don't give Lucian the answers that he is looking for or you all will be doomed." The candles went out, the bright blinding light was gone, and the lights came back on. I was shocked at what I heard, and I could not even find my voice to speak. The only thing that I knew now was that I was an essential piece to a puzzle that I had no idea how to unlock or keep locked, I was so confused.

"Are you ok?" Eva asked watching me. I don't know if she was waiting for me to run, scream or something entirely different.

The truth was I didn't know how to respond to her, so I settled for. "Maybe I should get home. My mom is probably worried about me." I said not looking at Eva and staring at the table. I could not even string together any emotions right now, the shock had taken over my body.

"I think you should come back tomorrow. We really need to talk more about this, and I will do some more research. However, where I'm going next, you had better not be here. Now go home and get some rest." She said placing a hand on my shoulder.

I slowly rose from my seat and walked towards the front door not saying anything. I opened and closed the door and walked the way home mulling everything over. The only thing I knew for sure was this whole thing was on me, a simple girl nothing extraordinary about me. I walked up to my front door, placed the key in the lock, and turned it. The lights were off, and it appeared as no one was home. But a small voice came from the kitchen.

"Lily is that you?" Mom's voice rang out.

"Yes, it is me, mom." I said as I closed and locked the door behind me and started for the kitchen. My mom was sitting in the dark with only the small glow of the light from the refrigerator door ice and water dispenser. She was playing with the tea bag in her mug wrapping the string around the handle of the mug. She had something on her mind. I could tell, and even though I just wanted to go to bed, I knew this was a conversation that just was not going to wait.

"Hey, mom what's up?" I said clearing my mind of what I had just learned. I didn't want her to know that I had something on my mind too. I certainly didn't want to have to tell her what Eva, or Jaxson rather told me.

"Nothing much dear, just been thinking about what you told me and I find it strange that we both had the same thing happen to us at about roughly the same age. How is that possible? I wonder if it also happened in the same location? What if we are cursed or something?" She said not looking up from her mug of hot tea.

I could see on her face that she was really bothered by this whole thing. From what I learned tonight, I would say that we were cursed, but I was not going to tell her that. Her questioning made me wonder why they didn't take her but I knew the answer to that, she was not the one Lucian was looking for. I wanted to tell her what I knew right now, but that would just make her worry more. Besides, I was still trying to wrap my own head around what I had heard tonight.

I settled for saying a whole lot of nothing except trying to put her more at ease. "Mom, we are not cursed, I'm sure that it was just a coincidence how things happened." I said as I sat down next to her and touched her hand trying to console her.

"Maybe but it seems too coincidental, but I suppose there is no sense in worrying about it right now." She said and took a sip of her tea. "I love you with all my heart. I guess I should go to bed I have a long day ahead of me tomorrow." She rose from her seat and kissed my forehead leaving her mug setting on the table.

"I love you too mom." Then she was gone to her room and in bed.

I sat there for a few seconds longer but quickly gave into my sleepiness. I stood and checked all the doors to make sure they were locked and then to my room. My bed felt comforting as I laid down on it. I went to shut off my bedside light knocking the book I had started reading on the floor. It was the latest vampire book. I groaned and left it where it was on the floor. Tomorrow I was going to throw out every vampire book I had. It didn't take me long to fall into a deep sleep. My dream started out sleeping with Bill, but when I turned to kiss him, it was not Bill anymore it was Lucian. He had his fangs bared at me he was pissed at me. I tried to get away from him, but he was obviously quicker than I was. He had me pinned up against a wall. "Tell me what the key is, and I will let you live." He said over and over again. Then he bit me and was draining me but stopped short of killing me because he knew that he needed me alive. He was punishing me, all I had to do is tell him what the key was, and he would release me. Only if I knew what the key was myself. The dream morphed into another time, and I was surrounded by people and vampires that I didn't know who they were. I saw them exchange something. It looked like the shiny black stone that got me into this mess in the first place. It looked like we were in some kind of cave or something. Then the dream faded into darkness and finally, my head was quiet allowing me some much-needed sleep.

∼CHAPTER 17∼

"Lily sweetie, I'm going to work, I'll see you in a little bit. Oh, and Bill called." She said, waking me up.

I laid there for a minute before getting out of bed and wondered if Bill left a call back number. I looked by the phone at the message pad, and all it said was I love you and will see you in a couple of days. There was not a call back number, and my heart sank a little. I really wanted to talk to him and let him know what I had found out, and maybe he could ask his sister if she knew anything about it. I made my way to the refrigerator to look and see what we had to eat. There was not much in here, but I found some eggs and some bacon and decided that I would have it. I cooked it sat down and ate it then cleaned up my mess. I looked down at my hair, and it looked dirty and tangled and needed to be washed and brushed. I made my way to the bathroom and into a hot steamy shower. I let the water roll over me closing my eyes letting the hot water soothe me. However, there in the darkness were the glowing red eyes again. I snapped my eyes open when I heard the phone ring. I got out of the shower and wrapped the towel around me, brushed my teeth and headed to my room to find something to wear. Standing staring into my closet, I found my favorite jean shorts and a gray tee shirt with a huge smiley face on it. I grabbed the brush from my dresser and sat down on the edge of my bed to brush my hair. After that was done, I picked up the phone to listen to the message.

It was Eva, "Lily you need to get over here right away I got something to tell you."

That was risky leaving a message, and something felt off about it since we had secretly met last night. She didn't even want my mom to know that I was with her. I erased the message, grabbed my key, and walked out the door. I walked down the blocks back to her house. When I got there, she was standing at the door waiting for me.

"Oh, good you got my message, please come in." She said.

But the whole thing still felt off to me. This just didn't seem like something she would do. Usually, she would have caught up with me on the street or at my mom's shop or waited for me to knock on the door. I eyed her speculatively, but she was not really giving me anything to go on. Except there it was she looked to the left away from me breaking our staring contest. I backed away until I was on the sidewalk.

"I would rather not." I said then paused thinking about another way. "How about you come out here, and we can go for a walk and talk."

She glanced around behind her then bolted out the door and grabbed my hand and we both ran from the house. Down to the corner bar and went inside.

Out of breath, I asked her "What was that all about?"

She nodded still trying to catch her breath. "Thank god your intuition is spot on. It is a good thing you didn't come in he was waiting for you."

I could not believe what I was hearing. He was here, oh no, how did he find me? Was the first thought through my head. Where do I hide from him? How do I hide from him? What am I going to do? Bill was still two days away not to mention the ten-hour drive that it took to get here.

"God help me." I whispered to myself.

I looked at Eva she seemed calm and relaxed. "Eva, we have to get out of here he will find us." She just stared at me, took my hand and led me to a table in the back by the kitchen door.

"You have to understand something Lily; he will find you no matter where you go or what you do. When he bit you and left those scars, you are connected to him somehow. I talked to Jaxson about this, and he said that this doesn't happen all the time but only when there is something special about the person. Every time you close your eyes what do you see?" She asked me.

I knew what she was getting at. Every time I closed my eyes, I saw him or the red glowing eyes in the darkness. The only time that it didn't happen was when I was with Bill. Somehow, Bill blocked out the connection, maybe because Bill and I had a stronger connection somehow, but I didn't have time to dwell on that right now.

"Eva, did you get a chance to find out anything else that I should know?" I asked hurriedly, not knowing how much time we had. I needed any information that she could give me.

"No, I didn't get a chance to find out anything else. He showed up shortly after you left. Why he didn't just go to your house, I don't know. Maybe your house is protected somehow, and he cannot get in. I don't have the answer for that either. All I know Lily is that you have to stay away from him he can't get whatever the key is. If he gets the key, then all the vampires on earth will pay." She said as the door to the bar opened. "Go get out of here, you must go now."

We were a bit hidden in the back corner, and it was a good thing the kitchen door was right there. I got up from my seat and quickly ran through the kitchen not even taking a glance to see if he was behind me. I ran for my life to my house. I opened the door, shut, and locked it. I knew that wouldn't keep him out unless Eva was right about he couldn't enter. I leaned up against the door just trying to breathe.

I called my mom to tell her to come home right now, but the phone rang and rang at the store. Then the thought crossed my mind. What if he was there with her I started to panic, but then a voice came over the phone.

"Hello, Voodoo Blues how may I help you?" She answered.

"Mom, are you ok?" I asked

She hesitated to answer for a split second. "Yeah, I'm fine. Then she hurried up and said take my box with you."

"What box, mom?" I said, but the line went dead.

I ran to her room and looked around on her dresser there was a note that said take this box. I grabbed the box and ran back to my room. I grabbed an old backpack and stuffed the box and some clothing into it. I then slung the pack over my shoulder and headed for the door. I thought that maybe if I left here, everyone would be safe. I knew that Bill was on his way, but I just could not risk waiting for him. I wished that I had his phone number so that I could call him and tell him that I was leaving. I walked to the door and was ready to turn the knob when I saw the silver Audi pull up.

He started to get out of the car. I yelled "get back in the car."

He looked at me like I was crazy but got back in the car. I shut and locked the door behind me and ran to the car. When I got to the street, I looked both ways just to see what was going on. About a block and a half down, I saw a dark cloaked figure walking towards me. Ok not walking now but running and fast, I ran to the car and climbed in.

"Hi swee…" I cut him off

"Drive and fast." I said and pointed at the figure that was half a block away now.

He threw the car in drive, squealed the tires and the car lurched forward. We started putting a bit of distance between the figure and us.

"What the hell is going on?" He asked practically spitting the words at me.

"I have so much to tell you… But first, how did you get back so soon? You were supposed to be gone for a few more days." I ask still shocked at his impeccable timing.

"I knew there was going to be problems. I was on my way to kill Lucian so that you could live in peace for the rest of your life. However, my sister called me and said she got word that he had left when I was just hours away from being home. I knew he was coming to get you I just hoped that I was not too late." He said as he reached for my hand. "I should have never left you unguarded." I could see the genuine look of shame on his face.

I was shocked by his words. He had left me to go kill Lucian; if that is not love, then I don't know what is. He could have gotten himself killed.

"Oh, Bill that is the sweetest thing anyone has done for me. I love you." I squeezed his hand as the love was overridden by anger. "I just have to ask, are you crazy? He could have killed you." My anger quickly replaced by the sadness of possibly losing him.

"Baby there are things that you don't know about me. First off, I'm a vampire and a werewolf. I have the power to take him out without even blinking. He has never met anyone like me before. I could kill him before he would even see it coming. Not to mention I have help from my sister and her husband. My sister is a famous vampire, and her husband is a well-known werewolf." He said as a matter of fact.

He was really trying to make me feel better about what he was off to do. I knew some of what he was telling me, but it still shocked me. He was also scaring me his tone was quick and furious. I hoped that he was not going to hurt me. This was the first time that I was afraid of him. The anger rolled off his tongue with every word he spat. I slowly pulled my hand away as his grip was getting too tight and threatening to break my hand.

He noticed quickly and calmed himself at once. "I'm sorry I didn't mean to frighten you. I just…" I hushed him with one finger to his lips.

I thought about what he had said again, there was no reason to fear him. He had been nothing but kind to me never once tried to hurt me, not to mention he had gone to kill my enemy. Therefore, I took a long deep, steadying breath. How could I be afraid of someone that was fighting for my honor? So, to speak. He stretched out his hand for me to take again. I hesitated a bit but took it swallowing my fear. I knew I was safe and that he would never hurt me. As I realized this a twinge of guilt ran through me.

"You don't have to be afraid of me." He said again. "I will not harm you, I'm the good guy." He said reassuring me. "Now can you tell me all that has happened in the day and a half that I was gone?"

I told him everything not leaving out any details about what Eva had said. I mentioned the box, that I had all but forgotten about, that my mom told me to take. When I was finished telling him, he was silent, and I assumed he was trying to figure things out. I had questions for him too, but I was not sure I should ask them right now. Questions about him being half vampire and half wolf. This sparked my curiosity, and I wanted to know more, but I had just given him a lot of information to think through. The only things I knew for certain right now was Lucian was after the key, and I had something to do with that. My boyfriend, even though I was not sure about that, was half werewolf and half vampire. Everything was starting to feel like some crazy dream that I just could not wake up from.

~CHAPTER 18~

I pulled the backpack up in my lap and unzipped it, slowly pulling the box out. The box was nothing extraordinary. It was just a plain wooden box that had collected dust over the years upon years of sitting on my mom's dresser. I tried to dust it off with the bottom of my shirt, but the dust just seemed to get pushed further down into the untreated wood. I opened the box, but there was nothing inside. Why did she want me to take an empty box? I closed the lid and turned it every which way looking to see if it was holding any kind of secrets. The more I examined the box though I still didn't see anything except an empty box. I turned the box upside down again hoping I missed something the first time.

"What are you looking for?" Bill asked startling me a bit. I was so concentrated on the box and getting it open that I almost forgot that he was there.

"I don't believe that my mom would send me away with this empty box. There has to be some kind of secret compartment." I said not taking my eyes off the box.

"May I try?" He asked, and I reluctantly hand the box over to him. After a few seconds of holding it, his hand began smoking, and he dropped it quickly. He shook his hand a couple of times shaking off the

pain. "I'm sorry I guess I can't help you with that."
He said.

"Are you allergic to wood or something?" I
asked trying to understand what just happened.

"No, I don't think so. Whatever is in that box
has been protected by something. I have never run
across anything like that before." He said and then
went on to say. "Everything you know about
vampires is a myth except for two things. We can be
killed by a stake to the heart, and we must drink blood
to stay alive."

What provoked him to say that? I had no idea.

"Well, I'm an exception to one of those rules.
Well kind of anyway. I do drink blood, but I can also
eat regular food the only problem is that regular food
doesn't make me as powerful as blood. That's why I
need to drink blood once in a while but not as often as
the rest of the vampires though."

Why was he telling me this stuff right now I
wondered, but then I got it, he was trying to comfort
me by telling me truths about vampires so that I
wouldn't be scared.

"What about werewolves?" I felt weird for
asking, but I wanted to learn more about what he is.

Like it or not I was going to have to deal with
all of this stuff that just a month ago was not real it
only existed in fairy tales. Then there was Eva and

her witchcraft or voodoo not sure which. All I knew was that it was time for me to start learning all that I could about what I'm dealing with. If I was ever going to stop Lucian from obtaining the key, whatever that maybe, I had better have a good handle on the do's and don'ts of vampires and werewolves.

"Well werewolves only have one weakness that I know of, and that is anything silver straight to the heart anything else will not work." He said showing me his palm where I'm assuming there should have been burn marks, but there was nothing there. I reached for his hand to get a closer look amazed that his hand didn't even have a mark.

"We have company." He said not taking his eyes off the road.

I started to turn to look out the back window, but he stopped me.

"Don't look, they are behaving right now and are just following us. I'm afraid if you look they will know that they have been spotted and who knows what they will do then."

I settled back in my seat and looked back through the mirror. I looked at the driver, but it was not Lucian driving.

"Are you sure it is them? That is not Lucian driving, and I have never seen that car before." I said.

"No, not one hundred percent sure but they have been following my every move for a while now." He replied.

"Maybe they just like the way you drive." I said and started to lightly laugh. He started laughing too. He got my dry sense of humor. It felt good to laugh for once, but it quickly came to an end and back to being a dangerous situation.

The rhythmic bump of the road and the soft music playing in the background was making my eyes droop, and I fought against the sleep that was coming, but it was no use.

"I'm sorry I fell asleep." I said even though I didn't really need to apologize. "Are they still following us?" I asked looking in the mirror, but it was too dark to make out the color of the car behind us.

"No, they turned off a few exits ago." He said.

That was good news I thought. "Well can we make a pit stop? I really need to use the restroom."

"Yes, we will stop at the next exit. We need to get gas anyway." Then my stomach growled. "Oh, and we should get you some food." He said as he veered off the highway down the exit ramp.

We pulled into the gas station and up to a pump. He dug into his pocket then handed me some money. "Please get yourself something to eat. Oh, and can you please bring me back some food too? I don't care what it is I'm starving. Unless you prefer I..."

He trailed off maybe realizing what he was going to say maybe would not have gone over so well. Then he smiled big with an apologetic look on his face. I was going to ask him what he was going to say but then decided to let it go for now my bladder was screaming at me. I got out of the car and walked towards the store. It dawned on me as I walked into the store what he was going to say unless you prefer I drink your blood. The thought of him putting his lips on me made my body ache with need, but right now I really needed to use the restroom. I finished my business in the bathroom and wandered through the store. I grabbed a bunch of junk food, hot dogs from the roller thing and a couple of drinks. I was in the process of paying for the items when I saw Bill waving his hand beckoning me to hurry up. The clerk stuffed everything in a bag for me, and I ran back to the car.

"What's the rush?" I said as I seated myself in the seat, pulled the door shut and put on the seatbelt. I feared that maybe he had spotted someone or something.

"Nothing I just couldn't wait to get you back in the car where you are safe." He said looking at me with a big smile that touched his ears.

My heart melted, and I felt the love emanating off of him. I leaned over and kissed his cheek, then proceeded to pass out food. I ate two small bags of chips, two hot dogs and washed it all down with a candy bar and a coke. Man, if I keep eating like this, I'm going to get fat. I would do anything for a home cooked meal right now.

I didn't want to start the next conversation, but it needed to happen. "Ok, so we really haven't talked about a plan yet. Lucian is just not going to stop until he kills me I think." Shivers ran down my spine as I thought about my untimely death.

Before he said anything, I leaned down and took the box out of my bag. I need it for a little bit of distraction. I knew there was more to this box than just a plain old dusty box. I opened the lid peering into the blackness. A nagging feeling in the pit of my stomach told me I was right about the box. On the left side of the box, I noticed something a small slit where the wood separated from the box a bit. Holding the box with my right, I waved my left-hand underneath but could not see anything except for blackness. Here was my ah-ha moment. There was a secret compartment, a false floor. I looked around for something to pry the box open with, but I could not find anything. Whatever was in this box was an essential piece of the puzzle. Then it dawned on me what if I call my mom she would be able to tell me how to open it. I looked over at his face, and he appeared to be deep in thought. I had almost forgotten that we were supposed to be having a conversation about my safety.

He moved his lips like he was getting ready to say something, but before he could, I asked. "Can I use your phone?" Without saying a word, he handed me the phone.

I looked at the time it was ten o'clock. She should be home. I dialed the number, and the phone rang twice. I was ready to start talking as soon as she said hi.

"Hello love, your mom and I are having a great time going through pictures of you, what a cute kid you were. When do you think you are going to be home? I would really hate to have to drink your mom's blood to get by." I started to unravel, the phone slid from my hand dropping in my lap. I sat there staring out the window for a second before I regained my composure and picked the phone back up. I choked back the tears that wanted to come. This was not the time to break.

As I put the phone back up to my ear, I heard my mom in the background. "I love you, don't come back."

That helped me to know that she was safe. Well at least for now anyway, and I found some peace in that and was able to find my voice. "I'm sorry that I ran." I said choking out the words fighting the tears that were coming. "I will return to you very shortly, please don't hurt her." I said and immediately started to fall apart. A shudder ran through me at the thought of him sucking her blood.

"Apology accepted but you have two days to come back otherwise…"

Then the phone went dead. I had lost the signal on the cell phone, but I knew what he was going to say.

"Don't worry we will save her." Bill said. "But first we need more information about why he wants you so bad."

I pulled my knees up to my chest, wrapped my arms around them not saying a word, and started to weep as the world fell away from me. Bill held on to my arm trying to console me. It did help a little but not enough to ease the pain I felt right now. My world was crumbling and falling down all around me. A picture of a wolf popped into my head, and it seemed like it could be a solution to the problem.

I managed to find my voice and ask. "Can't we just turn around and go back for her now? You could take him. Doesn't a werewolf trump a vampire?" I was trying to hold on to some kind of hope.

A sigh escaped him before he answered and I knew it was not going to be something I wanted to hear. "Depends on the circumstances and how old the vampire is and if they fought werewolves before. One of us would surely die in the process, I'm sure of that and I really rather it not be me. I also know according to my sister that he didn't leave his mansion alone. He left with three others. I would be outnumbered and

187

lose that fight for sure. Then he would have you. I cannot bear the thought of him having you. Lily, I cannot lose you. I love you. We have a connection, I felt it the first day that I met you."

I was crying even harder now but not just because I was sad about my mom but because I was happy too, he did love me, and I knew that he would do anything in his power to help me. His words gave me the strength to suck it up and stop crying. Sucking in a couple of deep breaths and steadying myself. I picked up the box from the floor where I had dropped it. A thought crossed my mind, and I placed the box back on the floor and began stomping it. It felt good to take my frustrations out on something. The box, however, appeared to be stronger than I was. I was starting to think that I could lite it on fire and nothing would happen to it. I picked the box up again expecting there to at least be a scratch, but nothing had happened to it.

"Oh, for the love of peat." I cried out.

What the hell was this box made of? This could not be your ordinary wood. I fumbled around with it some more turning it over and over looking for anything that would suggest how to open it. However, there was nothing. I closed my eyes letting my mind wander. I drifted back through my memories going back to when I was a small child. My mom clasped the box in her hand, and she was showing me something about the box. With a rush of enthusiasm, I did what she did in the memory. Opening the lid and placing my index fingers in the bottom corners, and then placed my middle fingers in the upper corners. With my fingers in place, I said. "Acik." Bingo the lid to the secret compartment sprang open. Inside two notes covered the bottom of the box and a black stone. I stared at the stone it seemed familiar. The more that I examined it I realized that it was almost identical to the one that I had found that took me to Lucian. I took out the first note being extra careful not to touch the stone and unfolded it. It was written in a different language that I had no clue how to read. I showed it to Bill, but he didn't know how to read it either. I pulled out the second note this one was in English. I carefully unfolded the letter and started to read.

My dear Lily,

If you are reading this, it means that they have found us and will not stop hunting us until we give them answers. I just want you to know that I knew this day would eventually come. I know all of this is a shock to you but your father and I did what we had to do to protect you. I just want you to know that I love you and I'm sorry that I kept this from you, but it was for your own good.

Love mom

I started to cry again feeling very crushed as I read the last few words, but my sadness quickly turned to anger. I was furious she had known that this was going to happen. Up until this point in my life, we shared everything. For whatever reason, she didn't see fit to tell me about this or to tell me one day you are going to be kidnapped by a vampire. I wanted to shout out what the hell mom. Then another thought occurred to me. How did she know this was going to happen? I had so many questions. However, I knew that I could not ask her right now. Especially since Lucian was with her. What if this was the key that Eva had talked about. I would be giving him what he wanted. Then everyone would be dead. This whole thing was becoming more frustrating by the second. I wanted to scream and yell and tear the note to shreds, but I took a couple of deep breaths, carefully folding the letter back up, and placing it into the box. Looking down into the all but empty box I stared at the stone. It shined in the dim light taunting me with its beauty to touch it. I felt the overwhelming need to touch it and before I knew it my hand was slowly edging its way towards it. Bill grabbed my hand jerking it away from the stone.

"Don't touch it. You don't know what it will do." He spat at me breathlessly.

I placed my hand on the outside of the box and started rotating the box a bit, watching the stone roll around the inside of the box on the black felt. Then I noticed something the stone had been broken. I could tell because one side was not shiny it was dull with what looked like little tiny white speckles. The rest of the stone was smooth, black as night and shiny. Why was it broken? Why would they not have left the whole stone for me to find? Whoever had broken the stone meant for me to find the other half but why? I had to shut down all of the questions that were starting to run rampant in my mind and start thinking about what was going on. I needed to stick to the facts, and maybe that would lead me to the answers. I found half a stone, and it transported me. Ok, check. I had a conversation with Eva where I was told that I am the key to vampires. My mom knew about this somehow, she said so in her note. None of this made any sense, and I could not make heads or tails out of any of it. However, something inside me said that I needed to find the other piece of the stone that was missing. This I somewhat already knew, and I already tried really hard to look in my memories for it, but really that only took me back to the spot where I found it. It didn't take me to what happened to it afterward. How was I ever going to find the other half of the stone? The rest of the trip back to the house consisted of me mulling all of this over and over in my mind searching for anything that would tie everything together. I tried to replay that day I was transported over and over hoping for some new information, but there was nothing. I knew there had to be one key element that would link all of this together but what. The more I thought about this, the more questions it posed. It was all crazy, and I was starting to question my sanity.

~CHAPTER 19~

We pulled up the long driveway back to the house that we had left a few days ago. I closed the box and stuffed it back into my backpack. Bill opened the car door for me to get out. We walked the short distance up to the door holding hands.

"Don't be afraid we would never hurt you." He said out of the blue.

That's bazar I thought but dismissed it. He opened the door to reveal Mrs. Woods, His sister and her husband Aidan, and two other people I didn't know. I tried to hide behind Bill not sure of the new people. I wondered if they were vampires or werewolves.

"Hi everyone," Bill said as he entered the room with me stuck to his back like glue. "Sam, I'm going to take Lily to her room and get her all settled in." Bill's sister nodded in approval.

We walked into a room beautifully decorated. All the colors were light, mostly whites and yellows. It was almost too happy of a room, especially for my mood. A huge bed sat in the middle of the room it boasted a puffy white comforter with a pale-yellow sheet folded over the comforter up by the pillows. On each side of the bed, dark wooden nightstands held up small lamps. The windows had white blinds overlaid by pale yellow sheer curtains. A dresser with a small flat screen TV on it stood opposite of the bed.

Bill pulled me into his arms before I got any more details about the room and squeezed me a bit. "Everything is going to be ok, you know. We… we are very experienced in this sort of thing. You should come and meet our guests they have been waiting all day to meet you."

"Are they vampire, werewolf or human?" I asked not caring how stupid that sounded, but something else stuck out to me from what he had said. "What do you mean you're experienced at this sort of thing?" I asked before he could answer my first question.

"Sweetie we have a lot of talking to do." He said sweetly in my ear. "But first we must go back out there with everyone." He said as he pulled away from me and grabbed my hand, gently pulling me to the door.

I didn't protest, even though I wanted too, I just let him drag me along. We walked into the living room and sat down on the couch where there was room.

The rather tall bigger man stood up and slowly walked towards me. He bowed and introduced himself. "Hello, I am Eric, it is a pleasure to meet you." Then he turned walking back to his seat and the woman sitting next to him rose and slowly walked over to me.

"Hello, I am Shannon the wife of Eric, it is a pleasure to meet you." She said and also bowed to me.

What the hell was going on here? I thought to myself why were they bowing to me. Bill wrapped his arms around me and pulled me closer to him in what I assumed to be protective move. I could feel him tense every time Eric or Shannon moved or even twitched. I got the feeling that he didn't trust these people and his reaction was making me anxious.

"So, Miss Lily, we have a lot to talk about," Eric said and smiled at me kindly.

Bill tensed, even more, he was like a spring that was slowly being wound tighter and tighter, I was afraid he was going to burst any second. I took a quick look at everyone, and they all seemed to be wearing a weary expression on their faces as well.

Eric started talking when I made eye contact with him again. "This is what I know about what is happening. A long, long time ago, back in the year one hundred and eighty-three, it was said that king Marcus traded his life to defend his people from certain death from the coming war. He had the best sorcerer cast a spell on him. He wanted to be the most powerful thing of all time. However, there was a price to pay. He would be damned to an eternity of drinking blood and would never die, but at the time, he didn't know it. Let me back up a bit though. He had the sorcerer take a black stone and place a spell on it. Then the stone was broken into two pieces. He sent his wife and child away with the black stones that would protect them from any magic or even arm to arm combat, it would basically protect them from everything. As long as they wore the stone, they were safe. But the stone was also cursed, but we will come back to this shortly."

I was all ears. He just had to be telling the truth. He knew about the black stone. I was excited I was hopefully going to get some answers to my questions.

"So back to Marcus, after sending his wife and child away, he gathered the sorcerer and the things that the sorcerer asked him to bring which included one human. Marcus had picked someone that had been placed in the dungeon of the castle. This man had been sentenced to die anyway. This man was a really bad man as the story goes. The man had killed villagers for fun and would drink and pour the blood over his body. The way that he was caught was one of the king's guards followed the man's bloody footprints to where he lived. Anyhow, Marcus didn't want to kill someone that was not already going to die he had too much compassion for his people. The townspeople said that the man Marcus chose was possessed by a demon. When the sorcerer did the magic, it is said that the demon was released from the man's body. At the time of the casting of the spell, it opened Marcus's soul, and the demon slipped in as the spell was being completed. Sealing the spirit or demon into his body creating a monster that would never die and would need blood to survive. Thus, creating the first vampire."

He paused looking around at everyone's faces it was apparent that no one knew the story. At this point, to me, it sounded more like hogwash but my experiences over the past month had me willing to try and believe this.

"Life went on, and Marcus won the war against his people, but he missed his wife and child. He knew though he could not be around his wife and child without harming them or at least that is what Marcus thought. He went back to the sorcerer and asked him to take the gift back so that he could have his wife and child back. A few years went by with the sorcerer trying to take his gift back, but it was not something that could be taken away he was completely and utterly stuck being the blood sucking demon that he was. Finally, Marcus could not take it anymore and went looking for his family. He found them in a small village they each wore half of the stone around their necks. When Marcus reached for his wife and child, his hand started burning. His wife seeing his hand burning from trying to touch her was saddened but knew that she had been protected from whatever he had become. He begged them to come back home with him though and promised that he would take care of them forever. It was said that they traveled home together and lived in the castle with him. He did all he could to hide his blood rage from them, and as far as the story goes, he was successful at it. After a while of being home, his wife decided that it was time for him to be able to touch her again. She longed for his touch. So, she went and seen that sorcerer hoping that maybe he could give her insight on what to do. The sorcerer told her to remove the stone around her neck and that Marcus would be able to touch her again. The sorcerer did caution her though and told her that he was not the man he used to be. The first thing she did was find her child and gave her half of the stone to the child hoping that the child would have extra protection from her father. However, in the meantime, Marcus had also gone to the sorcerer and asked if he could make his wife the same as him. The sorcerer told him there was a way, but he must have great control, or he would kill her. That night when she went to Marcus almost naked and not wearing the stone. Marcus got carried away and nearly killed his wife as the blood rage took hold of him. The child hearing the screams went running to help, but when she got there, she saw her mom lying on the floor with Marcus hovering over her feeding her his blood. He turned as the child came in and went after her but he could not touch her she was wearing her stone and had her mother's stone in her hand. Marcus fled the room, and the child ran to her mother and placed the stone on her. Somehow, this changed the stone. The stone absorbed the mixture of her mother's and Marcus's blood. The blood caused the stone to become the opposite of a repellent it became an attractant. Therefore, the human that possessed the royal blood and touched the stone would be transported to the King and queen. As for that last part, it is just hearsay because an heir has never been found to test that theory.

Anyway, the child ran from the castle when she realized what her mother and father had become. She left the stone that had been tainted with them, but she kept her stone for her protection in case her parents ever came looking for her. It is said that she had a long good life after that. When she was, old and passed on, she had given the stone to her daughter. Her daughter had the stone placed in something and had a spell put on it. She feared that if the stone got into the wrong hands that it may do more harm than good. Anyway, it was passed down from generation to generation until finally, it got to you. It just so happens that when your mother met your father and they created you. They created the same exact makeup of the original child, so you have magic blood running through your veins. When the stone is whole again, it is said that the person holding it would have all the power of the king and queen. Again, this is hearsay because we don't really know the truth, it is all part of the tale.

So now, you may be asking what this has to do with Lucian? Well, it is said that the mother was changed and she and Marcus ruled the vampire world together. Marcus never tried to make another vampire, but the Queen did. She was successful at it, always hoping that her long-lost child would come home so that they may live for forever together. But that never happened. Anyhow, the first Vampire that the queen made was Lucian, Marcus's longtime advisor or co-ruler if you will. His blood is the purest, a direct line, to the king and queen vampires. It is said that he is the only one left and that the king and queen had been destroyed long ago by his hand. Lucian sought the power that the king and queen had. The king and queen could do everything from reading minds to setting things on fire by just thinking about it. I don't know how much truth there is to that, but it seems to me that it is not true, but that is my opinion. Anyway, when Lucian left the palace, he took the mothers black stone with him. He wants to get all the powers that he thinks he deserves. He just wants to rule the world and everything in it. The only other thing that I can tell you is that it is said that if you kill Lucian, all vampires of the world will die too." He said finishing the story looking me straight in the eye. I felt like he was trying to decide if I believed him or not.

"Hum… Sounds familiar." Sam said grabbing his attention, and he looked at her now, then they both started laughing.

This gave me a second to analyze what he had just told us without him glaring at me. I got the feeling that some of the story was a lie and some were true, but I had no way to know what was what. I guess I just had to stick with what I knew about the stone. I started spinning a web of questions to ask, and before I forgot what they were, I started blurting them out as they came to me. "How did he know I was in New Orleans? I could have been anywhere in the world. Did he plant the stone himself where he knew I would find it? Why didn't he kill me when he had the chance? What else did he need from me?" I hoped that Eric would have the answers to these questions.

Eric slowly rose from the couch and inched his way towards me. Bill got up from his spot placing himself between Eric and me. "Eric, I advise that you sit back down." Bill's protective instincts were in full swing, and his coil was about to break. I wondered what Eric had done to make Bill act like this.

"I'm sorry I was just going to the window to look out. I thought I saw something move." He said calmly but immediately turned and sat back down next to his wife. After he sat, Sam moved closer to me, and Bill went to the window to look out then was back in a split second.

"I don't have the answers to those questions darling." Eric finally replied back to me after a few minutes. "We must really get going though. I will search around some more and see if I can get you more information." He said then he said good-bye and they were gone in a matter of seconds.

I snuggled into Bill and pulled his strong arm around me. I started to yawn, but I was forcing myself to try to stay awake.

He noticed that I was tired. "Come let's go lay down somewhere comfortable." He pulled me up, walked me back to the room, and laid down with me. When he thought that I was asleep, he got up. From the hall, I could hear him bickering with Sam.

"Why in the hell would you call on that asshole to help us? He has lied and cheated us before. What kind of personal gain is he getting out of this? You know that is how he operates." He said spitting the words at her angrily.

"Calm down brother, I didn't think that you were going to be back that quick, so I invited him here to pick his brain about the matter. I know that he is not trustworthy, but he is the only one that I know that knows the history. Next time I will bring in someone that we don't know." She spat back at him. "Look I'm sorry I put your little girl toy in danger." She said calming her voice a little bit.

"She is not just a girl toy, sister, I love her, and I hope that someday she will have me." He spat back at her. "I have been waiting a long time for this. I didn't say anything when you finally decided that Aidan was the one for you. I didn't say anything when you changed me to half vampire and brought the Cloaks down upon us."

"I'm sorry we both need to calm down we are all on edge. I need to go feed and clear my head we are going to have to come up with a plan to keep her safe. I will see you in a little bit, I love you." She said now in a calmer voice.

"I love you too," Bill said back to her then the doorknob rotated and the door opened.

I pretended to be asleep until Bill got back in the bed with me. I opened my eyes slightly and looked into his face. He looked like he wanted to cry but at the same time, he looked a little happy.

"What is eating at you?" I asked in a soft whisper acting like I hadn't heard him and his sister fighting.

He raised his hand to my face and gently touched my cheek. "Nothing, why are you not sleeping? Are you not tired anymore?" He asked.

I propped myself up on my elbow to look him square in the eye. "No, actually I'm hungry," I said, and my stomach followed that up right on cue, then we laughed.

He grabbed my hand and placed it on his chest. "Can you feel that?" He asked.

Feel what, I thought to myself there was nothing no heartbeat, not even a breath of air taken into his lungs. How do I put this gently back to him that I didn't feel anything without it coming out all wrong? I didn't want him to think that I felt nothing for him because that is not what I would mean.

"I don't have a heart that beats, and I don't have lungs that require air, but I still know how to love. I'm not a monster like Lucian. I can love you how you want to be loved. Please just let me try. I promise never to do anything you don't want. Please, I am begging you just let me love you. I will protect you with my life. I just can't stay away from you. I have waited years upon years for someone like you. Please let's fight whatever comes together." He said, and I saw the red tears flow from his eyes.

I wondered what had brought on this wave of emotions. We already knew that we loved each other, we had said this much before. He was begging me to let him into my life either for forever or until death do us part. I thought that we had made this perfectly clear a while ago, but maybe he needed more confirmation from me that I still felt that way about us. I already knew that he was not a monster like Lucian and that I could trust him with my heart. Something in that moment though had me linked to him, and I could feel his love for me. I pulled myself up to a sitting position and looked him in the eyes wiping his tears away. "I'm here right now, I trust you with my life. I love you back. But if I don't get some food soon, I will perish." I said trying to lighten the mood and it kind of worked. He smiled at me it was bright and would light up any dark tunnel. I wrapped my arms around his neck kissing him hoping that he could feel my love back.

∾CHAPTER 20∾

He jumped up out of bed and grabbed both of my hands pulling me to a standing position, wrapping his arms around me and kissing me passionately. I could feel his kiss in my groin and moving rapidly to my hands. I wanted to tear his clothing off. He stopped me though, by letting go of one of my hands and pulled me by the other to the door. Opened the door he pulled me down the hallway to the kitchen. We entered the kitchen to see Mrs. Woods standing there cooking some sausage, bacon, and eggs. My stomach growled at the smell.

"Can I help do anything, Mrs. Woods?" I asked as we entered the kitchen.

"You can get some plates down and set the table for three." She said pointing towards a cupboard.

Bill dropped my hand and walked over to the window. I did as Mrs. Woods asked and set three places at the table complete with forks, spoons, and knives. I poured two mugs of coffee for Mrs. Woods and me. I held out the pot towards Bill wordlessly asking if he would like some coffee. He waved his hand and shook his head no. I opened the fridge looking for some creamer but spotted the orange juice, and it sounded delicious at the moment. I Poured a small glass and took a sip. The juice would do until my coffee cooled down a bit since there was not any cold creamer just the powdered stuff by the coffee maker. As we sat down at the table we heard a wolf howl come from somewhere close outside, I turned in my chair to look outside but didn't see anything.

"I'm sorry I'm going to have to skip breakfast, I have to see what is going on out there." He said and kissed me then was out the door in a matter of seconds. The next thing I saw was a big grey wolf run by the window. The wolf paused a second to look at me through the window, and I knew that it was Bill. Bill disappeared into the woods, and I turned around and began to eat.

"So how are you holding up?" She asked.

I didn't know how to answer at first or really how I was holding up until she asked. A flood of emotions washed over me. I was happy yet sad, terrified but dealing with it, angry and surprised. The fact of the matter is that I just was not dealing with it at all right now. I started to break down and cry. My mom was Lucian's captive that was facing certain death if I didn't come back to him. The only reason that he wanted me was to rule the world, I discovered after yesterday's meeting with Eric. I knew that After Lucian was through with me, then he would kill me. If I killed Lucian somehow in the process, then Bill would die too according to yesterday's conversation. What was I going to do? Everything I loved or everyone that loved me would be gone. Mrs. Woods gently stroked my hand trying to calm me.

"You should eat, sugar. You need your strength for whatever path you decide to take." I wiped my tears from my eyes and took three huge gulps of air trying to calm myself. I had to try to keep a level head. "I think you should talk to Bill, let him know how you feel right now. I'm sure he feels the same way." She said, and half smiled at me. I finished my breakfast and sat at the table sipping my coffee just staring out into the woods that surrounded the house trying to find some kind of peace. I just wanted to go frolic in them, maybe find a quiet place to think about everything that was going on. I was lost in thought when the front door slammed back against the wall making the whole house shutter. I dropped my coffee, and it went everywhere.

"Lily, Lily, Lily, where are you?" I heard bill yell for me, he sounded panicked.

"I'm here," I said, but he had already found me.

"Get your things we have to go." He commanded.

"What? Why? What is going on?" I asked, but he didn't reply, grabbed my hand, and pulled me to my room.

"Just do as I ask please, I will tell you when we are safe." He said, and I knew right now was not the time to argue and just do what he asked. I hurried and grabbed the bag opened it to make sure the box was still inside, closed it and ran to his side.

Mrs. Woods was standing by the door with a gun in hand. I kind of admired her right now she was so fearless, unlike me. I wondered how long she had known about this secret world that surrounded humans. She had complete and utter trust in Bill, Sam, and Aidan and this made me believe that I was in good hands.

"Are you ready?" he said to the both of us. She nodded, and I did the same.

He swung the door open to reveal someone standing at the door. It was not anyone that I had recognized. "You know what to do Mrs. Woods," Bill said and changing to wolf and charging at the man.

I was shocked at how fast he turned and was tearing this person to shreds. As soon as he cleared a path for us, Mrs. Woods grabbed my hand and led me to the car. She got me in the car, dropped the keys in my lap, and shut the door before I could say anything. Then she placed herself in the back seat and closed the door, within a split-second Bill was in the car with the key in the ignition, and we were speeding down the long driveway to the road. When we hit the road, he finally started to calm down, but he was aggressively checking all the mirrors to see if we had been followed. We were on the highway in no time, and that is when he finally started to talk again.

"Lily, I'm so sorry that was close, I should have never left you unguarded for a second. If I would have been a few minutes later you…" He trailed off as the tears began to fall.

For the first time since we had been in the car, I looked over at him. There was blood on his face and hands. I wondered if the only person that he ever killed was the one on the porch. Then I wondered if maybe that was a person or vampire. Thinking back on it, that was most defiantly a vampire.

Whatever the case maybe I felt like I needed to keep him calm. "It's ok, everything's fine, I'm here," I said trying to comfort him lightly touching his arm then quickly looking away before he caught me staring at the blood on his face. It was a bit horrifying to look at.

"They came for you Lily, they were coming from every side." He said pausing to try and keep his composure. He was scared for the first time since I had met him.

"Where are Sam and Aidan?" I asked hoping that they were ok and trying to change the subject.

"They're fine they should be out of there by now. All they could do was slow them down a little to let me get to you so that we could have a chance." He said, and I could see the muscles in him tremble. I didn't know if that was a sign that he was going to shift into a wolf or not.

His phone rang, and he picked it up on the first ring. "Sam, are you guys ok?" He said as he answered the phone.

"Yup we are all good, no one is seriously hurt." I heard her say when Bill put the phone on speakerphone. "We will meet you at the place we discussed earlier." Then the phone went dead. I saw him breathe a sigh of relief.

"Where are we going?" I asked.

"We are going to my house." He said as he turned into a driveway. The house was not much but it was a cute little place. It was white with red wooden shutters with hearts carved into them. It looked like no one had been here in a long time judging by how high the grass is. He pulled up to the garage door and put the car in park. He looked as though he was pained. He pulled off his seat belt and went to open his door, but stopped pinching the bridge of his nose then released it.

"Stay here I better go check and make sure everything is safe. If you see anyone or anything you drive this car out of here don't wait for me." He said.

Then without another word he got out of the car and was gone around the back of the house in a flash. I looked around just looking for any sign of life, but there was nothing. The garage door started to open and the sound of the door at first made me jump. As the door opened and all I saw was his feet and legs I was scared that maybe it was not him. The door quickly revealed though that it was him, standing in the middle of the garage. As soon as the door was up enough for him to get out, he walked to the car, got in and pulled the car into the garage. He pushed the button in his hand to shut the door and then turned off the engine. No one moved until the door closed. I looked over at Bill and could see a fresh little red streak on his cheek where a tear had rolled down. He must have noticed I was looking at him and he quickly wiped it away almost like he was ashamed. I wondered what had him so upset. Mrs. Woods got out of the car first and opened the door for me, we walked around the car together and went in.

The kitchen decorated in a country apple theme, but it was not overwhelming just enough to be cute. I set my bag on the small round table then pulled a chair out to sit down. I took the box out of my bag and set it on the table in front of me. I opened it to reveal the small black stone and the notes. I wanted to touch the stone just to see if anything would happen. I got my fingers really close to it when I heard the door open then the noisy chatter of Bill, Sam, and Aidan. I pulled my fingers back from it and settled for pulling out the note that was written in a different language. Carefully unfolding it on the table. I stared at it wondering what it said.

"What do you have?" Sam's voice came from behind me. I jumped a bit, there I go again so dang jumpy.

"I don't really know, I wish I did," I said back turning to look up at Sam.

"May I?" She asked.

Taking the note setting it on the table pulling her phone out of her pocket and snapped a picture of it. Then she went and sat down across the table from me. Now she was doing it too, just sitting there staring at it. Then she placed the phone on the table and started to stare at me. Making me uncomfortable but I didn't say anything.

"Lily, you know my brother loves you." She said.

Holy crap she was going to give me the brother talk.

"Please don't do anything stupid, and don't hurt him he has been through enough. If you hurt him, I will kill you and will not hesitate." She said staring me down. Letting her fangs show a little.

I could tell that she was going to go on, but Bill came into the room just then. He pulled out a chair next to me placing his arm around me. I wanted to tell on her, she was scaring me but I shook it off knowing that she was just looking out for her brother.

"Everything good here?" He said eyeing his sister. "What are you gals talking about?"

"We were just discussing the letter." Sam said and pointed to it on the table. I eyed her, and she shot daggers back at me, so I just shook my head yes in agreement.

"Do you happen to know anyone that can translate this?" Bill asked his sister.

"I'm not sure, I was thinking about sending it to Eric to see if he could or knew someone that could. Of course, I wanted to talk to you about it first." She said.

"I guess it would be okay. We need answers. Did you find out who sent the band of vampires for us back at your house?" Bill asked.

"No, none of them would talk." She answered back.

Then picked up her phone and started punching in stuff. I assumed she was sending the picture to Eric via email or text message. She excused herself from the table and went to the little living room, finding her man and cuddling up to him. Bill sat right next to me and pulled himself closer to me. I rested my head on his shoulder, and that is when I noticed that he had taken a shower. His soap had a calming smell to it, so I just reminded myself to breathe. The next thing I knew he was waking me.

"Sweetie put this stuff away." He said.

I sleepily placed everything back in the box and back in my bag. When I was done, he picked up the bag and me carrying us to a room with a bed. He placed me on the very soft bed, covered me up, and that was it for me. I was sleeping in no time.

When I woke up, I was alone but could hear the quiet murmurs of everyone talking in the living room or kitchen. Even though I didn't want to move, I got up and quietly worked my way to the bathroom with my bag in hand. The shower in the corner looked incredibly inviting.

"Bill." I called from the bathroom door, and before I could blink, he was there.

"What is it are you okay?" He asked looking me up and down.

"No, I'm fine, can I take a shower?" I asked.

"Of course, there are towels under the sink there." He said pointing to the cupboard door under the sink. "Everything else is in the shower." He lingered at the door for a second, but then he gently shut the door.

I found the towels and hopped in the shower letting the water run over my skin. It felt like dancing in a warm rain almost like my shower at home. I missed home and my mom even though I was slightly upset at her. Then I wondered how she was doing and if Lucian was being somewhat nice to her. The tears came, and there was no stopping them. I wondered if Bill would let me try to call her. Then it dawned on me today was the day I was supposed to be home but I was nowhere even close. If we left right now, maybe I could make it. I wondered if Lucian really would kill my mom? My brain told me no and that he needed to keep her alive if he ever wanted to see me again. Now with a little more motivation than when I got in the shower, I hurried and washed. Got out and dried myself off quickly. I was a girl on a mission now. I had to find out what our plan was going to be. I opened my bag and started to pull out a pair of jeans and a tee shirt. However, when I did the box also fell and opened, spilling the contents onto the floor. The stone rolled to just millimeters away from my big toe. If I moved my toe even in the slightest the stone would be touching me. The draw to touch the stone came over me again, and I reached for it. This time picking the stone up and holding it in my hand. There was a sudden burst of light then everything went black for a second. I clasped the stone tightly in my palm, all the unsmooth edges dug into my hand. There in the darkness images started to go through my head. But they were going too fast for me to even really see what they were, it was more or less a blur of color. A knock on the door made everything disappear, and I quickly opened my eyes, placed the stone back in the box and shoved it back in my bag.

Bill's hushed voice rang through the door. "Are you ok in there?"

It took me a second to clear my mind and answer. "Yeah, I'm fine. I'll be out in a second."

I wanted to touch the stone again but decided that I had better get dressed. I threw on my clothing and rushed out of the bathroom with my bag in hand. I went out to where everyone was sitting at the kitchen table, placing my bag on the floor, and taking a seat next to Bill.

"We found out what the note says." Sam said looking up at me.

I looked back at her and then to Bill. No one was giving any initial clues to if it was bad or good. Then Sam took a deep breath, and Bill reached for my hand. Oh, this was going to be bad I gathered from this reaction. I braced myself.

"So, the note says that anyone in possession of this stone has protection from all vampires."

"Ok" I sighed that wasn't so bad. Then Sam looked away for a moment it looked as though she was trying to decide how to tell me what was next.

"Lily," She started then paused.

I wished she would hurry up and just tell me it couldn't be that bad.

"I'm sorry. She started again then pause again.

I could tell that this was the bad part.

"The note also promises that if the two bloodlines ever meet each other again that this person can either break the vampire curse or they can join it and become the queen of the vampires. It also says that the two halves of the stones must be joined back together. But the note doesn't say why. Eric suspects that if the stone is not joined back together than all the powers of the vampires are lost. I'm not so sure I believe that." She said a grim frown played on her lips.

I mulled over everything, but I still had questions that I was sure Sam didn't have the answers too. Questions that only I could answer according to Eva. I peeked over at Bill. He had his head hung, obviously displeased with what Sam had said. If I decided to kill all vampires, then Bill and his sister would die. I would lose the only people helping me through this and the love of my life. The thought of losing them saddened me. I had come to realize that not all vampires are bad apples like Lucian. There are good ones too that actually care about people. Bill could just have easily sent me on my way and back to Lucian, forever in prisoned by him. I had a decision to make, keep the vampires alive by becoming one or killing them all. I sat there staring at the wall weighing the pros and cons of being a vampire. So far, the only hang up I had about it was drinking blood. Coming up with no real conclusion about the vampire thing my mind switched over to the stone. I wondered if it could be destroyed, possibly leaving everyone as they are. Maybe Eva would know how to destroy it. If she could would that release me from my decision to become or not to become a vampire? As I thought about this, I was sure that if I decided to become a vampire I wanted Bill to be the one to change me. I idly wondered how long I had to make my decision.

"Sam, did the note happen to have a timeline?"

She looked at me for a long moment. I think she was trying to figure out where I was going with this. "No."

The room fell silent again. At that moment, I had made up my mind that I would become a vampire the only thing that was stopping me right now was the fact that I only had half of the stone.

Bill's phone buzzed against the table loudly jolting me from my thoughts. Bill picked it up to see who it was. "It is your mom's number." He whispered.

"Hello." Bill said putting the phone on speakerphone.

"You're late, I don't like waiting, bring me what is mine, unless the girl doesn't want to see her mother alive again."

Maybe he would negotiate with me I thought. "Lucian, could you be so kind to give me a little more time?" I was begging with the sweetest voice I could muster. "I promise, I will give you everything that you want from me. But, please just give me a little more time. I think I know how this is all going to end. I just want a little more time before that happens. Can I talk to my mom please?" I asked.

"Ok, I will give you a little more time, but if you are not here by sundown tomorrow night then your mom will die, I'm getting very hungry." He said with a snicker that sounded evil.

"Lily, are you ok?" I heard my mom's voice say.

"Yes, mom I'm ok. Say do you know how to use that black gumbo pot? I sure would like some right now." I said.

To anyone listening, I hoped that this would sound like small talk. However, I hoped my mom could pick up what I was trying to ask her. I was really asking her about how to use the black stone.

"No, I never use that one to make gumbo anymore. I use the purple one." She said back.

Translating this was a bit tougher. I think she was telling me that she never touched the black stone that I had in my possession. But she threw me off by saying purple one. I had to think about it for a second. What did I know that was purple? Then the image of Eva's house popped into my head, it had purple. I think she was implying that I should go talk to Eva.

"Oh, that purple pot that you got as a gift?" I said emphasizing the words purple and gift letting her know that I understood what she was telling me.

"Yes, that one, however, I can't seem to find it." She said.

Now she was telling me that Eva had gone somewhere to hide.

"Sweetheart, I think I may have left it at the church." She said telling me that Eva may be hiding at my mom's church.

"Mom, I promise I will get you out of this. I will see you tomorrow. I love you." I said holding back the tears that wanted to come.

"I love you too." I heard her say as Lucian was taking the phone away from her.

"There, you know she is ok, my love. Now what you must do is this. Be here by sunset, and you had better come alone. If you are not here by then your mom will die, I promise you that, or I could just kill her now." He said, and I heard my mom scream.

"No please, Lucian, I promise I will be there tomorrow." I said screaming back into the phone.

"One more thing darling it doesn't matter if you are messing with me about coming here. The fact of the matter is if I have to come looking for you we are going to have problems. You think about that." He said then hung up the phone.

I slowly placed the phone on the table staring at it. I could only imagine what he had in store for me if I didn't show up. I shook it off and pretended to not let it bother me. My sadness quickly turned to anger and despair, then to determination.

"What are we going to do?" I asked out loud.

"I thought you would never ask" Sam said. "Bill and you are going to take the car and make the trip back to New Orleans. The rest of us are going to follow, but we are going to take to the forests so that we can get there and scout ahead of you to see what we are up against. As soon as you go into that house and your mom is secure, then we will converge on the house and take them down one by one." She said, and I saw a flicker of fire from her index finger.

I could not believe what I was seeing but dismissed it for now. I would ask Bill about it while we were driving.

"We will meet you there with everyone that I can find and the pack." She said.

"Can we try something?" I asked.

"Try what?" Sam, looked at me speculatively.

I took the box out of my bag and set it on the table. "I think that this is the protection stone," I said glancing around at everyone's face, their faces ranged from no way, to what are you thinking, and finally anger when I looked at Bill. "Please just hear me out. I think that if we leave now, we should be able to find Eva and see if she can tell me for sure which one this is. I'm one hundred percent positive that if I touch it, you would not be able to touch me. Or maybe we don't have to find Eva and try it now if you're up to the challenge Sam." I said calling her out. I knew if I called her out specifically that maybe she would override everyone. More specifically Bill, because I knew he would say no.

She looked Bill in the eyes, basically telling him to shut up this was happening and he cannot stop it. "Yes, we can try it out right now." She finally said, her eyes never leaving Bill's face.

Despite his sister's looks. Bill still voiced his loud resounding "NO."

I rebutted. "But what if he tries to change me right then and there? I would rather be safe than sorry." I was trying to convince Bill that we should at least try by using facts. Also, I was giving him puppy dog eyes.

His face fell because he knew that it was a possibility that Lucian could turn me at that moment. "Ok we can try it, but I still don't like the idea." He said

I opened the box and hesitated a second before touching the stone again. Last time images flickered through my head, and I wondered if it would happen again. Despite that, I snatched it up holding it tight in my hand. I opened my eyes to see Sam eagerly waiting for me to say ok touch me. However, I had to get control of my thoughts first. I struggled but finally got my thoughts right after a few images flashed through my mind again. Same as last time they were going too fast for me to catch one single picture except for the last picture. A woman lying on the floor with blood surrounding her looking very much dead, but then she sat up and looked directly at me, mouthing some words that I could not make out.

I shook the image away and announced. "I'm ready now."

Sam reached for me and grabbed a hold of my hand. As soon as she did, her hand started to burn. The smoke flew up from her hand, and she quickly retracted it. Then Aidan reached for me touching my hand, but there was nothing. Mrs. Woods then reached for my hand, and again nothing happened. Bill was the last one that reached for me. He slowly took my hand. There was nothing at first but then his hand was also smoking and burning. I guessed that there was a delayed reaction because he was half vampire and half werewolf. I dropped the stone back into the box and reached for Bill's hand to see if he was ok.

"Well I think that she should wear that into the house to see Lucian, I think it will buy us some time to make our move." Sam, said, Bill and Aidan nodded in agreement. "Ok then it is settled, you guys should get going."

With that, we said our goodbyes. Bill went out ahead of me to make sure we were not going to have any problems. While he was scouting, Sam took my hand. "Please come back to us. Bill needs you. I'm sorry we didn't get off to a good start at first but my main goal in life is to protect my brother." She said then hugged me. "Wow, you smell good enough to eat." She said, and I instantly tried to pull away from her. I knew quickly that she was just joking with me when she smiled at me.

"Thanks, we will see you soon." I said and walked out the door after Bill said that it was all clear. We pulled out of the driveway and were on our way to save my mom and hopefully my life. The car ride was quiet, we both were in our own thoughts about how this was all going to go down.

~CHAPTER 21~

I broke the silence first.

"Bill, sweetie, I feel like you know a lot about me but I really don't know anything about you. Do you think since we have some time you could tell me your story?" I asked.

I really wanted to know all about my man. The one that I loved, I just felt like he was the one I was supposed to be with forever even though I had only known him for a week or two.

"I'll start from the beginning. I am the first-born of my family. We lived in New York back in the 1800's. My father was a well to do Lawyer, but some issues came up, and we ended up moving to Georgia where he bought a farm. Our whole family didn't really want to move but what they didn't know was that my father was going to be killed if we didn't. You see he had gotten caught up in a trial of wealthy men that had already committed murder. My father was trying to get the murderer put in jail. Anyway, my father was told that someone had placed a hit out on him. He didn't want to die and figured running away from the trial was the best thing for his family. He packed everything up and sold most everything else and bought our farm. He never practiced law again, and we lived off what we could from the farm.

I was somewhat of an inventor trying to make all our lives easier. My father, however, didn't like it and told me that I was trying to take the lazy way out of things. It was horrible he was always mad at me for something. Anyway, one day when he was mad at me I stormed off into the woods. While I was in the woods, I met a man. He offered me a life without my troubles. At that point in time, I was all for it since I didn't want to live with my overbearing father anymore. I asked the man if I could have a day or two to think about it. He said sure, and we split ways. Well at that time, too I was courting a lovely woman a few miles from the house. I went and talked to her about it, and she thought that it was a good idea but maybe I should think about it. I got up early the next day while everyone was still asleep and went out to the barn to work on another invention that I was sure would work. It was to help collect eggs. Anyway, I got it all setup, and it was working. The egg would go through a hole in the nest and down a tube and to a basket lined with straw. I watched as two eggs made their way down to the basket and it seemed to be working perfectly. Well, I walked away from it and started to clean the horse stalls. When I went back to check on it again a couple of the eggs had broken, and my dad was furious. He ripped down the contraption and told me that if I ever built another one that he would pack my bags and kick me off the farm. Obviously, I was pissed. I threw down the pitchfork and stormed out of the barn and back into the woods. I found the man in the same spot as last time. I do want you to know that my father was a good man he wasn't all bad we had good times too. Anyway, the man and I walked deep into the woods. Everything started to feel all wrong, as I calmed down from being angry. I began to think that maybe this is a mistake, but it was too late. The next thing I knew he turned into a werewolf and had scratched me. I instantly fell to the ground in pain, it burned like there was a hot branding iron stuck into my skin. Finally, I passed out from the pain. When I came to, I could see things differently. I looked down at my feet and noticed they were paws. I tried to yell help, but it came out as a howl. The next thing I knew the man was there again, calming me. Its ok I will teach you what you need to know, he told me. He showed me everything that I needed to know about being a wolf. I would go by the farm from time to time just to check on them. I wanted to go back, but he told me that I couldn't, that I would draw bad things to the farm that would kill my whole family. That is when I learned about vampires. The first vampire that I met was Jaxson. That was about the time my creator disappeared. Jaxson and I became the best of friends. I slowly found two others my creator made. The three of us banded together and ran together, me being the leader I guess because I was born first and I was tougher than the other two. Anyway, under the direction of Jaxson, we tried to keep the woods around our houses free of vampires. I think we were doing more of a service to Jaxson than to anyone else, but we did it anyway. We had been chasing one particular vampire around the woods she kept slipping by us. Well, it just so happened that one day my sister was in the wrong place at the wrong time. The vampire had pretty much drained her to the point of death. I howled for Jaxson to come because my sister was going to die if he didn't change her. I would have changed her to wolf, but she had already been bitten by the vampire, so I figured Jaxson had to change her. Obviously, he turned her for me and taught her the vampire way. I had to stay away from her for a few months just to be safe that she would not kill me."

I rudely interrupted his story. "I know that name, Jaxson. When I was at Eva's, and she called upon a spirit that is the spirits name." I said excitedly. He nodded at me in acknowledgment then proceeded on.

"However, things had gone all wrong. The vampire that bit my sister had been the wife of one of the elders. Well, they sent three vampires after us we called them the Cloaks. They were looking for the killer or killers that had murdered the wife. Long story short the wolves and I were the ones that did it, but somehow Jaxson was blamed and paid with his life. After that, my sister and I parted ways as she was dealing or not dealing so well with Jaxson's death. Not to mention the cloaks couldn't know I was involved or they would kill me too. Anyway, so we said a tearful goodbye to each other, and off she went spending the next two hundred years or so roaming before she came home. In the meantime, while she was away. I made my home in the park where we met, keeping vampires from coming in and killing the campers." He said, pausing thinking about what he should tell me next.

"I was married once, and we had a few good years together before she passed away from falling down the stairs. I have not been with anyone since. I know in my heart that I'm ready now though." He said and glanced over at me.

I reached for his hand not knowing what to say to that. I was a bit shocked and saddened by the news. "I'm sorry." I whispered fighting back the tears that want to come. I wanted to cry for him and with him.

He squeezed my hand in reply to say it is ok. He had given me a lot to chew on. I thought about all that he had said for a moment. The questions were firing up in my mind, and I wondered if I should ask them. I knew that he was half wolf and half vampire, but he didn't tell me how that all went down. Then I wondered if it was something that maybe, I didn't need to know right now. I mulled the question over in my mind.

"Can I ask you a question?" I said still not sure if I should ask or not. I didn't wait for his reply, and the words just shot out of my mouth. "How is it that you are half wolf and half vampire?" Then I bit down on my lip hoping that he didn't mind me asking.

"Well long story short we had another run-in with the cloaks years later. I got bit by a vampire and my sister was the one that saved me that time." He said.

He gave me the short answer, but I knew there was more to the story, but I was satisfied for now.

"Well, you shared your story with me it is my turn to share something about me with you." I said and looked at his face to see if I could tell what he was thinking, but I was horrible at reading faces sometimes, so I started anyway. "I was born January twenty-first of the year one thousand nine hundred and ninety-two to my wonderful parents. The house that we live in is that house where I was born and raised. I am an only child. My dad was killed when I was four. A man shot him in the heart while I stood there helplessly. The man wanted my dad's money but became impatient and just shot my dad. He was going to shoot me too but people came around the corner, and he ran. I have nightmares about it from time to time still. Other than that, I went to public school and graduated the top of my class. I am currently going to college to become a Mechanical Engineer. I am only a semester or two from graduating. My life up until now has been relatively uneventful." I said looking up at him through my lashes. I felt compelled to spill my soul at that point. Besides I could be dead in a couple of hours anyway. "I wish I could say that I had never been kissed or have had sex, but that would be a lie. I did whatever I had too to stay alive when I was with Lucian." I said, and I could see the pain on Bill's face even though he tried hard to mask it. I felt the pain rush through my body as well but swallowed it back down. I did feel a little better to admit that to someone than keeping it all bottled up. "I'm sorry maybe I should have kept that to myself." I said feeling kind of guilty.

"No, it is ok, for us to be together we should share the good and bad with each other. I'm just sorry you had to go through that." He said, and I instantly felt better for telling him.

"Bill, I love you. I just want you to know that no matter what happens I will always love you. I know that it may sound strange since we really haven't had the time to get to know each other, but I just feel like it was love at first sight for me." I said and wanted to kiss him right then.

He must have felt the same way because he pulled the car to the side of the road and took both of my hands in his. "Lily, I love you too, I don't think that you are foolish in any way because I feel that way too. When this is all over, I am planning to ask for your hand in marriage." Then he kissed me softly on the lips as tears gushed from my eyes.

I whispered against his lips "When you do ask, my answer will be yes."

Then we somehow wound up in the back seat of the car making love to each other. This was how sex was supposed to feel when you loved one another. My mind was blown. After some time of lying there naked in the back seat just cuddling, we decided that we had better get a move on. We had burnt up the better part of an hour. Neither one of us wanted to do anything but the phone rang, and he had to answer it. It was his sister telling him to get a move on that she knew what we were doing. He jumped up quickly looking out of the windows then his sister laughed,

and I heard her say. "I really didn't, but I do now."
Bill was very displeased with her antics and hung up
on her but then started to laugh, I too laughed. We
pulled our clothes back on and jumped back in the
front seats. The sun was beating down on me through
the window, and it felt good. Leaning my head
against his shoulder, my eyes started to become
heavy.

∿CHAPTER 22∿

"Lily, sweetheart we are here."

I woke up in enough time to see the New Orleans city limits sign.

"I think Eva may be at the church that my mom goes too. Have you heard anything else from your sister? Maybe we should call her and tell her to meet us there." I said as my mind kicked into overdrive trying to think of every little detail. He picked up the phone, dialed her up, and with my help gave her directions to my mom's church.

"Can you go into the church?" I asked.

Bill immediately started laughing. Then realized that it was a bona fide question I was asking him.

"No, it doesn't hurt us to go into a church that is a myth." He said then added "Sorry."

We pulled up to the church and met Sam at the front door. We walked in together and didn't make it very far before Eva got our attention and pulled us over to a hallway and into a room shutting the door.

"What the hell are you guys doing here?" She said. Sam gathered her into a hug and mumbled.

"Thank you." I looked at Bill, but he looked just as confused as I did. "Can you help us again?" Sam asked releasing her. It was evident at that point that Sam already knew Eva somehow.

Eva looked at me first then at each of us in the room before speaking. "You need to take her far away from here and never return. Keep running and never look back. Life as you know it is over."

"But Eva, there must be some way? He has my mom, and is going to kill her if I don't go back tonight." I rebutted "Please" I begged.

She looked up at me then down to the ground. I knew what she was thinking at that moment, and her words came out in a whisper. "Just let her go."

"No, no, no." I screamed back at her. There was no way that I was going to let Lucian kill my mom.

She turned away from me. "I'm sorry, but it must be done. He cannot have you."

I looked up to see Sam staring at her in disbelief. Then when she looked at me, I realized that the help that they were going to provide going forward was to keep me away from Lucian. They would hide me somewhere with Bill, which I wouldn't mind. The problem with that would be that my mom would be dead. And It would be all because of me and these people. My so-called friends that had promised to help free her. I just could not deal with this idea at all right now let alone the rest of my life. The guilt alone would drive me insane. I would eventually end up in an insane asylum. Where they would give me a nice room with four padded walls with a padded floor and ceiling to boot. I'm sure they would give me a nice jacket to wear as well. I had to sit down as the weight of the situation pushed on me. My knees felt a lot like Jell-O. However, I knew that I had to do something to save my mom no matter what Eva said. I slowly pulled myself together and lifted the heavy weight that was crippling me. I knew that I had to somehow ditch everyone, get the stone and save my mom. I wondered for a moment if the stone would protect us both. I didn't see why not, and I had to try. It was obvious to me that our original plan had been thrown out the window. I looked up at Bill's face it was drawn in a hard line to almost a frown. I smiled back at him when he looked at me, and the corners of his mouth lifted a little. Sam had walked over to Eva and had put an arm around her. Their backs facing us and they were in a deep, hushed conversation. I took one last look at Bill's face memorizing every detail. My eyes wanted to fill with tears; I knew what this was going to do to him. He wanted to marry me. I took a slight step back from him and slowly edged my way towards the door.

"I need to use the restroom." I announced and silently slipped out of the door into the hallway.

I ran with all I had to the car, thankfully it was unlocked, I grabbed my bag and ran. By the time, I got to my block I was sure they knew I was missing and knew where I was headed. I hoped that they would come after me, but at the same time, I hoped they didn't. I slowly approached the house grabbing the stone out of my bag and holding it in my hand then shoving my hand into my pocket. I knew I had to touch my mom before he touched me. If I failed at this I knew that he would use her as a bargaining chip, and I knew that I would give in. How was I going to do this, so that didn't happen? Then I wondered what part of the house she was in. If she were in the living room, I would have a slim chance of getting to her, but if she was in the kitchen, my odds were worse. I decided to look in the windows and see if I could see her. I looked in all the windows but there was no sign of her anywhere. Therefore, that meant that she was either in her room or in the bathroom. Then I saw her, she had come out of her room into the kitchen. However, I didn't see any signs of Lucian. I grasped the stone again in my pocket and checked the handle on the back door it was unlocked. It was odd to me, but I decided not to think anything of it. I rushed in and put my arm around my mom keeping my hand that clasped the stone shoved in my pocket. My mom, started to cry as she realized that I had come for her.

Lucian's voice called to me. "There is my girl." Then he moved towards my mom and me. "Your little heartfelt reunion is over." He said reaching for me.

I squeezed the stone hard in my pocket so hard that it felt like it was going to either break my hand or make it bleed. When he touched me, his hand started to sizzle, and he was forced to pull his hand back.

"Well, well, well what do we have here? Looks like someone has been busy. So, what do you know my love?"

My blood ran cold as he called me, love. I pictured his face like a snake's face as he hissed at his wound. A jolt of terror ran through me as I saw his fangs elongate. He was trying to shake me, and I knew it. I summoned the strength within me and was able to steady myself quickly. I held on tightly to my mom as he made a move to grab her arm. When he came into contact with her his hand sizzled again. My plan was working, I felt triumphant, I was going to beat him and walk out of here with her. I inched us closer and closer to the door and freedom. He noticed my movement and placed himself in front of the door. I knew all I had to do was touch him and he would move but I would have to take the stone out of my pocket, or I would have to let my mom go. If I let her go, then she would be vulnerable to him. If I used the hand with the stone in it, I might accidentally drop the stone, or he could knock it from my hand, and it would be over for the both of us. I should have made a necklace for it then I would have both my hands free. You know what they say hindsight is always twenty, twenty. I decided that maybe the front door was the answer, so I started pushing my mom towards that door, but again he quickly moved into our path. This was a game that I was not going to win and knew it. He was faster than me, and he could do this all night long. I could not even stay awake as long as he could play this game. I started to think about other options, the big windows. We could smash through the window. He may follow us, but at least we would not be trapped. I was going to smash through the window, but then it was as if he could read my mind and blocked the way. I could hear what sounded like a dogfight outside and was starting to wonder if that was Bill and Aidan. If it was, they needed my help. I made a split-second decision that led to my demise. I went for the door not taking my hand off my mom for a second. I moved to touch Lucian's face with the hand that clasped the stone, I had to get him out of my way. In return for my motion, he also brought his arm up. In what I thought was a move to stop me but I was wrong. I noticed all too late that his hand held the other half of the stone. My arm already in motion it was too late to recoil or stop it. The two stones collided and it shimmered like we had poured black fairy dust on it. Weird looking black tendrils appeared. It was kind of like when your hair gets static, and it is drawn to everything. I watched in horror and tried to pull back, but the stone pulled its self together. It was done the stone was whole again. I let go of it immediately and backed away from Lucian putting my mom behind me.

"Now you are mine." He said with an evil grin then reached out grabbing my arm and pulling me close to him. Putting the stone in my hand. All the protection power was gone.

My mom stood on the other side of the room shaking. I wanted to go to her and comfort her, but I didn't know if Lucian would let me.

"I know I have been a shit, but could you please let me say goodbye." I managed to shyly ask.

"Sure, I'm not that insensitive." He growled sarcastically.

I wrapped both of my arms around my mom and whispered a tearful goodbye. Then all of a sudden, Lucian picked me up pulling me away from her, out of the back door, where he flung me over his shoulder and ran away with me. This was it my life was over now. The whole time that I had spent with him before, he had never said anything about the black stone. I wondered how he knew about it. Nevertheless, at the same time, I knew that answer. This was Marcus's partner in crime, of course, he would know about the stones. How would he know to put them back together to void the protection? I pondered as he ran with me through the woods.

Every now and again, a branch would scrape my back, shooting pain through my body. The last branch that scraped my back made me cry out in pain.

"Lucian, please, you're hurting me." I said, but he didn't slow down.

I tried biting him, but that didn't do a thing. Then I started punching him, but that didn't even faze him. Then he stopped setting me down on my feet. I could see a road and a car sitting there.

"Now we are going to walk to the car, and you are going to get in like a good little girl. Please don't make me kill you right here right now." The look in his eyes was that of pure malice, he had meant what he said.

He grabbed my hand tightly almost too hard it was hurting my hand. If he tightened his grip anymore, I'm pretty sure that my hand would break. We climbed down the embankment. When we got to the car, he opened the door for me to get in. I was a good girl got in the car and then scooted to the other side and tried to open that door, but he was in front of it and shaking his head no. I released the door handle and started to rub my hand it was throbbing slightly from the grip that he had had on it. The passenger side door opened and he eased into the backseat with me. I had not noticed the driver until now. He scooched closer to me put his arm around me as our driver sped off. I thought about jumping out of the car door, but I would have to get Lucian to let me go first. I wondered if I would die if I jumped out of the moving car. Then the thought crossed my mind what if I did die. Would that save everyone from what was going to happen? Of course, it would the little devil said inside my head. Then there was the angel saying what about Bill and your mom? Could they make it without you? Of course, they would I thought. Then again, the angel was there saying Lucian is never going to stop unless he is dead, your mom and Bill will never be safe. You will find a way out of this you will see. The angel won over the devil this time and I hoped I was not making a mistake that I would regret. I watched the miles tick by watching every turn we made and I realized that we were not headed back to his mansion we were heading somewhere else. I looked up at Lucian; he was playing with the stone, rolling it around in his hand. I didn't remember giving it back to him but really the last hour was a blur anyway.

"May I?" I asked pointing to the stone.

He looked at me then back at the stone, then handed it to me without hesitation. I tried to split it apart, but that was a failed effort. It just was not coming back apart. I rolled it around in my hand then cupped it in both hands. It sparkled and shined like a black diamond. I wondered what kind of secrets it was holding. I stared intently at it, but nothing was happening. I closed my eyes and rested my head back against Lucian's arm trying to concentrate on the stone, but I was just too distracted by Lucian and what he might do to me in a vulnerable state. I just could not clear my mind and let the stone talk to me, I needed to be alone with it. I'm sure that he would not let that happen though. I tried repeatedly, but it was no use. He took the stone from me and pulled my arm up across his face.

"Oh, you smell so good. I can't wait to get you home!"

I tried to jerk my hand away, but it was no use. His iron grip was no match for my weak body. He kissed the inside of my wrist and down my arm a little bit and whispered.

"Maybe just a little taste." I wanted to protest, but it was too late I could feel his fangs pushing on my arm and then breaking the skin. I could feel my veins collapsing with every sucking sound that he made. I wanted to scream out in protest, but I just was not going to give him that satisfaction. I turned my head and clenched my mouth and my eyes shut. I tried to think of anything that made me happy. After a few more gulps of my blood, he let go of my arm.

"Oh, you taste so good." He licked his lips and placed a cloth on my arm where he had bitten me. He applied a small amount of pressure to get the blood to stop flowing. Then he wrapped me in an iron-tight hug and pulled me to his chest. I protested, but it was as if he could not hear me. I had no choice but to go along with it. I became extremely tired after that and fought off sleep in every way that I could think of, but it was no use it was coming no matter what. My eyelids drooped down over my eyes.

∾CHAPTER 23∾

Looking around the chamber that I was in it appeared to be an old castle. In the room was a huge bed fit for a king. A fireplace roared against the far wall spreading a low light to the room. The chamber door opened and a couple with their faces pressed together, in the thralls of passion walked in. They were undressing each other without taking their mouths apart. The man gently pushed the woman on the bed and began kissing her inner thigh. Then there was blood running from her thigh, but she didn't seem to notice. He kissed her belly next leaving a trail of blood from her leg to her lips. As things heated up and they were climaxing he bit the woman's neck. She screamed and then went limp. He had not noticed until he was done, that he had killed her. He screamed and shook her hard looking for some sign of life. There was nothing. He reached for the sword above the bed and kneeling over her putting the sword to his throat. Blood squirted from his neck all over the woman that he killed. Nevertheless, as soon as the blade was removed the cut healed and he was still living. He threw his hand up to the sky and screamed. The door burst open and in walked a little girl. She was horrified by the scene. He reached for the girl with his bloody hands, but when he touched her, he started to burn. The girl shouted something at him, and he fled the room. She ran to the woman tears

dripping from her eyes. "mommy, mommy wake up."
She repeated several times. I don't know how long
the girl stayed with her, but the girl finally placed a
part of the stone on the woman's chest. The stone
started to glow red from within and then out words
making a red flash go through the room before it
turned back to the shiny black stone. The girl looked
down at her mom that was now burning by her touch.
She ran from the room knowing what had happened
to her mom. It was just like what Eric had said it was.
I stood in the room for a few more minutes. The man
came back for the woman I'm assuming his wife at
this point with another man in tow. This man was
dressed in a brown cloak holding a wooden staff.
Judging from the story, Eric had told this must have
been the sorcerer. The man pointed to his wife. The
sorcerer went over to the woman and placed his hand
on her chest. Then all of a sudden, the woman
grabbed the sorcerer and faster than he could protect
himself, bled the pour man dry. The man was
overjoyed and kissed her over and over again. The
stone fell to the ground rolling away from the two of
them. The room started to fade away focused on the
stone. I saw a hand come out of the darkness picking
up the stone. That was it. I opened my eyes to Lucian
staring at me as if he was expecting me to say
something.

"Can we stop I really, really need to use the
restroom." I said but then quickly realized that we
were not in the car anymore. "Where are we?" I
asked, but he didn't reply he just stared at me like he
was waiting for me to tell him something.

I frowned at him I had nothing to say to him. I turned my head away from his gaze. He must have realized I was not or didn't have anything to say to him. He released me, and I quickly found the bathroom. I pondered about telling him the dream but decided that I needed to analyze it myself before I gave up any information. Most importantly, I needed him to tell me more about what he was planning on doing to me. I knew exactly how to do that. I must have lingered too long in the bathroom though. The door quickly opened with a swish, and he popped his head around the corner. An embarrassed smile crossed my face along with please go away. He turned and placed himself in the doorway not looking at me so that I could finish. When the toilet flushed signaling I was done, he turned to face me again. He had a small smile on his face that almost touched his eyes. He held out a hand for me to take. I did without saying anything. He pulled us over to a couch and flipped on the television. Well so far, this room was not as nice as the old one, but at least this one had entertainment. He sat in the corner of the couch and pulled me down into his lap.

He stroked my cheek gently with his hand. "I missed this." He whispered against my skin as he gently caressed my neck with his lips.

I felt nothing for him, but this was not going to get me anywhere but dead. I placed my hand on his cheek and slowly and gently guided his lips to mine.

I closed my eyes and whispered back "me too."

He took a deep breath and finally relaxed a bit under me. I moved a bit, rested my head on his arm exposing my full throat to him, and whispered. "Would you like another little taste?"

I closed my eyes trying to conceal my hatred at what I was doing. Trying to block out how I really felt about him. I felt his slow kisses on my neck, and then I heard the pop of my skin breaking away and letting the blood flow out into his mouth. He took a few sips and then quit. He carried me to the bed, where he cuddled me, touching me everywhere. I let everything fall away from me at that point blocking everything from my mind. After it was over and I could see the blood on my body, I wanted to take a shower. I felt dirty in every sense of the word. I missed my man, my half wolf half vampire. He would never have treated me like this. The tears were coming, and I didn't want to give him the satisfaction of me crying.

"May I please take a shower?"

I didn't wait for his answer but just got up, started walking but my legs were weak, and I could barely stand, but I managed to make it to the shower. In the shower, I just stood against the wall letting the water wash over me. I was hoping the dirtiness of it would fall away. The tears began to flow, but after a few minutes of crying, I gave myself a pep talk. Lily, you can do this you have all you need to beat him it just comes down to a matter of when and how. You will beat this. This is just some shit you have to go through to get back to your mom and Bill. Bill the love of my life the man that asked me to marry him. I just had to make it through. I could not make him a widow again. I grabbed the washcloth and the soap and scrubbed my body clean. When I got out of the shower, it was time to play. Play Lucian's game the way he wants to play it. I danced out of the bathroom brushing my hair.

He looked at me curiously. I hopped up on the bed then on top of him putting my hands on his wrists. It felt like I had control but he could still move too easy for me to have any control. However, I pretended anyway. I looked him in the eyes and asked the question I wanted to know the answer to the most.

"What are your plans for me? I hope it involves us forever." I said eyeing him seductively. He eyed me back trying to figure out my angle, but I must have been hiding it well. He flipped us over without even trying, and I was now pinned to the bed.

"Well, you see my darling; I plan on changing you to vampire, and then you will rule as queen with me your king."

"Well, what are you waiting for?" I taunted showing him my full neck again.

"Oh, my darling the time is not right just yet. We have another few days before that happens."

"What happens in a few days?" I asked back.

"You shall see." He said being vague.

Whatever was going to happen was in a few days so between now and then I needed to find a way out of this. My stomach growled just then, and he heard it as well. He jumped to his feet and went straight to the phone. This room had a phone, and I put two and two together we were in a hotel. I don't know what kind of hotel we were in but it was nice and didn't appear to be a hotel room at all, it looked more like an apartment. I was listening as he ordered a bunch of stuff off the menu, everything from fried chicken to salad and soup. I thought about throwing a fit when the room service came, in hopes, they would get me out of here but all that would do is get him or her killed. I could threaten to kill myself, but all that would do is get me tied up for sure. A knock on the door pulled me out of my thoughts, and my stomach growled, as I smelt the food waft in through the open door. As I waited for a couple of people to push the carts into the room one last thought occurred to me. I had a few days to figure out what all this was about and I intended to do so. I just had to find a way to get Lucian to tell me what was happening.

I opened all of the lids to everything that had been brought. I took a bite or more of everything and then sat down on the small couch stuffed to the max. Lucian was reading a book or at least pretending to read a book. I could not see the title because his hand was covering it. I sighed and sunk into the couch watching him to see if he was going to look up at me, he didn't. I sighed louder this time, but still, he didn't respond. So, I took matters into my own hands and pushed the book out of my way so that I could sit on his lap facing him. He looked into my eyes with a small smile toying with his lips.

"I remember a time not too long ago when it was just you and I." I said and smiled back at him.

He closed the book and set it down on the table next to the couch. He wrapped his arms around me and pulled me in close to him.

"I just wanted to say that I was sorry for running, I was scared. I should have come back to you sooner I missed you. I always feel safe with you. Please find it in your heart to forgive me."

I leaned into his lips and softly kissed him then his cheek and down his neck. I was hoping that this would soften him up to tell me what was going to happen and why. I had not forgotten about Bill, and I truly would rather be in his arms than here with Lucian. I started to cry but stopped myself. Lucian's hand gently wiped the tear away from my cheek.

"It is going to be ok." Then he trailed kisses down my cheek and to my neck. "You are here with me now, and I can see how sorry you really are." He whispered against my neck hesitating and drinking in my smell.

He licked the wounds from earlier then pulled back from me a bit. I thought he was going to bite me again but instead threw his head back against the couch and closed his eyes. It looked as though he was fighting with something in his mind.

"Lily, my love." He said in a pained voice.

Then he picked both of us up caring me like I was a feather to the bed. Oh, crap this is not what I wanted to do. I just wanted him to give me information about my future. However, he surprised me again and laid beside me nuzzling his face in my hair. He pulled out the black stone and placed it on my chest. I caught it before it rolled off me and onto the floor.

"Tell me what do you see?"

∾CHAPTER 24∾

I clasped the stone with both hands and pressed it into my chest. I didn't see anything though except the ceiling. I tried again, but still, there was nothing. "Lucian, maybe if I sit up I could see."

He removed his arm from around me to let me sit up. I closed my eyes and sat like I was meditating. I concentrated really hard on the stone and pushed everything else out of my mind. Slowly an image started to appear. It was a woman and a man sitting on golden thrones. The woman was dressed in a fancy red gown with a red veil covering her hair. The veil was attached to a beautiful crown that held huge pearls that wrapped around three huge red rubies. The gown was mostly red velvet except for the wide white ribbons that had intricate embroidered floral patterns running the length of the gown. The man wore a red velvet robe that concealed him completely. He wore a crown of gold full of precious gems, red velvet boasted slightly above the gold and covered his head. I glanced around at the room. It was lit by dim burning candles. The more that I observed the room, the more I realized that this was not in a castle but more of a modern-day house.

Both the man and the woman were staring at me as I looked into their faces finally the man spoke.

"I am Marcus!" his deep baritone voice boomed through the small room.

I instantly recognized the name. This was the king and queen vampire, and I quickly bowed to the both of them to show my respect.

"Get up child." The woman's soft voice said. "Never mind him he has been waiting centuries to say that." The woman got up from her throne and started towards me.

I stumbled backward a little bit not sure of her intentions.

"Don't be afraid I'm not going to hurt you." She slowly extended her hand for me to take. I cautiously took her hand. "I have a gift for you."

She slowly pulled her hand out from behind her back and waited for me to extend my hand under her hand to receive the gift. However, there was nothing in her hand instead; she latched on to my arm. I was terrified and tried to struggle away from her, but it was no use. Marcus at that point rose from his throne and approached me now.

He ran his fingers through my hair and down the side of my neck. "It looks like we have a bad vampire on our hands." He said looking at the woman then back to me.

I started to protest, "I'm not…" The woman silenced me though by placing a finger to my lips. Then after a second more, they released me.

"Could it be?" The man said staring at me.

"Of course, it is you, dummy. Can't you smell our blood running through her veins?" She asked the man.

I saw him sniff the air and then ponder the smell for a second. "I don't believe it our princess is finally home."

What me a princess I was thinking. No, I'm just an ordinary girl from New Orleans. Then he came towards me as if he was going to do something, but the queen stopped him.

"I know that you are not my Aylin, she died a long, long time ago. However, you do have our blood flowing through your succulent veins, and I accept you as our child. We would like to give you the gift of forever." She said and stared at me waiting for me to accept the gift.

"I came here seeking answers." I said trying to change the subject. My now mother figure looked at me strangely but didn't say anything. "I have a problem you see, and I don't know what way to go. There is this vampire named Lucian. He wants something from me, but I don't know what it is." I looked at the both of them, and the kings face filled with rage.

"Please, my daughter let me turn you now. Lucian is no good… oooh if I ever get my hands on him…" He said, and he started towards me again.

I put up my hands. "Wait, wait, I'm not sure that is a good idea. He is with me now. I don't know how this is working, but I have the black stone."

He looked at me funny but stopped his advance.

"You have to get away from him. He is after the power that the stone possesses. If he gets ahold of the stone and spills your blood on it, he will have all of the powers of every vampire in the world. Your blood is the key to all the vampires of the world's undoing. With simply a thought, he could kill all or any vampire. The human race would be at his beckon call. Where are you we shall come for you and get back what rightfully belongs to us!" He was serious.

"I don't know except for that I'm in some sort of hotel. Please hurry I have only a few days left." I said as everything faded away.

I felt drained as I opened my eyes to see the hotel room again. That was an intense meeting. Everything seemed so surreal.

"Well, my darling, what did you see?" He asked intently gazing into my eyes.

I knew that I could not tell him what or who I saw. This was something that I had to keep from him.

I remembered being told that this man supposedly killed the king and queen. Their recent warning still ringing in my ears.

"Nothing much really, just a lot of still pictures of a king and queen." I lied, shaking my head. "None of this makes any sense."

I dropped the stone on the bed. He wrapped his arms around me and pulled me in close to his chest. "I'm sure that I will end up dead when all this is done."

I tried to push away from him, but it was like pushing against iron bars he had absolutely no give to him. I started to cry. I was trying to pull out all the stops I needed him to tell me what his plan was for me.

"Darling don't cry, it all will be over soon. You will see we are going to have a wonderful life together. Maybe a nice hot bath will help you relax." He released me and was off to the bathroom and running water.

I looked at the stone then to the door and thought for half a second that I could make a break for it but I was positive that I would not get far. If he caught me then all of the things that I had done up until now would be all in vain and he surely would not trust me to tell me anything. Not to mention I'm sure he had guards posted outside the door. I eyed the stone again and lightly touched it stroking it a bit. I could see a dim red light start to appear and was focused on it. I had seen it emit the red light before when it was put back together but not since then. I moved my hand away from it and the light dissipated. I was reaching back for it when Lucian called me from the bathroom. I ignored him and reached for the stone again. After a second of me touching it, it started to glow again. It was mesmerizing somehow. Lucian startled me when he placed a hand on my shoulder. I let go of the stone instantly dropping it back to the bed. He didn't say anything just scooped me up and carried me to the bathroom. He set me down on my feet and I proceeded to undress and quickly get in the hot tub. It was almost too hot, and I could feel my skin turning red. I sunk down into the water until it was touching my chin. I paid no attention to anything else in the room and just stared into space. Not really seeing anything just thinking about all that I had seen and done the past month or so. My thoughts rested on Bill and it was almost as if I could see him standing there, and could feel his arms around me again. He wanted to marry me. He loved me. I felt a pain of sadness run through me. Man, I really screwed this one up. He had no idea where I was or even how to save me from Lucian. All I could do was tell him I was sorry over and over in my head. Then there was my mom. She would have given up her life to save mine. I knew though that I would have done the same thing if circumstances were reversed. Now I was leaving her to walk this world alone, but on the same token, if he would have killed her, I would be the one walking this world alone. Now the entire vampire world's fate rested on my shoulders. My beloved Bill and his sister could possibly die even without trying to save me. I could feel a gaping hole rip through my chest. I had made a mess of everything. Everyone that I loved was going to die unless by some miraculous feet I freed myself. I thought about suicide again, and this option was becoming the only way out. I shut the thought down though it was too tempting to try. I just promised myself that there would be a way out and the opportunity would present it's self soon I just needed to focus. Lucian's voice broke the silence and brought me back to earth.

"May I?" He said gesturing to the tub, I didn't say anything but moved to make room for him behind me. He squeezed in, and I leaned back against his iron-hard body. Hating every second of it I wished I was here with Bill.

"Please, please, please tell me what your plan is for me." I begged, I hated not knowing what his intentions were.

"Well ok, you have confessed a few things, and I think that maybe you deserve to know what I plan on doing with you. First, you are going to become my wife in a few days. Then I'm going to change you." That was all he said.

I knew better though I was putting all the pieces to the puzzle together. He was going to marry me, change me then kill me. The only answer I didn't have was about the stone. And, why he wanted to wait a few days. I started to ask, but he shut me down with a kiss. The next thing I knew he was drinking from me being careful not to spill a drop. When he pulled his mouth away from me, I saw a little dribble of blood start to roll down his lip. I don't know what I was thinking but I licked it off him. He gave me a strange look at first but then he smiled and nodded. As if to say good job, you are going to make an excellent vampire. The blood tasted like I put some metal keys in my mouth, but that quickly turned into sweetness like I drank some syrup. It was not too bad I thought. What the hell was I thinking? There is no way in a million years I would have even thought about putting blood in my mouth. I was shocked at myself. I have not ever put a cut finger or anything that was dripping blood in my mouth. I jumped back from him, stood up and jumped out of the tub. I had to get away from him to think. I wrapped the towel around me and left the bathroom quickly. I paced back in forth between the coffee table and the couch. Ok, Lily what the hell were you doing? Did he make you do that? Why, how could you? The better question was why did you like the taste. This is the one that shocked me the most. What the hell was going on with me?

"Ouch…" I cried out when my pinky toe hit the coffee table leg. I started to fall as the pain of my toe took over my body. Lucian was there to catch me. I pulled my foot up to examine my toe. It looked fine it just was jammed.

"Lily, are you ok?"

"Yeah, yeah, I'm fine." Then I pulled myself up to my feet. My toe still hurt but the pain was rapidly going away.

"Do you want to talk about it?" Lucian asked.

My first thought was my toe but then my brain caught up with what I was initially doing. I shook my head no and turned away from him cradling my face in my hands.

"Well, I think it was cool. You're going to make an awesome vampire."

I was too embarrassed to look at him, but my brain did catch the words awesome and vampire. So, I now knew that he planned to change me.

"Oh, I want to change you right now." He said.

"What are you waiting for, do it now." I said back pulling my hair to one side and exposing my neck to him. I felt him touch my shoulder then he started kissing it. He trailed kisses up my neck to a point, I could feel his fangs slightly touching my skin, and I froze in place waiting for the pain of the puncture to come. He pulled away and lightly laughed.

"Oh, you are making this too easy. I have to wait a few more days and then you will be mine." He whispered in my ear wrapping his arms around me.

"Lucian, what happens in a few days?" I asked very softly and sweetly. Hoping that he would tell me, hoping maybe he would spill the beans.

"My love, I'm going to turn you. You see it is a special day. It is the same day the king made the queen, and since you are going to be my queen, I want it to be a special day for you too. It is also when the stone will be at maximum strength and will give you all the power of every vampire in the world and together we will be powerful and rule the world all of the living and the undead." Then he groaned in my ear, spun me to face him, and kissed my lips.

∾CHAPTER 25∾

Now that I knew, his plan and why the day was important it was time to make my escape plan. How exactly was I going to do that? He was not going to let me out of his sight. Somewhere in my thoughts, I fell asleep but not a deep sleep. Therefore, when he got up and move from under me, I listened to what he was doing. Then I heard the door open and shut. I quickly got up and looked around for him. He was nowhere to be found though. I put my ear to the door and didn't hear any movement or talking in the hall. This was my chance. I called room service to come pick up all the trays that had been left. They were there on the double. I learned that there was a guard outside the door. He let her in with a little hesitation and closed the door quickly. A quick uppercut to the jaw and she was lying on the floor unconscious. I grabbed the stone and threw on her clothing. Here I go, I hoped that this was going to work. I pushed the cart out into the hall and walked away from the guard who called out have a nice day. I turned the corner of the hallway and spotted the elevator bank, ditched the cart, and ran to the elevator bank. I pushed the button rapidly and repeatedly. Please God get me out of here. The elevator finally stopped on my floor, and I got in. The elevator was empty, and I pushed the button labeled L. Then the close doors button. While the doors slowly closed I kept pressing the button, trying to will the elevator to be faster. However, no matter how many times I pushed the close door button the doors still went at their own pace. I was thankful that the elevator itself was not as slow as the doors and it quickly lowered me to the lobby and dinged as the doors opened. I peeked out to see if he was there anywhere. I didn't see him and I wanted to start running for the door but I had to be cautious, he could be anywhere. If he were around, he would see me for sure. I stepped out of the elevator and took another quick look around. I still didn't see him. I started walking towards the front doors and to my freedom when I saw him. Luckily there was a hallway to my left, and I quickly turned down the hallway walking away from him. I quickly ducked into the first open room. It was a laundry room. If he had seen me, he would be here in a few short seconds. I heard the ding of the elevator doors then heard them clank shut and decided that this was it. It was now or never. I peeked around the door, and the hallway was empty. I ran towards the end of the hall to the door on the side of the building. I was in luck there was a car running with no one standing around it. I checked the door it was unlocked. I threw the car in reverse backing out of the parking space. Slammed the car into drive and away I went. I drove at a fast pace down the winding road that was lined with woods. There was nothing but woods around me, he could still catch me if he figured out what I had done quick enough. He could run through the woods without being seen. Finally, after what felt like an eternity, I came to an intersection and saw a street sign that said Lake Oconee. There was nothing around I decided to go right. I passed a couple of hotels and came to another intersection. By the way, it appeared this was a major road. I decided to take another right. I spotted a road sign in the headlights. It said interstate twenty-eight miles. Woohoo! I had chosen the right direction. I drove as fast as I could down the road until I hit the highway. I was sure that I made it in record time from that intersection to the highway. I was just happy that there were not any cops around to slow me down.

Once on the highway, I gunned it and drove as fast as I could handle. I had to stop though, I had no idea where I was or even how to get home from here. I saw the lights of a little town and decided to stop and ask for directions. The gas station clerk was accommodating and told me that I was just outside of Atlanta and to keep heading west on twenty until I got to fifty-nine. I hoped that I had enough gas to get there. Then something dawned on me. Lucian probably knew I was gone by now and was on his way to my mom's house knowing that is where I would go. I was not going to make it before him if he ran there. I pushed the button on the mirror that had a phone symbol. A voice came over the speakers saying how may I direct your call. I gave the person the phone number and waited as the phone rang. No one answered though. I pushed the button again and had the person dial the number to the store. It rang twice before my mom answer the phone.

"Hi, mom. I need you to do something. Get the hell out of town, call Bill and tell him that I'm ok and I am on my way home. Oh, and get Eva. I'm bringing a world of shit with me." I said and waited for her to reply, but she was silent. "Mom, are you there?"

"Yes, yes, I'm here. I will do as you ask." She sounded funny to me though.

"Mom, what is going on?"

"Nothing dear, I'm just shocked to hear from you, I thought for sure you would be dead by now."

That was a bleak outlook, but I guess she was right. "Look, mom, I'm fine, but I need you to get your things and Eva and meet me at the bus station. I don't think he would look for you there. I'm coming to get you. Please tell Bill I'm sorry."

"Ok, ok, I got it I will see you at the bus station." She said happier this time. I think it had finally sunk in that I was ok.

"Love you see you soon." I said, and we hung up the phone.

I turned on the radio and changed the stations until I got to a metal station and heard serenity by Godsmack. I really could use some serenity right now. It would be nice to visit a beach with the love of my life. Laying on a blanket and enjoying some sun. I drove as fast as I possibly could, and I was making good time. I didn't think about anything except for driving. I crossed the Louisiana state line and knew it was just a matter of a few hours until I got to my mom. The hours flew by and the next thing I knew I was getting off the expressway. The gas gage was almost on E, and I thanked God for getting me this far. I thought about Bill and hoped that he would be there and that I would be safely back in his arms. I pulled up to the bus station and instantly saw my mom and Eva sitting on a bench. Behind them stood my man, I pulled up by them and got out of the car. My mom and Eva eyed me for a minute then wrapped their arms around me. I looked up at Bill, but the expression on his face was unreadable.

"Come let's take my car." He said pointing to where it sat a few rows away. "Let's go now." He said looking around, and I was getting the feeling that he was sensing something. He grabbed my arm and started to pull me towards his car.

"Wait, wait, I have to get something." I said as I struggled against his grip on my arm. He reluctantly let me go but didn't leave my side for a split second.

"Let's go he is here." He said and looked everywhere trying to spot him. He held on to me tightly while pulling me along with him to the car. My mom and Eva had already gotten in. As soon as he got in, he floored it, and the tires squealed against the pavement lurching the car forward and making me feel like I was glued to the seat. I looked around trying to spot anything out of the ordinary but didn't see anything. As we approached the highway and got on, some of the tension in Bills shoulders relaxed, but it was not entirely gone.

Then without warning, he unleashed. "That was the most dangerous, stupid thing that you have ever done. Why, why, why did you do it?" The words were like venom spewing out of his mouth. Each one stinging a little deeper than the last, then I burst into tears and just uncontrollably started to cry.

"If I would have lost you…" He said in a quieter slightly calmer voice and reached for my hand. "I'm sorry I just…" I looked up at him now the anger that was on his face had turned into pure sadness. The red trails on his face were proof of that.

"I'm sorry, I just wanted…" Tears filled my eyes again. I knew that I shouldn't have done what I did. Sadness filled me to the brim and overtook me.

He reached for my hand then patted it a little. I think he was trying to tell me that it was ok. My mom who sat behind me placed her hand on my shoulder; she was trying to comfort me. If I had been in the backseat with her, she would have wrapped her arms around me and held me close to her. Eva was chanting something I could not make heads or tails of. Eva was lost in her own world.

"Where are we going?" My mom asked after a few minutes.

"The only place that I know is safe from all of this, my home." Bill replied back to her.

Then the car went silent, and we all fell asleep except for Bill. I could feel him holding my hand not willing to let me go for a second.

∾CHAPTER 26∾

In my dream, I saw the queen and king again, they were in a different place now. I looked around the room and recognized it from the room that I had just escaped from. I didn't know if they could not see me this time because they didn't look at me or even acknowledge my presence. Looking around the room, I saw the devastation that I had left behind. There was blood flung on the walls, and two people lay dead on the floor. The maid and the guard, Lucian had massacred them. I drifted out of that scene to the scene of the queen lying on the floor in a pool of her own blood. The child placing the stone on her mother and it started to glow red. The red light filling the room after the child had run. The light then seemed to swirl around the room. An image of a sorcerer standing by her caught my attention. He was chanting something, but I could not understand the words. Siyah sihirli vermek ona the guc. The faster he chanted the words, the faster the red swirled around the room. Finally, it was sucked back into the stone, and the light went out as the king entered the room. She was coming to at that point and let out a shrill scream. The king gently lifted her off the floor, but she was not having it and jumped away from him. In the process, she grabbed the sorcerer letting the bloodlust take over, draining him dry before he even had a chance to get away. The Stone fell to the floor and rolled out of the picture. The image faded away into blackness. The red floating eyes were there.

"Lilly, Lilly, wake up." I felt hands on me gently shaking me. My eyes popped open, and everyone was staring at me.

Why was everyone staring at me? I was going to ask but then quickly realized that we were pulling into Bills garage. Bill turned off the car and got out along with everyone else and went in the house. I sat in the car for a few minutes trying to gain my composure and wipe the sleep from my eyes.

A few seconds passed before Bill came around and opened my door. "Are you coming in?" He asked eying me.

"Of course." I smiled looking up at him.

He reached for my hand and pulled me out of the car, wrapping me in his arms holding me tight to his body. "I thought that I would never see you again." He said kissing the top of my head.

I started to say I was sorry again but shut my mouth before anything came out. "I understand why you did it though." He said as he pulled back to see my face. Then he noticed the bite marks on my neck and I could see the anger shoot through him. The anger was not for me but for Lucian. Then his face softened as he noticed my face again. "I'm going to kill that prick. I promise you that." Then he pulled us into the house.

Sam looked up as we walked in and gave me the I want to kill you look. Then she looked away and went back to talking to my mom and Eva. We didn't join them though, we walked past them down the hall and too what I assumed was Bill's room. He pulled me into the bed next to him and wrapped me up in him. He kissed the wounds on my neck but didn't say anything.

"He is going to come for me, you know." I said softly, trying to be quiet stating the obvious.

He didn't say anything and just continued to stroke my hair. It was obvious to me that he didn't want to talk about any of it right now. That was fine with me too. I just laid there with the man that I loved and took in his beauty, touch, and smell. Wishing that we could stay like this for forever with no more trouble.

A knock on the door startled both of us. "Brother, we need to talk to her too you know, the sooner, the better." Sam's perturbed voice came from the other side of the door.

"We will be there soon." He spat the words back at her. He was mad that she had interrupted our moment.

He placed his hand over my heart but didn't say anything. I wondered what he was doing, but I didn't want to ask and ruin the moment. Furthermore, I didn't need any more information rolling around in my head. I would ask him later though. Then he sprang to his feet pulling me with him.

"We should…" I silenced him with a kiss.

I hoped by kissing him, he would forget about going out there and we could stay right here. I knew all they wanted to do was pick my brain for information. I could feel the stone in my pocket at that point and it felt hot and heavy. I dropped my arm to retrieve it from my pocket. When I pulled it out of my pocket, it was emitting a small red light. I held it out for Bill to see too. He blankly stared at it not saying anything. Then there was a knock on the door again, but this time she didn't say anything and burst through the door. She grabbed my wrist and pulled me from the room. She gently but roughly sat me down in a chair with my hand on the table to show everyone the stone that was emitting the small red light. Bill protested at the way she was treating me, but that fell on deaf ears as everyone stared at the stone. I placed the stone on the table out of my hand, and the light went out. Everyone just stared in silence except for Eva. She had her eyes closed and was moving her lips but not making a sound. It almost looked as if she was praying. My mom stared at me now with her mouth hanging open. I could tell she was thinking what the hell. Sam and Aidan stared at the stone. Bill grabbed my hand in both of his and just held on to me. Freeing one hand I moved to touch the stone again, and everyone yelled "no" unanimously. I slowly pulled my hand back from the stone and placed it back in Bill's.

Sam was the first to speak. "Ok, Lily, what the hell is going on?" She said her words coming out in a hiss.

I looked at my mom, then to Mrs. Woods and finally Eva. I could tell they all had the same question on their minds. Well except for Eva, she still had her eyes closed, saying something but without sound. Bill wrapped an arm around me and pulled me close to him. They all wanted to know what I knew about the stone. I wondered why Eva had not told them already. She seemed to know everything. I opened my mouth to speak but shut it again before any words escaped, how was I going to explain this when I didn't really understand any of this myself. I was getting ready to speak when the room went dark except for the bright light that emanated from behind me. I had seen this happen only one other time and that was with Eva. I knew that she had called on her spirit friend again.

"Hello, Sam." The deep booming voice said. Sam looked at Aidan, who was looking at her.

"Hello Jaxson, what are you doing here?" She said back to the voice. She sounded calm and collected now.

"I have come to warn you trouble is coming your way. You are way outnumbered." Jaxson said.

"Do you have any words of wisdom for us?" She asked him back and almost looked as though she was going to cry. Right then I got the feeling that she knew Jaxson as well but perhaps in a different way than Eva.

"No, other than run, get as far away from here as you possibly can, leave the girl and let them have her." He said, and it was obvious at that point I meant nothing to him, or there was no way out without heavy casualties.

Then he was gone, back to where he had come from before anyone could say anything else. I looked at Eva, and now she was staring at me too. My mom looked shocked underlined with panic. Sam stared at Bill, and he stared back at her.

Aidan had turned and was staring out of the window into the yard. He rose from his seat and started to back up away from the window slowly, then more quickly. Something out there had startled him. We all had our eyes fixed on the big picture window, but I could not see what he saw. I could not see anything, but Sam and Bill seemed to be able to see something. Bill jumped in front of me as if he was protecting me from something. I tried looking around him, but Aidan was in my way. I grabbed the stone and put it back in my pocket. Then without warning, they started pushing us all backward away from the window. I caught a glimpse of three black figures that had red glowing eyes. They looked like something straight from hell. Bill grabbed my arm and my mom's arm leading us to the garage and practically throwing us in the car. Aiden, Sam, Eva and Mrs. Woods shortly joined us. They placed the four of us in the middle between Sam and Aidan. Bill threw the car into reverse and backed out of the garage crashing through the door. We were down the driveway and on the road in seconds. We saw the figures appear in the road behind us, but they didn't chase us. No one was talking as we watched them disappear out of sight.

Sam relaxed into the seat and pinched the bridge of her nose. Aidan didn't relax instead he kept staring behind us. The heat that was radiating off him was making me sweat. I had to get away from him before he spontaneously combusted. I climbed into the front seat leaving my poor mother sitting between a vampire and a werewolf and sitting partially on Eva who was squashed between Mrs. Woods and Sam. Still, no one was saying anything about what we had seen. This was driving me crazy, and I was just about to ask when Aidan said something.

"What in the hell are they doing here? I thought we…"

"I thought so too. But apparently, these ones are either new or…" Sam also abandoned her thought.

I waited for Bill to say something but he stared at the road, with an expression on his face that I didn't recognize. I wanted to ask him what his thoughts were but settled for reaching for his hand instead. I knew he would tell me when he was ready. We pulled into the park where this had all begun. The park boasted a huge sign on the gates that said closed. I could see the thick chain and huge padlock that kept the gates closed. I watched as Bill grabbed the heavy chain and pulled one of the links apart with little effort. He made it look so easy almost like it was made out of plastic. Sam jumped into the driver's seat and pulled the car through the gates. I watched as Bill closed the gate and squashed the chain link back together, again making it look like nothing. Bill looked at Sam and then he exploded into wolf form and ran into the woods. Where the hell was he going, I needed him to be here with me. Sam drove up to the cabins past the burnt remains of the store.

"Stay." Sam said as Aidan and her got out of the car and walked around a couple of times.

Mrs. Woods and Eva got out of the car and were walking around too. Sam came and opened my door. Sam held onto my wrist pulling me into the cabin first. We were all ushered into the cabin quickly. Aidan kept Mrs. Woods, Eva, and my mom moving into the cabin. I collapsed onto the couch with my mom beside me.

"When will Bill be back?" I asked needing him right now. He was the only thing keeping me sane.

Sam turned and smirked at me, but didn't say anything. She just stood there staring at me puzzled. Then she turned and faced the door like she was expecting someone. I got the feeling that she was not going to tell me anything.

"Ok, I usually wouldn't do this but, I will tell you what I know if you tell me what you know." She said as she turned and looked at me.

She slowly extended her hand to me, so that we could shake on it. I thought about it for a short second then extended my hand and shook hers.

"Ok, start talking." She said as soon as we were not touching anymore. So, I told her what I had seen, and experienced over the last couple of days. The only thing that I left out was the story about talking to the king and queen. For whatever reason, I felt she didn't need to know that. I did tell her about Lucian's plan and how he was going to change me and that he was waiting for the same day the vampire queen had been born. She took all the information in and thought about it for a few seconds before she started to talk.

"Those cloaked figures that you just saw, well we have seen them before. It has been a long time since then, and we thought that we had killed them, but it appears they are back. I don't know how they are involved with this but; if they are involved, it is bad." She said.

I got the feeling that she was not telling me the whole story, I was going to ask when the door opened, and Bill stood in the doorway. I ran to him wrapping myself around him. He too wrapped his arms around me, but it felt as though something between us had changed. I slowly let him go and pulled back from him a bit. I looked him in the eyes, and that is when I saw it, fear, terror, and agony. I was going to tell him that it was going to be all right but knew that one he didn't want to hear it and two I honestly didn't know if everything was going to be all right. All I knew was this was bad, and I had not seen him act like this before now.

"Can we talk?" I asked, looking him in the eyes pulling him into the room, and shutting the door. "Bill, tomorrow is the day that he was going to change me. I know that he will be coming for me and in case he gets me I want you to spend one last night with me." I asked looking down at my feet, hoping that he would say yes. He pulled me up to him and kissed me slowly, but I could tell by his kiss that he was trying to let me down easy.

"Lily, baby, I'm sorry, but we must have a plan for tomorrow. I hope you understand, I love you, and we will be together tomorrow night and many nights after that." He kissed my forehead and led me out of the room. I felt like my world was ending, even my man didn't want me right now.

I sat on the couch between my mom and Eva. Everyone else sat at the table discussing a plan of attack. Every angle that was presented had some kind of flaw. It got me thinking about what if I was not a weak human then I could defend myself. Leading me to my next thought, what if Bill or Sam just turned me now and we could skip this whole nightmare. Seamed like the logical answer to me anyway.

I just blurted it out without thinking any more about it. "Guys what if you just change me now and save us all the hassle. Bill, Sam, one of you could just change me, and all our problems are solved." I said standing up, ready to do it right now.

"What if that is what Lucian wants to happen, then what?" Sam snapped at me.

She had a valid point, but at least I would not be a weak little human, maybe I could even kill him myself. That would be satisfying.

"Bill?" I called upon waiting for him to answer.

"I'm going to have to go with Sam on this one, I'm sorry." He said, but he would not look at me.

Disgusted with them I got up and went to the room slamming the door behind me. I paced back and forth. Why, why, why wouldn't they just change me themselves and save everyone the battle. I heard a knock on the door but chose to ignore it, hoping that whoever it was would just go away. However, Bill opened the door and walked into the room. I was to mad to even acknowledge that he was there at first. He caught me mid-stride in his arms.

He kissed my forehead. "Sam and I are going scouting, and we both need to drink too. We will not be gone long and are leaving you in the care of Aidan and the pack. Just do as they ask, please." He kissed my lips and started to pull away.

"Here drink me." I said and pulled my head to one side exposing my neck to him.

He leaned in and kiss me gently, and I thought for a minute that he was going to do it but then he pulled away and left me standing there looking foolish. I felt like my blood was not good enough for him and that saddened me right down to my core.

Maybe I was foolish for thinking that he loved me. I stood there for a few seconds longer after he had left, then made my way to the living room with everyone else. I made a plan and hoped that Aidan would go along with it.

"Aidan, how long does it take to make a werewolf?" I asked letting the words fall from my mouth trying not to give my plan away.

He looked at me funny for a second but answered my question. "It takes about twenty minutes. Why?" He asked eyeing me.

"What do you think about changing me into one? I don't want to be fragile just waiting here for Lucian to come get me. I would like to fight back." I said trying to make him understand where I was coming from.

"I don't know, Bill and Sam would be very angry at me." He said and frowned at the thought. "Maybe you should ask Bill to do it." He said even though he had been part of the conversation earlier.

"Please, Aidan, please, I want you to change me to a werewolf at least I would not be defenseless." I begged him over and over again.

I could tell now that he was not going to budge on his answer. Well, there goes my plan out the window. I sat there sulking and trying to think of an angle that I could use to get him to do it, but I was coming up with nothing. I wished that I were a vampire right now so that I could bend him to my will. I pulled the stone from my pocket and rolled it over and over in my hand. The dim red light filled the stone again. I was thinking about Aidan and him turning me still. He abruptly turned and glared at me.

"Fine, I'll do it!"

He turned to wolf and quickly scratched me hard making me drop the stone on the ground. He then turned back to human, and I think I heard him say, "What have I done."

Then everything went black, and the scratch mark on my arm burned red hot. It felt like I had been branded by a branding iron. The darkness faded and turned into a forest. A glimpse of a rust colored wolf that seemed to be taunting me appeared. I had the overwhelming feeling that I had to catch the wolf. I chased it but I just was not fast enough to catch it, I had to trick it. I pretended to give up and walk away from the wolf. I used a vine that I had pulled down along the way and made a noose out of it. I started to run again away from the wolf, and it seemed to follow. Then without warning, I ran smack dap into Lucian. He grabbed me by my throat and lifted me off the ground. The wolf charged and bit off his arm that was holding me, knocking both of us to the ground. The wolf recovered quickly and was over me in seconds protecting me. Then everything went black again, and pain ripped through me changing my heartbeat and raising my body temperature.

"Lily, Lily, come on Lily, snap out of it." I heard a panicked Aidan cry and shake me.

I slowly opened my eyes looking him right in the eye. "Thank you." I whispered. I was now a werewolf thanks to my friend. I could not help but feel invincible right now.

"He is going to kill me you know." Aidan said back to me, standing up and folding his hands behind his head as he started pacing.

He was furious with me, but I wondered what had made him change his mind. I looked around the room at my mom, Eva and Mrs. Woods. They all had the same expression on their faces. Their mouths gaped open looking like they wanted to ask me the question of, what did you do. I grabbed the stone and ran to the bathroom. I looked myself in the mirror trying to come to terms with what just happened. I somehow made a werewolf that was not going to turn me to turn me, and I think it was because of the stone. I felt the power of the stone growing. The power felt good, and I wanted to use it some more. What could I use it on now, I wonder if it would make me rich, or if it would bring people back from the dead. I was mesmerized by the stone and the power that coursed through it and into me. My thoughts turned dark, what if I used it to kill humans and everything and everyone in my way by just a wave of a hand? The idea started to root deeper and deeper, taking all that was good out of me. An image of my dad standing in the kitchen making me pancakes popped into my head. I was a little child sitting at the table waiting for him to put the pancakes on my plate. When he turned around his face was grey and wrinkled, he had no eyes or nose, and his lips were black. He smiled, and I screamed. I must have dropped the stone because I heard it rattle around the porcelain as it bounced around the sink. I stood up straight and looked into the mirror trying to catch my breath. I was about to reach for the stone to pick it up and place it in my pocket when the door flew open and Bill's hands were on my arms squaring me up with his body.

"Why did you do it?" He asked tightening his grip on my upper arms. I knew that he already knew what I had done. He was furious with me.

"Bill, I just, I mean, I…" Then I started to cry. "I'm sorry, I never meant to."

"Well you seem to be ok but, you owe everyone an apology especially Aidan." He said and pulled me into him again. Then led me out of the bathroom to the living room where I had to face the music of my actions.

"Everyone, I'm sorry, I just wanted to be not so fragile. I need to be able to fight off Lucian when he comes. I just don't think it is fair that you guys take all the risks for me." I said through tears that were still streaming down my face.

I glanced around the room at everyone. The only person that didn't look like they accepted my apology was Eva. She knew something else was at work here. I felt the stone in my pocket shift, and she looked down at it. She was telling me that she knew what I had done, and she was disapproving of it. She looked like she was going to say something when Bill's phone rang. He flipped the phone open and without saying anything, the voice, Lucian's voice, was on the other end.

"Listen here, half-breed." He spat the words at Bill. "I want the girl back and now. I will give you until tomorrow night to send her out, or I'm coming in after her. Did you like the little gift I sent you at your house?" Then loud booming laughter came across the receiver, and Bill held it away from his ear. "They will be with me when I come for her. I will get back what you have stolen from me." Before Bill could say anything, the phone went dead.

Bill looked at Sam and Aidan. His face turned red with anger. Bill grabbed my arm and pulled me outside of the cabin. Sam and Aidan joined us quickly. Bill didn't say anything and changed to wolf and Aidan followed suit. I knew then why Bill brought me out here, he wanted me to be a wolf. I tried to think about the wolf inside and let it tear through me, but nothing was happening. Bill fazed back to human. "Think of your happy place." Random happy moments ran through my mind, but still, nothing was happening. I just could not shift to the wolf. I tried other memories and thoughts too, but they didn't work either. Finally, a picture of Lucian's face floated into view. That was the one thing that I was out to kill, and I transformed into the wolf. I let out a giant howl that was piercing to my own ears. My vision was clear, and I could see many little details. I could hear for what seemed like an eternity. I heard the pitter patter of other small feet and rodents gnawing on bark. This was very distracting and disorienting to me. I was going to have to listen to certain things if I didn't all the noise would drive me crazy. I could smell animals in the forest, but I was not sure what smell went with what. Then I could smell her, Sam, as she stood behind me. She smelled like dried blood and old sweaty gym socks but as she noticed I was smelling her the scent changed to that of dried blood and roses. Bill came over, put his head to mine, and made a whimpering sound. I had no idea what the whimper meant at first, but then the words popped into my head. He said that he loved me. I mimicked the sound back to him. He made another sound, which translated into follow me. So, I did, and we loped through the woods. I was starting to realize what all the smells were, earth, trees, water, and each animal that we crossed paths with. Aidan and Sam who didn't let me out of their sights for a second flanked us. Then Bill must have said something and they veered off leaving us alone. Bill came to me again and put his head on me like he was giving me a hug.

Then he said to faze back through a bunch of short quiet barks. Think of your saddest thought he was saying. I tried that but quickly realized that it was not working. So, my unhappy thought got me in here, so maybe my happy thought would pull me out. So, I thought of Bill and his smile, him holding me. I slowly turned back to human. This was so messed up, and I wondered if any of the others were like me, I had to think of the opposite thing to shift.

He put his arms around me and pulled me close to his body. "I'm still a little upset with you for tricking Aidan. I never wanted this for you. I'm not sure this is even going to help us in the long run." He pulled me down to the ground with him, turning me to face out away from him. I sat between his legs leaning back against his chest. "Lily, can you tell me why you did it?"

I sat up wrapping my arms around my legs, I felt a bit embarrassed. Maybe it was more guilt than anything really. "Bill, I…" I was trying to find the right words to say. I didn't want to tell him that I had used the stone, but there was no other way, so I blurted it out. "I used the stone." I knew if I stopped on any one of those words that I would have choked and not said it. "I didn't know that would happen. I just wanted to be able to help the cause and be able to fight if I needed too." I said a little more relaxed but still on edge.

I was waiting for him to say something but he didn't, he just wrapped his arms around me and pulled me tight to him.

We sat there in the silence for a few moments. "Come we should go it is getting late, and we need to be up early. I'll race ya." He said then in a matter of a second he was out from behind me and had changed to the wolf.

He turned and looked at me antagonizing me with his eyes. I changed to wolf, and we were off on a dead run back to the cabin. As we approached the cabin, I could hear bickering back and forth. We walked in to see everyone sitting around the table talking and from what I gathered it was about tomorrow. Bill pulled up a chair and sat down with me sitting on his lap.

My mom said. "We should run."

Eva said. "We were all going to die."

Mrs. Woods was quiet. Sam was trying to talk strategy with Aidan and everyone else. Aidan was listening, but I could tell he was ready to explode from the stress.

"Everyone please just shut up and listen to what Sam has to say. If anyone can get us all out alive, it would be her." I said and amazingly enough, everyone quieted and looked at Sam. Sam glanced at me and smiled.

"Ok everyone here is the plan. Mrs. Woods is going to take you two and go far away from here." She pointed at my mom and Eva. They started to protest, but I shot them both a look telling them to shut up and just do as they are told.

Sam looked at Bill and me now. "Here is the plan for you Lily, in a small circular clearing in the woods you are going to stand there and wait for Lucian. All the other wolves will surround you to protect you and mask your wolf smell. However, there will be stakes on every tree around you. You are going to try to kill him. Bill started to protest, but

Sam somehow quieted him down. Aidan and I will help whoever is in trouble." Then she sat back in her chair closed her eyes and pretended as if she had left the building.

As I sat there, the realness of the situation started to weigh on me. Tomorrow would either be my last day on this planet or the first day of forever with a man that didn't want anything from me except for the powers that I would gain. I knew that I could and would not take the stone with me, in fact, I needed someone to take it and bury it or destroy it. I looked over at Eva; she was just staring off into space. Then I wondered if I could trust her with the stone and possibly, just maybe she could destroy it. I reached for the stone in my pocket and felt it move a bit. I needed her to be alone though. I didn't want everyone knowing what I was doing with the stone. I briefly looked at Sam but wondered if the power would go to her head. I was not sure that I could trust Sam to destroy it. I know it was not fair for me to think this way but the fact was that she had not liked me from the start and was only being nice to me for her brother's sake. Slowly everyone started to excuse themselves from the table. When my mom and Eva excused themselves, I followed them to the couch. I pretended like I was going to spend the last little bit of time I had with my mom and Eva. Bill, Sam, and Aidan all excused themselves outside. Maybe they had sensed that I wanted some alone time with my mom. My mom fell asleep quickly though. I looked at Eva, and she was still awake but fading fast. "pst…pst…" I whisper to her trying not to make too much noise. When I had her attention, I pointed to the bathroom. She got up and walked to the bathroom. I waited for a second then also got up and went to the bathroom. I didn't say anything but placed the stone in her hand to take. She went to say something, but I shushed her, I didn't want anyone to know that I had given her the stone. We filed back out of the bathroom and back to the couches where we could relax and await orders.

Somewhere in the tick-tock of the clock and the eerie silence, I somehow managed to fall asleep.

∾CHAPTER 27∾

A picture of a meadow appeared, and I was walking through it holding someone's hand. But when I looked up to see the face there was nothing there, I looked at the body for clues as to whom I might be walking with, but for whatever reason, I couldn't see that either. I looked around me. The green grass and flowers that grew here absorbed the bright sunshine. The scene was beautiful, picturesque, like a painting done by Shirley Novak. A glance behind though told a different story, it was dark, pitch black. As I moved forward, the darkness followed me consuming all that was nice and good. I wondered if the darkness would stop if I stopped moving, so I tried it. The darkness just kept coming it was not stopping for anything. It wanted to consume me. I started to run away from it, but it just kept coming and faster now. I could see a pinhole of light left when I woke myself up by gasping for air.

A voice and arms came from somewhere, and they were holding me. "It's ok, it was just a dream." Bill's voice said soothing me. I relaxed into him still panting a bit.

"I need to clear my mind is it possible to go for a run?" I asked.

"Ok, but we have to stay close."

Outside the front door, I changed to wolf and started to run a small loop around the cabin. I was around about four times before Bill joined me. Then he led the way and I just merely followed him. We ran at top speed, the wind through my fur coat felt delightful. It was almost like a million fingers caressing my skin at once. I felt all my muscles stretch and contract with every stride. The wind whistled around my ears drowning out any thought that I had in my head. This was nice very nice. Just to be lost in the nothingness. Bill stopped dead in front of me, and I had not been paying attention and ran right into him knocking both of us to the ground.

"I'm so sorry." I said through a few short barks. He rested his head on mine in a gesture saying apology accepted. He had led us to the top of a hill that overlooked the land. It was amazing. Everything looked so small from here. The moon was full overhead, and for whatever reason, it made me what to howl and let everything go, so I did. I took in as much air as my lungs would hold, pointed my nose to the moon and let out the most beautiful, graceful, and loud as I could muster howl. I heard Bill join in for a second but he let me finish. I felt like I could do this all night. The stress of everything was just rolling off me with every howl. Even though I wanted to stay, we had to go, but we phased back to human and walked hand and hand towards the cabin.

"Lily, I think I like you being a wolf." He said with a giggle. "I love you, you know. How about we get married right now?" He asked pulling us to a stop and turning me to face him.

"We don't have anyone that can marry us right now." I rebutted, I was not ready for this, I didn't want to be the next dead wife. "You know I love you, and I do want to marry you but how about after this is over. Besides we need to get back to the cabin my mom, Eva and Mrs. Woods should be leaving soon, and I want to say goodbye." I said, but I could tell that I hurt him a bit. I leaned in and kissed him. "Please understand I love you, I really do, but I want it to be forever. What if something goes wrong tomorrow? I don't want to be... well, you know." I said hoping that he would understand, I could not even make the word dead come out of my mouth. His face brightened, and he pulled me in for a kiss. Then playfully he tickled me, and we ended up on the ground.

"Race you back." Then without warning, he was the wolf and running away from me. I quickly scrambled to my feet, changing to the wolf, and perused him aggressively. This had turned into a giant game of hide and go seek.

Back at the cabin, the moon was getting low in the sky and was setting to make way for the sun. Mrs. Woods had stuff packed in the car and was ready to go. Where they were going no one really knew. Sam said that she wanted to keep it a secret just in case.

I gently woke my mom and held her in my arms for a moment. "I love you, I will see you soon." I said with confidence.

I just could not let her know that I may die for whatever this was. I walked her to the car and watched as she climbed in shut the door and put her seatbelt on.

Eva walked by me just then, and I grabbed her arm so that she would give me a hug. While we were hugging, I whispered. "Do you have it?" She didn't say anything back but just nodded her head yes. "I hope we have the power to destroy him." I said putting emphasis on the word destroy, I hoped that she got the idea to destroy the stone.

I watched as she took her place next to my mom. Then they sped away. I wanted to cry but knew that I had to just let it go for now. I needed to build a mental wall to block out all emotions and focus on the task of killing Lucian. Bill and I stood with each other for a short time before it was time to go in. The sun cast a fiery glow across the ground, making me feel sadder reminding me that my time was short.

Bill and I spent the rest of the day wrapped up with each other. We held each other tightly all day. The day went by too quickly, and soon the sun was starting to set, and it was time to face death.

Bill and I walked hand and hand to the small circular clearing. He kissed me one more time then disappeared into the woods. As I stood there waiting, I looked around at the trees and just as Sam had said there was a wooden stake affixed to them. The plan, I was supposed to stand here surrounded by wolves until the moment was right. Then run towards him grabbing a steak and plunging into his heart ultimately killing him. I waited for any sound, but I just didn't hear anything, my blood boiled and the wolf was scratching at me to come out. Then all at once, the wolves were there surrounding me, and I knew that it was almost time now. The more I thought about him, the more I wanted to change to the wolf, but I knew that I could not do that. He could not know about the wolf, well at least not right away. Then I wondered how this would mess up his plans. Maybe since I was not purely human anymore, he would leave me alone. Perhaps nothing would be the same. Maybe now he could not change me and get the power that he wanted. This is what I was hoping for at this moment. The wolf boiled faster inside me now just waiting to be unleashed. I heard movement to my left and felt the pull of Lucian.

His voice sang through the trees. "Are you ready, my love?"

I looked in the direction that I thought he was going to appear, but I didn't see anything. A snarl behind me indicated that Lucian was behind me instead of in front of me. I whipped around to face him. The wolves were backing up and making the circle tighter around me. Standing to the left of Lucian was one of the dark cloaked figures, and on the right, was another one. I remembered there had been three and instantly wondered where the third one was. Then it dawned on me that maybe Lucian was the third one. Anyhow, I didn't have time to dwell on that right now. I needed to get down to the task at hand. How was I going to grab a stake and get to Lucian to kill him?

"Don't you look radiant; I thought you might have dressed up for the occasion." He said smirking at me. "I guess we will just have to fix you up first. Come, my love." He said and stuck his hand out for me to take.

The wolves started snarling, snapping and growling at him. He ignored them though and took a step forward. The wolves shrank the circle around me again. He was almost in line with one of the steaks now, and I knew that I could not let him get much farther. I started to run towards him now. I ran between two of the wolves straight for the steak in the tree. I grabbed it, whirled in a circle Steak out and pointed towards him. Then I dropped the steak, and the next thing I knew I was growling and barking in his face but something was restraining me from both sides. Something touched me, and I whimpered and instantly changed back to human. Shit, shit, shit, I had really messed this thing up, damn the wolf.

I was laying on the ground in pain while Lucian stood over me. "Pick her up." He said to the others.

I could not feel my feet, so I was relying on them one hundred percent to hold me up. Whatever it was that touch me had paralyzed me.

Once I was up and facing him, he said. "Well, well, well, look who thought the wolf would save her soul." He placed his hand gently under my chin and pulled my head up to meet his eyes. "This is not going to protect you from my gift. This causes no complication to us at all. The only thing I get is the bonus of having a pet." Then he laughed the most horrifying and evil laugh he could muster. "You got the stone, my bride?"

This was going to be how I stopped him.

"Actually, Lucian, I don't have it I lost it on the way to New Orleans." I said and started to giggle to myself. He was furious, I could almost see the steam coming out of his ears. Then he calmed himself, and it seemed that he remembered something about the stone. "No matter, come bring her."

I found some inner strength and started to wiggle against my restraints. I got one arm free and tried for the second one.

"Lily, stop fighting, or all of your friends will die." He showed me a gun with a shiny silver bullet in the chamber. "Yeah, my whole entourage has them." Come peacefully, or they die, and they know it.

I walked with my head hung staring at the ground, he had outsmarted us again. Now I was sure to face his full wrath. I was sure to be tied up and immobilized until he turned me. Even after that, I was not sure that he would ever let me roam freely.

"Lucian, may I talk to you?" I said, and I sounded tired and exhausted to myself. "What is your plan for me? Are you going to lock me up and keep me there forever? Are you going to kill me?"

I wanted to know the answers, but then again, I didn't want to know. Maybe it was just better not to know my fate right now. "Never mind don't answer that." I said and could feel the tears coming to my eyes.

I would never see anyone again, and I had hoped that I did everything right to get into heaven with my dad. I prayed for the first time in a long time in hopes that there was forgiveness.

We were crossing out of the park when Lucian was struck by something and went flying. Then I heard the familiar sounds of growls behind me. I could see fire light up the woods as someone was throwing fireballs at Lucian. The guards that had been holding me were now trying to get away from the attacking wolves and the firefight. I quickly changed to wolf and charged at Lucian. This was my chance to take him down. I leapt up to his face grabbing it in my teeth and started shaking him. He was too strong though and threw me back from him. I regained my composure and went after him again this time snagging his arm. He put his other arm around me and started dragging us both backward away from the fight. He saw an opportunity and bit me. He was quickly draining the blood out of me. My wolf could not sustain, and I changed back to human. I could feel his fangs deep into my skin and sucking out my life in huge gulps. I was fading fast and could only see a small light in the center of my vision. He was sucking the life out of me. Just as I was going to close my eyes and slip into the darkness, he stopped. My body fell to the ground with a thud. I don't know what happened next, but all I knew was that I was teetering on the edge of being alive and dying. Just one more small gulp of my blood would have done me in. I gasped for air like a fish out of water.

"Lily, Lily, Lily, baby come back to me." I could hear Bill's voice frantically calling and talking to me. "Stay with me, baby. Sam, can you fix it?" I heard him say.

Then I felt a few droplets of something on my lips, and it rolled down my tongue and to my throat. Then there was nothing, no noise, no nothing. It was just dark and scary. Then pictures of the king and queen ran through my mind again, and I knew what was happening to me. I was back in the room where I had first met them again. They both got up to greet me. Our beautiful daughter is finally come home. Please take these gifts that we have been waiting a long time to give you. I could see what looked like red bullets fly through the air one by one they pierced into me. I was not expecting the pain that came along with them. The first one dropped me to my knees. The next ones made me a helpless pile on the floor. I think I counted eight in all, but with the pain, I could not concentrate. When that was done, they each came over to me and placed their arms over my lips and told me to drink from them. So, I did as I was told and the pain dissipated quickly and was gone. As I lay there on the floor, they went back to their thrones and watched as I slowly got to my knees, then to my feet. When I was standing again, they both bid me farewell. Please come back soon and see us, all you need to do is follow your heart to find us. With that, it was over, and I opened my eyes to the blackened sky of night. My head resting on something but was not sure what it was at first but when I looked up, I saw Bill's face staring back at me. I clenched my throat as the burning seared through me. Bill picked me up and carried me back to the cabin. Someone had brought humans to the cabin. The smell of human filled my nose, and the luscious blood sang to me. It took me a few seconds to drink them dry and regain control over my body. My thoughts cleared and I could now stand on my own. I slept all of the next day and awoke with a hunger that was enough to drive a sane person insane. All I knew for a few days was sleep and blood, rinse and repeat.

"Baby, what do you say we get married now?" Bill asked me after a few days when I was finally more awake than I had been.

"Yes, yes, yes!" I exclaimed, and now that everything was over I was ready and couldn't think of a day without him by my side.

We had a simple little wedding in the woods, mostly just the family and the pack. He took me to see my mom and Eva a couple of times as they got back to their normal way of life. My mom had met someone and was living life to the fullest. I guess the near-death experience had done her some good. Making her realize that life is to short not to. She eventually sold the store for a nice chunk of change and traveled around the world.

Now that the threat to the campers was over, we reopened the park and rebuilt Mrs. Wood's store. Bill and I moved back to his house and we lived there happily just the two of us. Sam and I got along a little better these days, I would be pushing it if I said we were really close friends, but at least we were friends. For some reason, she still thought I was going to hurt her brother. That is a sister and brothers love though. They always are looking out for each other. I also got to meet Aidan and Sam's daughter Kate, my new niece. What a beautiful pre-college teenage girl.

Sam and Bill killed Lucian; at least that is what they tell me. As far as the stone, Eva said that she was successful at destroying it. She even showed me a pile of ash supposedly that's all that is left of the stone. All though it didn't matter if I would have had the stone or not because the queen and king still gave me all the gifts. I wondered many times what the purpose of the stone was, and I should have talked to Eva about it, but at the time, I was just glad to be rid of it. The gifts that the queen and king gave me were awesome. I would play with them when I was alone. This was a secret that I kept from Bill, I didn't want him to know how powerful I really was. In the transition to vampire, I lost the wolf somehow and it kind of sucked. I really liked the time that Bill and I howled at the moon together.

I was out for a drink last week without Bill, and I could have sworn that I saw three cloaked figures moving in the darkened alleys of the city. They looked up at me with their red glowing eyes. I blinked and then they were gone. I don't know if I had really seen them or if it was a vision. That is one thing that I was having a hard time getting used to, the visions. I would see things that were not there. However, for some nagging reason, this didn't feel like one of those visions. I ran towards the place that I had seen them, but I didn't see anyone lurking. I turned and ran back the way that I had come. When I got to the end of the alley an evil laugh echoed through the alley, taking me by surprise. I knew then that I would see them again someday soon.